This Time with Love

A Christian Romance

Kimberly Rae Jordan

THREE**STRAND**
P R E S S

À CORD OF THREE STRANDS IS NOT EASILY BROKEN.

A man, a woman & their God.
Three Strand Press publishes Christian Romance stories that intertwine love, faith and
family.
Always clean. Always heartwarming. Always uplifting.

Chapter One

E RIC McKinley slumped into the cavernous easy chair near a large glass window, the low murmur of conversation swirling around him. With his head resting on the back of the chair, he stared out at the snow-covered landscape, the absence of trees being the only indication of where the lake lay. Even though it was just past five o'clock, the colors of nature were easing into shades of gray as twilight descended. Daylight didn't hang around too long in the midst of winter in Minnesota. Unfortunately, the dreary world beyond the window did nothing to lighten his mood.

"What's up, man?"

Eric looked away from the window to see his best friend, Trent Hause, settle into the chair across from him. Trent was a reformed hacker who now headed up the virtual security division of BlackThorpe Security while Eric worked in the corporate division. Given the six year age gap between them, they were an unlikely pair, but their friendship worked for them.

Trent pulled off the bright red ski cap he'd been wearing. His brown hair stood on end, but he didn't bother to try to tame it. "Where's Mel?"

Just the question Eric didn't want to have to answer at that moment. He gave one version of the truth. "She ended up having to work."

Trent shook his head. "That's the problem with being in a profession that works twenty-four seven. Is she going to make it at all?"

"Doubt it." Eric stared out the window again.

When his foot was jostled, he looked back at Trent.

"Is Mel not being here what has you so bummed? This isn't like you."

"That and the fact that she broke up with me." The words slipped out before Eric could stop them.

Trent gave a low whistle as his eyebrows shot up. "She broke up with you? Good gravy, man, what's up with that?"

Eric lifted one shoulder in a halfhearted shrug. "I haven't a clue."

"She didn't give you a reason?" Trent leaned forward, propping his elbows on his knees. "That doesn't sound like Mel."

"She gave a reason." Eric rubbed a hand across his forehead. "Something about us not connecting like she wanted. I know we've both been busy, but she wasn't interested in trying to work it out apparently."

"And she won't even meet to talk it over with you?"

"Oh, she will. We agreed to get together when I get back to the city, but she made it pretty clear it was only to give a definite end to things, not to try to patch things up."

Trent flopped back into the chair with a huff. "Wow, that's kind of a downer way to start the New Year."

Eric arched a brow at his friend. "You think?"

They sat without speaking for a couple of minutes before Trent said, "Are you going to stick around?"

"I guess. Not much to do at home since I cleared my schedule to be here."

"And maybe you'll meet someone interesting."

Eric shot Trent an exasperated look. "My girlfriend just dumped me, man. I'm not looking for someone interesting. Something tells me I should take this weekend to figure out what on earth is wrong with me."

Trent gave him a lopsided grin. "Can I start the list?"

Eric kicked Trent's boot. "You've stuck with me longer than most of my girlfriends, so I think I must be doing something right in the friend arena. My trouble seems to come from being a boyfriend."

"Well, from what I hear from the ladies, it's not your looks, so it must be a personality defect."

"A personality defect." Eric couldn't help but laugh. If nothing else, he could always count on Trent to lift his spirits. "That's a good one."

"What have your other girlfriends said? Is there a consistent theme in the excuses they give when they dump you?"

Eric winced. He didn't really want to be reminded of just how often he'd been dumped in the past five years. Was he really that bad a guy? Since he'd recommitted himself to Christ, he liked to think that he'd improved remarkably, but clearly there was something wrong somewhere. A *defect*, to use Trent's term.

"They've given a variety of reasons. We're not right for each other. I travel too much. I'm not letting them get close. I hold myself apart from them."

Trent's brow crinkled. "Too bad women don't come with a handbook. Would help immensely."

Eric agreed one hundred percent with his friend. Trying to make sense of the opposite sex gave him a headache. "It's just a waste of time and energy trying figure out what Melanie means until we can actually talk it over."

"So you're going to try to enjoy the weekend in spite of this latest downturn in your social life?" Trent waved his hand toward the room at large. "I think it's going to be a great retreat. We've already got a good crowd here with representation from five different churches."

Eric let his gaze roam the room. People stood in clusters of three and four throughout the large meeting room of the camp's main lodge. He recognized a few of the people—the ones who had come from his own church. This was his first time at this particular camp, but he found the décor similar to places he'd been before. Log walls, large windows, old furniture. There was a piano in the corner that looked like it had been made before he was born—maybe even before his dad had been born. From his vantage point, he could see clusters of framed photographs on the wall, but Eric couldn't tell what they were pictures of. At some point during the weekend he'd take the time to have a look at them.

His gaze snagged on a woman talking with a tall, slender man. There was something familiar about her. Something familiar in the profile of her face, in the tilt of her head. She had long blonde hair that ended about midway down her back. From this distance, it looked like she had a cell phone clutched in her hand, and she was gesturing to the man with it.

The rigid postures on both of them made it pretty clear that the conversation wasn't an easy-going, friendly one. Eric felt a spark of sympathy for the man. It appeared that he wasn't the only one having a less than perfect weekend. He wondered if the guy was having as much trouble understanding his woman as Eric was Melanie.

Trent stood up and thumped him on the knee. "I'm going to find out when supper is. I'm starving."

Eric nodded absently to his friend while keeping his attention on the couple who were still tangled in their intense discussion. In apparent frustration, the woman looked away from her companion, and Eric caught a glimpse of her face.

Recognition slammed into his gut with the force of a sledgehammer.

Of all the places—of all the times—he never dreamed he'd find her like this.

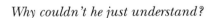

Why couldn't he just understand?

Staci Moore gripped the phone in her hand, trying her best to keep from stamping her feet. Her frustration with Vince was outweighed only by her frustration at not being able to get hold of Miriam so she could check on Sarah. Was it because he was a man that he didn't understand her concern? He acted as if she was being completely unreasonable in wanting to make sure her daughter was okay. It had been with a great deal of reluctance that she'd agreed to come on this singles retreat over the New Year. She hadn't even been here two hours and was already regretting her decision.

4

"This weekend is not going to be enjoyable at all if you spend the whole time worrying about Sarah. She's fine."

Staci swung back around to face Vince. When she saw the boredom on his face, it was all she could do not to walk away, get into her car and leave the camp. She'd hoped that during their time out here, she'd have a chance to get to know Vince better. They'd been on three dates so far, and he'd been the ultimate gentleman with her. Too bad that wasn't carrying over in his attitude toward Sarah. She didn't need the rest of the weekend to know that this wasn't going to work between them.

"Vince, I'm going to keep trying to get hold of Miriam. Maybe it would be better if you just found someone else to hang around with for now."

"C'mon, Staci, don't be like that." He grabbed her arm in a grip that was just a little too tight for her liking. "I'm just trying to get you to relax. If you spend the whole weekend worrying, no one will have a good time."

"I'm sorry you feel that way." Staci jerked her arm away. "But this is the first time we've been apart. I don't stop being a mother just because I'm not with her."

"Fine." Vince took a step back. "Don't come looking for me if you get bored."

Staci shot him an angry look. "Somehow I don't think you need to be concerned about that."

As she watched Vince stride away, Staci felt a measure of regret that this first foray into serious dating in over half a decade had gone so poorly. She hadn't figured that her first dating experience after all these years away from it would end in marriage. However, it would have been nice if it had been a pleasant relationship with someone who respected her—not just as a woman, but as a mother.

Staci turned her phone over to look at the display. It still showed a signal so at least that was a bonus. She wasn't stuck in the middle of nowhere with no cell service. Now if only Miriam would answer the phone.

The swell of conversation in the room grew as more people joined the crowd already there. Knowing any conversation on the phone would be impossible with the noise, Staci left the main meeting room and headed for the dining room. Though there was some activity there, it wasn't as loud.

She tapped the screen for the fifth time in the past fifteen minutes. This time the phone rang four times before it finally connected on the other end. Miriam sounded winded when she answered.

The older woman's breathlessness concerned her. "Is everything okay, Miriam?"

"Everything is great. Sarah wanted a bath, so we've been in the bathroom for the past half hour."

Staci smiled. Yes, her daughter did love the water. Showers were a frequent occurrence, but baths were a special reward. She was glad to hear that Sarah was okay and having a good time.

"I was just concerned because I couldn't get an answer on the phone."

"I'm sorry, Staci," Miriam said, regret clear in her voice. "I forgot to take the phone into the bathroom with me and didn't want to leave Sarah alone to answer it. You know, with her being smaller and all."

Staci understood and appreciated Miriam's concern. "Not a problem. Just glad to hear that all is well. Don't let Sarah twist you too far around her finger."

"Oh, my dear, you know that warning comes way too late," Miriam said with a warm laugh.

Staci felt her heart lighten at Miriam's words. Not everyone could see past Sarah's physical differences to the sweet spirit within her. Miriam had absolutely doted on the child since she'd begun attending the same church as Staci three years ago. And as much as Miriam loved Sarah, the little girl adored the woman who had become a surrogate grandmother to her.

"Is Sarah up for a chat?" Staci asked. Bedtime was in about an hour, so Sarah was probably having a snack and watching her favorite show on television.

"Yes, I think she'd like to talk with you."

Staci could hear murmurs in the background and then Sarah's sweet voice said, "Hi, Mama."

Staci swallowed before answering. "How are you doing, baby?"

"Fine. I had a bath."

"I heard. Are you having fun with Miss Miriam?"

"Oh, yes." Even without seeing her, Staci could imagine Sarah nodding, her dark brown curls dancing. "We're having sundaes."

Staci smiled when she heard Miriam laughing in the background. Yeah, Sarah was working her charm for sure. "Eat a couple of bites for me, okay?"

"Okay."

"I'll let you get back to your ice cream now. Remember Mama loves you. Be good for Miss Miriam."

"I will," Sarah reassured her. "I love you, too."

"Sleep well, baby." Staci blinked rapidly, thinking of the precious bedtime routine she'd be missing. "Let me talk to Miss Miriam again, okay?"

"You're not mad about the ice cream, are you?" Miriam asked when she got back on the phone.

"No. Not at all. You two enjoy yourselves." Staci paused. "Listen, my cell phone gets service out here and my battery is fully charged, so if you need to get hold of me for any reason—any reason at all—please don't hesitate to call."

"I'd tell you not to worry, but I have a feeling you still will, so just remember that God is taking care of us here just like He is you there."

Staci took comfort in Miriam's reminder. God had opened the door for her to come to this retreat. She still wasn't sure why. But she needed to remember that she had been willing to trust in His will—even just this morning—though now her weakness was being preyed upon. Doubts and worries plagued her.

"Thank you for watching her, Miriam. I couldn't have come up here with anyone else taking care of her."

"You go and enjoy yourself. Make some new friends and watch for opportunities the Lord might send your way to broaden your horizons and strengthen your faith."

Staci ended the call feeling much more at peace than she had a few minutes ago. Maybe Vince had been right in cajoling her to lighten up. Perhaps she owed him an apology.

Perhaps…

"Ana?"

The name.

The voice.

The past.

It all came crashing down on her.

Clutching her phone, Staci turned, hoping—praying—it was all in her imagination. Or maybe it was just a dream. She'd wake up in her own bed, her past still safely behind her. But there before her stood the man she'd left six years ago. The one who hadn't wanted to be a husband or a father. This was not the things dreams were made of. This was her worst nightmare.

What was he doing here? He'd said more than once during their time together that hell would freeze over before he moved back to Minnesota. Last she'd heard, that hadn't happened. Her alarm at his presence here in Minnesota equaled her shock at running into him at a Christian singles' retreat.

"Ana? Is that really you?" He stared at her with astonishment that was surely mirrored on her own face.

His dark hair was a little longer than he'd worn it back then but his brown eyes were familiar and it looked like he still enjoyed working out. The jeans and sweater he wore were a little more casual than his previous style but he looked good as ever. Too good.

All Staci could think of was to escape.

"What are you doing here? Where have you been?" He shot the questions at her as he stepped toward her.

It took everything within Staci to not step back, away from him.

He moved closer. "Why did you just disappear?"

Staci could have answered all of his questions with just one sentence, but she wasn't going to. Six years ago he'd made the decision to not be a permanent part of her life. She owed him no explanations.

She took a quick breath to steady her nerves, drawing on everything she'd ever learned about maintaining her composure. "Eric. What a surprise."

His dark eyes narrowed, leaving no doubts about his displeasure with her response.

"*Eric. What a surprise?* That's all you have to say? It's been six years since you walked out on me without even a word of goodbye, and that's all the greeting I get?"

Staci crossed her arms, willing the trembling in her extremities to cease. She could not let him see how much this encounter upset her. The snack she'd eaten in the car on the way up churned in her stomach. Moisture flooded her mouth. Staci had to swallow several times before she could respond. "As I recall, you made it clear that night that there was no future for us. I figured that was our goodbye."

"I didn't know that just because I reinforced my position regarding marriage—a position, I might add, you knew about from almost the beginning of our relationship—that you would just walk away from what we had as soon as I left on my business trip."

Staci swallowed hard, trying to keep from throwing up all over his shoes. She had to be so careful of what she told him. Of what she revealed of that time. "What we had was a relationship I could no longer be part of because I had become a Christian."

Eric stared at her. "Are you telling me that the last night when we talked you were already a Christian?"

Staci nodded. "I knew I couldn't continue the relationship as it was. If marriage wasn't an option then the relationship was over for me."

It had been so much more than that, but Staci didn't want to get into a discussion. The more they discussed, the greater the possibility she would say something she didn't want to. This was a slippery slope she had to get off. Fast.

"The past is the past, Eric. There's no need for us to dwell on it." Staci took a step back. "I guess I'll probably see you around."

Before Eric could respond, Staci slipped out of the dining room and brushed past people to get to the entrance of the lodge. As she stepped out of the building, she realized she'd forgotten her jacket, but even the cold could not turn her back. She raced over the packed snow on the path leading to the cabins. She heard Eric call her name, but didn't slow down or stop. Didn't even glance over her shoulder.

The past had to stay in the past. The taint from her life six years ago must never touch Sarah. She would do what she must to keep that from happening. The woman she'd been back then was gone. And she must never, ever be allowed to return.

Her boots slipped on the snow, and she fell to her knees. Panic swamped her. She couldn't allow Eric to catch up with her. Staci scrambled to regain her footing. As soon as she was on her feet once again, she bolted for the door of the cabin, and the safety that lay behind it.

Eric stood on the porch of the lodge watching Ana make her mad dash to a cabin off to the left of the main building. His breath caught when she fell, and he started to go after her, but then stopped. He could find her. It wasn't as if he didn't know which cabin she disappeared into. Right then, however, he was still trying to come to terms with the fact that after six long years, he had once again come face to face with Miss Anastacia Stapleton.

His breath came in visible puffs in the cold air as he shoved his hands into the pockets of his jeans. Eric gazed at the cabin where Ana had gone, his mind full of questions. And memories. So many memories.

He'd immediately seen the changes in her. The short and sassy way she'd worn her hair had given way to long blonde strands. Would it still be silky soft if he ran his fingers through it? She didn't have the waif-like look of six years ago either—the look that had been so popular in the circles in which they moved. If he had to pick one word to describe the changes in her since they'd been apart, he'd pick *soft*.

Memories he'd tried hard to suppress over the years came rolling through his mind like tumbleweeds in the desert. Seeing her again after so long had set them free once more. He couldn't ignore them. They just kept right on coming.

The battle with his thoughts raged. He didn't want to think of their more intimate times together. But they had been together nearly two years, and there was no denying that their physical relationship was really what had held them together. Over the years, he'd come to realize there hadn't been much substance to what they'd had but that hadn't stopped him from wanting to find her.

Eric rubbed his forehead, glad for the chill that invaded his body from the cold winter wind.

What was he to do now? No matter what Ana said, things weren't finished between them. Had it just been his unwillingness to marry her that had sent her away? But why go into hiding? There was no doubt in his mind that she had disappeared with the purpose of never being found by him.

Her agent had blocked him at every turn when he'd come back from his engineering assignment in Africa. Bribing hadn't even worked. For all intents and purposes, Ana had vanished off the face of the earth. He'd spent a small fortune trying to track her down. He'd given up trying to find her three years ago, and now here she was. At a Christian singles' retreat. In Minnesota. The very last place he would have ever thought he'd run into her.

Eric gave his head a shake. "Very funny sense of humor you've got there, God."

And it wasn't helping his ego any to be reminded of his biggest failure in the relationship department on the very same day his latest failure had occurred. Though he had stopped his search for Ana, he'd never had a sense of closure on things with her. He would have that opportunity now, and maybe, while he was at it, he could see if Ana could tell him what it was that made him bad news to the women he dated. After all, she was the woman who had stuck with him the longest. If anyone could point out his *defect,* it would be her.

He supposed that his break-up with Melanie now had an upside—he could focus his attention on Ana without feeling like he was neglecting Mel. Eric also felt certain there was more to Ana's need to disappear than she was letting on, and he had every intention of finding out what it was.

Chapter Two

S TACI paced the small room. Bunk bed to the door. Door to the wall. And back again. She could have stayed in the main area of the cabin and had more space to move, but somehow she felt safer with two doors between her and Eric should he decide to come looking for her. Which was ridiculous really, since neither door had a lock on it.

Only one option remained in this situation—she had to leave. She could disappear without having to actually leave the city. Eric only knew her as Anastacia Stapleton not Staci Moore, which was what she went by now. He could ask until he was blue in the face, but no one would ever be able to connect the two for him.

Staci grabbed her bag and put it on the lower bunk. She'd only pulled out a few items earlier so packing to leave wouldn't take long at all. As she shoved her things back into the bag, it dawned on her that Eric had seen which cabin she'd gone into. He would be able to discover the name she used now without too much difficulty.

Her frantic movements stilled.

Clearly, running away this time wasn't going to work. Best to stay and see if she could get the situation to the point where he accepted the past and was willing to leave her alone. Staci sank down on the bed, ducking her head to avoid getting a whack from the upper bunk.

She heard the front door of the cabin open. "Staci? You here?"

The bedroom door was the next to swing open. Her friend, Denise, stood there, concern written all over her face. "Why are you hiding out in here? Philip said he saw you take off like the hounds of hell were after you."

"I wasn't feeling well."

"You left this." Denise tossed the coat she was carrying onto a nearby chair then sat down next to Staci on the bunk bed. "Are you missing Sarah?"

"Of course, but it's my stomach that's bothering me." She pressed a hand to her abdomen. Thankfully, that wasn't a lie.

"You're wanting to go home, right?" Denise stood, crossing her arms. "You promised you'd try to stick this out."

"I'm not going home," Staci said, making up her mind just as the words spilled out. "I'll pass on dinner, but hopefully I'll feel up to joining the group later on."

"Are you sure?" Denise laid a hand on Staci's forehead. "At least you don't seem to have a fever."

Staci allowed a small smile to curve her lips. "Thanks, Mom."

Denise's gaze went to the bag on the bed. "I'll leave you in peace to rest as long as you don't sneak off."

"I won't." Staci stood, picked up the bag and dropped it on the floor. "I'm going to lie down."

"I'll be back in a while to check on you." Denise gave her a hug. "I know it's rough being away from Sarah. I'm proud of you."

Staci watched her friend leave the room. She felt bad for allowing Denise to think it was all about missing Sarah. But it was necessary to keep the past where it belonged, so she couldn't confide in her friend about Eric. She'd been honest to all who had asked about Sarah's father. She'd told people that she'd become a Christian and that Sarah's father hadn't been interested in marriage so they'd gone their separate ways. She had only found out about the pregnancy after she'd left LA—and Sarah's father—behind.

There was no way she wanted to introduce Eric as Sarah's father. For if Eric ever found out about Sarah, their whole life would change—and not necessarily for the better.

Even though he'd become a Christian, there were aspects of Eric's personality that Staci doubted would ever change. He had always been a perfectionist and never left anything undone. He'd always focused on how perfect she was. Her body was perfect. Her appearance was perfect. Her playing was perfect. The desire to keep that level of perfection in order to please him had just about done her in. And though she didn't care what he thought about the changes in her, she had no idea how he'd react to meeting his daughter. In the eyes of the world, her little girl was anything but perfect. Staci wasn't going to give him the opportunity to reject her because of that.

It was absolutely necessary that she convince him that this thing between them was done. Finished. Over.

Eric glanced around the room at the tables filled with people. Dinner was well underway, but there was no sign of Ana. He saw the man she'd been with earlier, but she wasn't among the group at his table.

"Lookin' for someone?" Trent spoke over his shoulder.

Eric glanced at him. "Finished eating already?"

"Nope. Got waylaid. Should we find a couple of seats?"

Fairly certain that Ana wasn't coming to dinner, Eric nodded and followed Trent as he weaved his way among the tables to the one where people from their church sat. The bowls of food on the table were nearly empty, but there was enough left for the two of them to get at least one helping. That was fine for him since his appetite had long since fled, but he had a feeling it would barely put a dent in Trent's hollow leg.

"Attention, everyone!" A man stood at a microphone in the corner of the room. "We need your help cleaning up. Please scrape your plates into an empty bowl on the table and stack them. All the dishes need to be cleared off to the metal racks that are being wheeled out of the kitchen. Once we're done here, let's move into the meeting room for some fellowship."

The noise level in the room increased significantly with the screech of chairs and clatter of dishes and silverware. Eric took a couple more bites of food before handing his plate over to be scraped. He helped gather up the glasses and placed them on the rack.

"Let's go," Trent said to him once the tables were all cleared and the racks were wheeled back into the kitchen.

People began to fill every available seat in the main meeting room. Eric and Trent snagged two on the far side of the room. As luck would have it, his seat gave him a perfect view of the door. And a perfect view of Ana when she walked in a few minutes later. She'd changed into a thick pink sweater and blue jeans. Her hair was pulled back, making her look more like the Ana of six years ago.

He watched as she looked around the room. Their gazes met. Eric waited for her to look away. There was no change of expression on her face, just a blink, and their connection broke as her gaze continued to travel the room. Had their relationship really been reduced to a quick glance?

Eric frowned.

He wasn't sure why, but he hadn't wanted to believe her when she'd said it was over, that she'd moved past him. But from all appearances, she was telling the truth. But what about him? He'd searched but never had the closure of finding her and figuring out what had gone wrong. And even though he'd heard her explanation of what had prompted her departure, it wasn't over for him. Not by a long shot.

Without another look in his direction, she walked to a group of people kitty-corner to where he sat. It was with interest that he watched who she interacted with. A woman with a passel of black curls smiled as Ana approached. There were two ways to skin this cat. He'd prefer to go directly to Ana, but, if necessary, he'd find another way to get the answers he needed. He always did.

The ancient piano sounded amazingly good as the pianist began to play. Eric wondered why Ana wasn't the one at the keys. There wasn't any doubt in his mind that no one in the room played even half as well as she did.

The program progressed with lots of singing and then a short devotional. Eric had to force himself to keep his attention on the leader of the meeting and not on Ana. There would be time for that later.

As soon as the meeting ended, everyone was invited to hang around and play games, chat or partake of yet more food that had been laid out for them in the dining room. Though Trent, along with a large group of other men, made a beeline for the food, Eric lingered behind, waiting to see what Ana would do, where she would go.

She sat for several minutes talking with the black-haired woman, a tall man with dark blond hair standing over them. His hand rested on the nape of the woman's neck as he looked around the room. Eric averted his gaze, not wanting the man to know he was staring at them.

Out of the corner of his eye, Eric watched for Ana to stand. It wasn't long before she and the woman both stood and made their way out of the meeting area. He followed them and ended up in the dining room.

Eric bided his time, waiting for the moment when she'd be alone. He was fairly certain that she'd go out of her way to not let that happen, but he was patient. When he wanted something bad enough, he could wait.

While he waited, Eric grabbed a small paper plate and filled it with a handful of chips and a couple of slices of cheese. A cup of coffee rounded off the snack quite nicely.

He wandered the room, chatting with a few people he recognized from church. All the while he kept an eye on Ana and her small group of friends. As he dumped his empty plate and cup into the garbage, he saw the black-haired woman and her man head back to the main room. When Ana approached a table and took a couple of things, Eric didn't give her any opportunity to escape this time.

"Ana?" To her credit, she didn't show any signs of tension at the sound of his voice.

She turned to him, no expression on her face. "Eric. How are you enjoying the retreat so far?"

For a moment, Eric wanted to say something—anything—to rattle her composure. But if this was how she wanted to play it, he'd do it her way. "It's not too bad. My first time at something like this. How about you?"

Ana hesitated. "Yes. My first time, too. I'm glad the forecast is nice for the next couple of days."

His patience dropped almost to zero at her comment. "Is this what we're reduced to, Ana? Talking about the weather?"

"I'm not sure we have anything else to discuss," Ana said as she dropped her napkin into the garbage can.

Eric realized in that moment that not everything about Ana had changed. The steely composure she had when performing and the guard she'd rarely let down—even around him—were still firmly in place. Getting any answers from her was going to be a challenge. That may have been daunting to any other man, but Eric liked challenges.

"I just want to know why you left like you did," Eric said.

Ana turned toward him. "I told you earlier. I knew our relationship couldn't continue as it was since I had become a Christian. You made it fairly clear that marriage was not something you were interested in. That kind of left me in a difficult spot."

"Okay, so that explains why you ended the relationship, but why did you go into hiding? Even your agent wouldn't tell me where you were."

Ana glanced away from him, and Eric saw a tiny crack in her composure. But when their gazes met again, it was gone. "I figured it would be difficult for me to be around you. Either the temptation would be too great and I'd give in or I'd have to watch you get involved with other women. I wasn't strong enough to deal with either of those situations back then. The simplest solution was to leave."

"I looked for you," Eric told her, suddenly finding it important that she know that.

Ana's head dipped. "I know. Bethany told me that you'd contacted her. I'm sorry it didn't end better. I took the easy way out, I know that.

But since then I've managed to build a life for myself, and I'm assuming you have, too."

"So does that mean we can't keep in contact with each other?"

"What we had between us…" Eric saw a flush rise on Ana's cheeks. "Well, that side of things was always a strong connection. I don't want to find out if that is still true. I will not put myself into a situation that could lead to something we'd both regret."

Eric wanted to argue with her, but he understood what she was saying—he just didn't like it very much. He took a step back from her. "I wouldn't try to convince you to do anything like that now. My life has changed as well since we were together." Even as he said the words, Eric knew that she would be a big temptation for him, too. Just seeing her again, he felt that pull. It surprised him with its strength after so many years apart. "Well, maybe if God wills it, we'll run into each other again sometime."

Ana didn't respond, just stared at him with her big blue eyes before turning and walking away.

Staci blinked then blinked again. Moisture threatened to flood her eyes and spill down her cheeks. It shouldn't have been this hard. Their relationship had ended six years ago. That should have been more than enough time for her feelings to disappear. But looking at him again, seeing all the things that had attracted her to him in the first place, made it hard to deny the fact that she still felt…something for him.

But right now protecting her little girl was more important than anything else. Sarah, her precious daughter, who would never grow taller than three or four feet. Who would have to live a life filled with challenges because of some people's inability to accept those who weren't like them. Staci couldn't chance that Eric would react in a similar way.

She knew perfection was important to him. He hadn't just wanted that from her, he'd held himself to that same standard.

Working out regularly. Dressing immaculately and always having his hair perfectly groomed. From the looks of him now, that was still how he lived his life. He may have been wearing jeans, but they would no doubt be expensive brand name ones, and the white long sleeve cotton shirt he wore with them had been perfectly pressed.

I wonder what he thinks of me now. She finally allowed herself to entertain the thought that had been on the edges of her mind since seeing him again. Staci knew her body had filled out—pregnancy tended to do that. She hadn't fought to lose the remainder of the weight she'd gained while pregnant. In fact, she'd kind of enjoyed having a few more curves. In those first couple of years, it had seemed very important to become the total opposite of the person she'd once been. That had included growing her hair out and keeping the extra weight.

For too long she'd worked to present the image everyone else thought she should. Staci liked herself better now. But if Eric's idea of perfection was who she had been, maybe it was as much for her own sake as Sarah's that she couldn't let him back into her life. A lot of things may have changed, but rejection by the man she loved was something she could handle only once in her lifetime.

"Hey. You feeling sick again?"

She had been so lost in her thoughts, Staci hadn't seen Denise approach. She gave her friend a weak smile—it was all she could muster up at that point. "Yeah. I think I'm going to go back to the cabin and lie down."

"You don't feel up to staying for the late night fellowship?"

Staci shook her head. "I want to enjoy tomorrow, so I think I'll call it a night and get some extra rest."

"Okay. I'll try to be quiet when I come in."

"No problem. I brought ear plugs."

Denise gave her one last look before allowing Philip to lead her away. Staci pulled her jacket on and left the lodge. The night was clear so the stars stood in vivid contrast to the black sky. At any other time, she would have enjoyed the sight, but tonight she wanted nothing more than to burrow beneath the blankets on her bed and retreat from the world.

Once in her room, Staci changed into a pair of sweats and a large t-shirt. She spread out the sleeping bag and blanket she'd brought along. They'd all had to come with their own bedding since the camp was not outfitted with enough for their whole group. Staci turned off the overhead light and left the door open just a crack so a little light from the main room shone in. She slid into the sleeping bag and plumped her pillow.

Curled up on the lumpy mattress, Staci allowed herself to indulge in a wash of tears. It had been quite some time since she'd cried. And it would be a while before she'd do it again. Tonight, and only tonight, would she allow herself to feel the pain of lost love.

Tomorrow she had to be strong, but in the semi-dark of the room, so far from home, she cried for what might have been.

Overnight, Eric had decided that he wouldn't look for Ana, wouldn't seek her out. Yet the minute he walked into the dining room for breakfast the next morning, his gaze circled the room—searching.

He found her friends first then saw her sitting next to them. Her blonde hair was braided and hung over her shoulder. She wore a dark blue sweater that stood in vivid contrast to her hair and no doubt brought out the blue of her eyes. He'd always loved her in blue. It was a color that looked perfect on her.

He took a step in her direction then halted. He couldn't push her. She had disappeared once, she could do it again. It seemed that perhaps the best way to do this was to get to know the woman and man she spent time with. Though she had made her argument about not staying in contact, he wasn't able to completely let her go. All he needed was a conduit, a channel, to keep up to date on what was going on in her life. Eric couldn't bear the thought of completely losing contact with her again. Seeing her had brought every other relationship he'd had with a woman into sharp focus. She was the reason he'd never been able to connect with them the way they wanted. How could he when the shadow of Ana lingered in his heart?

He spent the rest of the day waiting for the opportunity to talk with Ana's friends. He didn't know if Ana was trying to avoid him because he didn't give her the chance to. True to her request, he left her alone.

Chapter Three

STACI spent the day on pins and needles. She kept an eye on Eric, ready to move if he approached her. It was almost anti-climactic when he never came near her. She had stuck close to Denise and Philip most the day, just in case, but as dinner ended, Ana decided to take some time to go back to the cabin and freshen up. The next part of the evening would last until midnight when they rang in the New Year all together.

She took a few minutes to phone Miriam and Sarah. They were having a grand time watching videos and eating popcorn. Miriam assured her that Sarah would be in bed well before midnight.

"Are you going to be all alone when the clock strikes midnight?" Staci asked.

"I certainly hope so," Miriam replied with a chuckle. "I plan to be in bed."

"You're not staying up?" "I've rung in enough new years that I'm not worried about missing this one."

"Thank you, Miriam." Staci finished the call and hung up. She flopped back onto the bed and stared up at the bunk above her. Initials had been etched into the wood. She reached up and traced the rough lines, wondering about the person who had carved them.

As a child, she'd never been allowed to attend a camp like this. This would have been considered a frivolous waste of time. If it hadn't revolved around school work or her music, it hadn't been allowed. That she'd ever had the courage to break free from her parents still amazed her. And breaking free from them had given her the strength to break free from Eric, too.

Staci rubbed a hand over her eyes. She curled onto her side, seeing her daughter in her mind. Her eyes were the same dark brown as Eric's. He may not have been in her life, but not one day during the past six years had gone by without her thinking of him. How could she not when her daughter was a constant reminder?

Wary of giving in to the emotions of the night before, Staci sat up. She went to the small bathroom in the cabin to splash water on her face. Taking a deep breath, she stared at herself in the mirror. Dark circles beneath her eyes showed the lack of sleep she'd had the night before. Tonight would probably not be any better. Chances were, she wouldn't sleep well until she was safely back home. Away from Eric. Away from her past.

Not wanting Denise to come in search of her, Staci only took a few minutes to fix her makeup and hair. The walk back to the lodge was cold, but refreshing. She felt more rejuvenated when she walked into the warmth of the lodge. Immediately, she spotted Eric sitting near the fireplace with a man who had spiky dark blond hair and was wearing a bright red shirt. Their gazes met, but he didn't get up or do anything to make her feel threatened.

Had he truly gotten the message?

Staci glanced around to find Denise and Philip. They were seated with others from their church, and she made her way across the crowded room to join them. Before she could say anything, the worship team invited the group gathered there to sing with them.

If it hadn't been for her turmoil over Eric, Staci would have thoroughly enjoyed the evening. She loved music and right then the choruses and hymns they sang were soothing. She closed her eyes and tried to let all her concerns slip away. As the minutes ticked by, Staci found herself relaxing. This would all work out, she was sure it would.

Midnight drew closer and as it did, memories began to work their way into her mind.

A kiss.

A touch.

The start of a new year with the man she loved.

Would she ever experience that again?

"Let the countdown begin!" the leader encouraged them. "Ten… nine…eight…"

Staci joined in the count as they headed into the New Year. Once the clock over the fireplace began to strike midnight, people all around the room cheered and began to hug each other. To her right, Denise and Philip shared a kiss. Fighting a jab of jealousy, Staci looked away from them and right into Eric's gaze.

In his expression, she saw the shared remembrance of years past. Her heart clenched with a bittersweet yearning. The two New Year's Eves she'd spent with him had been her happiest up to that point. And now, as they shared the memories through a glance across a crowded room, it reinforced the very reason why they couldn't be around each other.

Breathless at the memory, Staci looked away. She touched the base of her neck and the necklace she still wore after all these years. Beneath the texture of her sweater, she felt the shape of the pendant. It was a musical note with a diamond inset in it. His gift to her for their last Christmas together. Only she hadn't known—and neither had he—that was what it was.

Swallowing, Staci turned away and gave Denise a hug. "Happy New Year!"

A few others in their group joined them for hugs as well. It took about ten minutes for the noise to dim. When things had finally settled down, some of the people began to leave the room. Others settled back into their seats, chatting with those around them.

"I'm going to the cabin. Are you hanging around here?" Staci asked Denise.

"Yeah, but I'll walk with you. I want to grab something."

Arm in arm they left the lodge. "So, we met a friend of yours tonight. Although he knew you as Ana."

She should have known that he wouldn't just leave her alone. "That's an old nickname."

They had reached the steps of the porch and climbed up together. Denise opened the door and warmth rushed out to greet them. Once inside, Denise turned to her. "How do you get Ana from Staci?"

"My full name is Anastacia."

Denise stared at her for a long moment then something sparked in her expression, and her eyes widened. "*The* Anastacia?"

"I suppose that depends on who you're talking about." Staci tried to put off the inevitable revelation. How on earth had Denise made the connection from just the name? Though it wasn't a surprisingly common name, it also wasn't that rare.

"The pianist. I have all your CDs."

Staci nodded. "Yes. I know."

"I've always thought there was something vaguely familiar about you but could never put my finger on it. You look different from the pictures I've seen of you." Her brows drew together as she scowled. "Why didn't you tell me? How could you keep such a secret?"

"It wasn't that I wanted to keep it a secret, it was just part of a life that I was trying to leave behind."

"And Eric is part of that life?"

"Yes. He was an old friend." *That* was an understatement. "It was a bit of a shock to see him again."

"Philip recognized him."

Staci shot her a startled look. "Recognized Eric?"

Denise nodded. "There was lots of footage of him following his release."

"Release? From what?" Staci was beginning to wonder if they really had met her Eric.

Denise gave her a quizzical look. "You don't know? He was kidnaped while in Iraq three or four years ago. He was released a little while later."

A sick feeling flooded Staci. She hadn't known. In the years following Sarah's birth, her world had narrowed considerably. She'd rarely watched the news. All that had been important at that time was setting up her new life and adapting to the fact that her daughter needed special attention.

She pressed a hand to her stomach. "I had no idea."

"He wasn't sure if he'd get a chance to talk to you before the retreat was over, so he just wanted to know what church we were from. Said he might stop by."

The walls pressed in on Staci. She should have known better. In the time they'd been together, Eric had never, ever given up on something.

Was running her only option once again?

Denise touched her arm. "I'm sorry. I didn't mean to upset you with that news. I just assumed you knew."

Staci gave her a weak smile. "It's not your fault. I cut off contact with all my friends in LA when I became a Christian. My life had to change then, and it meant leaving behind all the people I knew. Making a clean break was the best thing I could do."

"I understand." Denise reached out and gave her a hug.

Staci gathered herself together. "You need to get back to Philip. He's going to be wondering where you are."

"You're going to be okay?"

"I always am." She gave Denise what she hoped was a reassuring smile. "I'm going to head out first thing in the morning."

"Missing your girl?"

"More than I thought possible." Staci covered her mouth to hide a yawn.

"I guess it's good you insisted on bringing your own car then."

"Yep." Desperately needing to be alone, she gave her friend another hug and sent her on her way.

Tremors set in as soon as Denise left the cabin. Staci walked to the room on shaking legs. She barely made it to the bed before they gave out from under her. A cacophony of emotion thundered through her.

Fear led the way.

The next morning, Eric wasn't surprised to not see Ana…Staci. He had a hard time thinking of her as Staci. To him, she'd always be Ana, but if he hoped to fit into her world, he needed to begin calling her by what she wanted to be known as now.

After breakfast, most of the people began packing up and leaving. Some planned to stay and enjoy the day, but Eric was among those heading back to the Twin Cities early. He had unfinished business that needed tending. First up was Melanie. When he'd called before leaving the camp, she'd agreed to meet with him for lunch.

Since it was on his way, he stopped by his folks' place in Rogers to check on them.

"Eric! Happy New Year!" his mom said when she let him in the back door of the house.

The warmth of her greeting created a welcome that embraced Eric. He let out a deep breath and felt tension he hadn't even recognized ease from his shoulders.

"Want a cup of coffee?"

"That would be great." Eric watched as his mom got a mug from the cupboard and filled it with coffee. With quick movements, she added a teaspoon of sugar, a splash of cream and gave it a stir. She set in front of him. "Just as you like it."

"Thanks, Mom." Eric took a swallow. It still surprised him that not only were his parents back in his life, but he was enjoying a relationship with them in a way he never thought he would. "Dad not here?"

Caroline McKinley set a plate containing several cookies and a couple of muffins in front of him. "He's at Victoria's. She needed help putting together that bookcase we gave her for Christmas. Did you need to talk to him?"

"No. I just thought he'd be here." Eric took another sip of his coffee. He set the mug on the table and ran his fingers along the smooth edge of the handle. "I found Ana."

"Really?" His mom abandoned the cloth she'd been using to wipe the counter and came to sit across from Eric. "I thought you'd given up on that."

Eric stared at his mom, wondering as he did, that he'd never recognized her quiet strength when he was younger. All he'd seen was how she took his dad back after he'd cheated on her. He'd humiliated her—more than just the affair. They'd had to leave their mission assignment in Africa and eventually the mission altogether because of what his father had done. He'd hated him for years because of all that had happened since it had robbed them of the life they'd loved. He and his younger sister, Brooke, had loved Africa and their adjustment back to life in the US had been rough.

His mom's face showed the years. Lines bracketed her eyes and mouth. Her hair had long since turned gray. Yet there was a peaceful beauty about her that Eric had never seen in anyone else. He mourned the years he'd foolishly spent far away from his family, hoping to distance himself from all they believed in. God had been gracious in giving him another chance instead of abandoning him to his bad choices and lifestyle.

His mom reached over and placed her hand over his briefly. "Are you okay? Was there something wrong with Ana?"

"Staci," Eric said. "She goes by Staci now."

"Is Staci okay? How did you find her?"

"Surprisingly enough, we kind of found each other." Eric took a cookie from the plate and bit into it. He swallowed, took a swig of the coffee and said, "I ran into her at the singles' retreat I was just at."

Caroline pulled back, her faded blue eyes wide. "Really? Wow. That certainly was a turn we couldn't have anticipated." A slow smile lifted the corners of her mouth. "What was she like?"

"Different. Six years has changed us both."

"Well, I know it has changed you for the better," his mom pointed out. "How about her?"

"Two days at a retreat with dozens of other people wasn't exactly the ideal place to chat. And then let's not forget her reluctance to actually talk to me."

Caroline gave a slow nod of her head. "She wasn't happy to see you."

"I guess you could say that. Shocked, for sure."

His mom got up and poured herself a cup of coffee. She put double in hers what she'd put in his and rejoined him at the table where she took a cookie for herself. "Maybe she needs time to get used to the idea of seeing you again. You yourself said she must have had a good reason for disappearing like she did."

"Actually, Mom, I believe I said that she must have *thought* she had a good reason to disappear."

"You don't know her mind, son." His mom gave him a stern look. "Are you going to give her a chance to explain, or just judge her without hearing her side?"

Eric sighed and slumped back in his chair. "Old habits are hard to break."

His mom's expression softened. "I know, but you need to keep trying to break it. She's still young, Eric, be gentle with her."

"Actually, she's not that young anymore." Eric smiled at his mom. "And it's just like you to defend someone you've never even met."

"I'm hoping that will change."

He didn't have the heart to tell her how unlikely that was. Though he hoped that eventually Ana…Staci might decide to give them a shot at friendship.

"I gotta run, Mom. I'm meeting Melanie for lunch."

"How is Melanie?" His mom stood and took their cups to the sink.

"Not sure but since she decided it's best we go our separate ways, I'd imagine she's doing better." Eric placed his hands on the table and pushed up to a standing position.

His mom turned from the sink, her hands dripping water onto the floor. "You're just full of cheery news today. What happened with Melanie?"

"She felt that we weren't as close as we should have been. I guess she feels I was being distant from her."

"Is she right?" Trust his mom to ask the one question he didn't want to answer. Given the events of the past couple of days, the answer would most likely have to be yes.

"I guess we need to talk about it a little more before I can answer that question."

His mom gave him a hug. "I'll pray for you two. And for Staci, too."

As he sat with cup of coffee number four of the day waiting for Melanie to arrive, Eric realized that his goal for this meeting had changed. When Mel had initially agreed to meet with him, Eric had been determined to win her back. But now...now he just wanted to apologize that he hadn't been able to be what she'd needed.

"Eric." Melanie slid into the booth across from him. She pulled off the knitted cap she wore and ran her hair through her short blonde hair. Her blue eyes were serious as she regarded him. "How was the weekend?"

"Interesting," Eric told her, not really wanting to get into the details of all that had gone on. "Most of it was enjoyable."

"I'm glad." Melanie looked up as the waitress approached their table. "I'll have a glass of iced tea and the grilled chicken salad with ranch dressing."

Eric waited for the waitress to write Mel's order down. "I'll have a cheeseburger and fries." He lifted his cup. "And a refill, please."

Once the waitress had left them, Melanie leaned forward, her arms resting on the table. "Listen, I need to apologize for how I ended things. I shouldn't have done it on the phone, and my timing was a bit off, too."

"Is there ever a good way to end things?" Eric asked.

Melanie shrugged. "I suppose not. But I am sorry."

Eric sat back in the booth. "I'm not here to get you to change your mind. I just wanted to apologize for not being able to give you the relationship you wanted."

The relief on Melanie's face hit him like a hammer in the gut. He had been unaware of how unhappy she'd been with him. Clearly, he was more dense and oblivious than he thought.

"Your heart wasn't in it." Melanie picked up her knife and turned it over and over between her fingers. "If I had to guess, I'd say your heart belongs to someone else. I don't want to take second place to another woman in my man's life."

Chapter Four

ERIC tossed the Styrofoam take-out container onto the counter in his kitchen. After Mel's statement about not taking second place to some other woman in his life, conversation had died. How exactly could he respond to that? He could no longer deny her observation since seeing Ana—Staci—again.

He jerked the fridge open and grabbed a can of soda. After popping the tab, Eric took a swallow and removed a plate from the cupboard. He set the can down and opened the take-out box. After putting the burger and fries on the plate, he nuked it for several seconds.

Leaning a hip against the counter, Eric crossed his arms and mulled over the meeting with Mel. It could have gone worse. At least she hadn't ranted and raved or dumped water on his head. Their meeting had just…ended.

When the microwave beeped, Eric pulled the plate out, grabbed the can of soda and headed for his office. He hadn't bothered to tell Melanie about Ana. *Staci*. Actually, in this case, Ana was the right name, because *she* was the woman he'd never had closure with. The Staci he'd met at the retreat wasn't the same woman Ana had been.

Eric rubbed his forehead. Too many names. Too many personalities. Too many women!

He picked up a fry, realized he'd forgotten to bring some ketchup, and tossed it back onto the plate.

His intent wasn't to get back with Staci—at least he didn't think it was. When he'd first discovered she'd disappeared, he'd wanted to find her in order to continue what they'd had together. But when he'd stopped his search, he'd moved on. He'd dated—okay, not successfully—but at least he'd tried. Staci was part of his past. An important part and one he needed to resolve apparently, before he could have success in any future relationship.

Unfortunately, he couldn't deny the biggest draw to Staci was physical, and he just didn't trust himself. The spark was still there, but physical intimacy was nothing to base a solid relationship on. And their previous intimacy would only interfere in anything they tried to build now. No, all he wanted from Staci were some solid answers and closure.

Eric turned on his computer, taking bites of his burger as he waited for it to boot up. Slow and easy was the best way to approach things with Staci. In a surprising turn of events, he now had an appointment with Staci's friend Philip on Friday. It was one way to keep himself in Staci's life—even if it was just on the outskirts. And since there wasn't a new relationship on the horizon, he had some time to figure out how best to deal with her.

Opening his email, he found several messages from his supervisor at BlackThorpe. His plans for the week changed upon the opening of the first one. It looked like his trip to New York had been moved up. The three guys he was supposed to meet with before their departure to Africa needed to leave sooner than expected. The next three emails were actually from his boss' secretary with information on his flight and where he'd be staying and his itinerary once he got to New York.

At least he'd be back for his appointment on Friday with Philip. And maybe it was good he had something to keep him occupied for the next few days. Though he doubted anything could really keep his thoughts from Staci and the tangled mess of their past.

Staci folded a tiny t-shirt and placed on the top of the pile. Her suitcase sat open on the window seat in her bedroom. Open, but empty. She hadn't put the suitcase away after emptying it upon her return from the retreat. But she still hadn't actually put anything back into it. Though there were piles of clothes around it, she hadn't packed them yet.

She sat down on the edge of the bed and took a deep breath. All week she'd been trying to figure out what to do. All week she'd been waiting to hear from Eric. Yet here it was Friday and still no word from him.

What did that mean? Was he really going to leave her alone?

"Mama?"

Staci looked up to see her daughter standing in the doorway of her room. "Hey, sweetheart." She waved her in. "Did you have a good nap?"

"I didn't want a nap," Sarah told her indignantly.

Staci just smiled. She ran her hand over Sarah's soft, dark curls. The little girl leaned against her leg and stared at the piles of clothes. "Are we goin' somewhere?"

"I'm not sure. Right now, I'm just sorting stuff." Staci picked Sarah up and sat her on her lap, an action made easier by the little girl's small stature due to her dwarfism. "Would you like to go on a trip?"

"Maybe. On television, there's a Disney boat. That would be fun."

Staci nodded. "That would be." She was fortunate to be in the financial position of being able to take her daughter on such a trip. And maybe now would be a stellar time to get out of Dodge.

Sarah slid off her lap and headed for a nearby pile. She plucked a dress from mid-pile causing the clothes to tumble onto the floor. "I wanna wear this." She held it up to her shoulders. "It's my favorite dress."

Staci motioned her to come back over. She helped her take off her shirt and pants and slid the dress over her head. It took just a second to zip up the back. "You look beautiful." She folded the recently rejected clothes and set them beside her on the bed. "Are your legs hurting you?"

Sarah shook her head emphatically. "No. I don't need medicine."

Staci watched as her daughter sashayed out of the room as only a five-year-old little person could. Surely there was no one in the world who wouldn't fall in love with her beautiful little face and bubbly personality. But what would Eric think? Mr. Perfection. Would he have a problem with the fact that his daughter was a little person? She'd always be stared at. They'd discovered that already and she wasn't even six years old. There would be physical things she could never do, but Staci had chosen early on to focus on all the things that Sarah could do.

Her refrigerator was covered with amazing pictures that Sarah had drawn. They cooked together. They danced together. They read together. Staci was determined that Sarah's life would be so rich and full that she'd never regret the things she wouldn't be able to do. One of the things she did long to give Sarah was a father and maybe a brother or sister down the road.

It had been Sarah's regular requests for a sibling that had finally spurred Staci towards trying out the dating scene again. Though the few guys she'd gone out with had been nice, none of them had stirred her emotions. Vince had seemed promising, but events at the retreat had shown her otherwise.

How could she think of ripping Sarah away from the stability they'd developed in their life here in Minneapolis? Staci stood and left her room. She found Sarah seated on the floor of the living room, her dress spread out all around her, eating a banana. For now, the children's program on the television would keep her occupied.

As she stood there watching her, Staci knew she couldn't take this all away from her daughter. If Eric did show up, she would try her best to keep Sarah's existence from him. If he did find out and couldn't accept Sarah for who she was, Staci would make sure that Sarah never knew her father had rejected her.

And it would be Eric's loss in the end.

Eric pulled into the underground garage of his apartment block with a sigh of relief. It had been one of his busier weeks, with his trip to New York and his attempt to get caught up once he got back. He'd been tempted to put off his appointment with Philip, but the pressure he'd been under lately at BlackThorpe made him go ahead with it.

He entered his apartment and went to his office to put away his briefcase. The trip to New York—though busy—had been enjoyable. He'd gotten to spend hours talking about a place he loved, a culture he was well-versed in. Though he'd only been nine when they'd left Africa, Eric had continued to expand his knowledge of the continent and all the countries it contained.

When he'd graduated from high school, Eric hadn't been able to afford college on his own, but he knew he had to get away from his family. Particularly his dad. Joining the military had seemed like the logical thing at that point. And being on active duty, he was able to get some discounted tuition rates to study what he really wanted to get into. Armed with his courses in international security and his military experience, he'd been approached by one of the men he'd served under to join their company in LA, offering security to corporations working overseas. He'd left the military and joined that company, eager to use his knowledge. He had been good at his job and they had paid him well for it.

But then had come the day when none of his knowledge, none of his experience, had been enough to keep him from being taken hostage by a rebel group in Iraq. He had taken unnecessary risks—an all too common practice since Ana had left him—and had paid for it when he'd agreed to take someone else's place at a meeting and then hadn't arranged for proper security. He had known better, but he simply hadn't cared. But God had had plans for him.

After being released by his captors, his spiritual revelation had led him back to his family in Minneapolis. That had meant leaving the company in LA, but it hadn't taken long for BlackThorpe to approach him so he hadn't been unemployed for long. His job with them had been a bit different. Rather than going out into the field as security, he'd been given assignments that involved educating businessmen and other people traveling into areas with sensitive security issues. It had worked for him so far. Though it had still involved travel, the risk was lower.

But he'd been hearing murmurs lately from his supervisor that he was going to be sent on a longer assignment. Right then, the idea didn't sit well with him. Part of his agreement with Marcus Black when he'd hired him had been that there would be no long-term assignments. Since nothing official had come through yet, Eric was just biding his time. He really didn't want to end up working hands-on security for three or more months, which is what he'd been hearing.

The buzzer for the security door went, drawing him back to the present. He left his office and made his way down the hallway to the foyer.

"Yo!"

"Yo? Let me in, Eric."

Grinning, Eric pressed the button to let her in. He opened the door and leaned against the door jamb waiting for the elevator to arrive on his floor. When it did, Victoria stepped out, a large pizza box in her hands. "Hey, Eric, have time for some supper?"

Eric smiled and took the box from her. "Pizza? With you? Anytime." He stepped back so she could come into the apartment. As they walked through to the kitchen, he noticed her limp was a bit more pronounced. "How's the pain these days?"

Victoria slid onto a chair at the table just off the kitchen. "Some days are better than others. They're talking hip surgery now."

"How do you feel about that?" Eric asked as he put the pizza box on the table and went to get a couple of sodas from the fridge and two plates.

She didn't answer him until he sat back down across from her. "I have a hard time contemplating another surgery. The one on my back was not fun."

"But the results were worth it though, weren't they?" Eric opened the box and lifted a piece out and set it on a plate for Victoria then took one for himself.

"Yes, for sure. I'm just weary of pain, you know?" Victoria reached across and patted his hand. "You wanna say grace?"

After he had said a prayer for the food, they spent a few minutes in silence as they ate their pizza. Eric looked at his sister and marveled again at the fact that she was actually speaking to him. After the way he'd treated her…he didn't deserve to have any sort of relationship with her. It spoke of her goodness and God's grace that he had a second chance with this sister.

She was ten years his junior but had a spiritual maturity that far outpaced his. She'd been born seven months after they'd come home from Africa. His nine-year-old mind hadn't been able to grasp all that had been going on then. First having to leave Africa so abruptly then having a sister who required so much extra attention—all it had said to him was that God was mad at them. Otherwise, why would He have let it all happen?

At fourteen, he'd finally understood everything. Then he viewed all that had happened as a punishment for his dad's sin. And he'd hated him for it.

"Do you think I should have the surgery?" Victoria asked as she laid the crust of her pizza down.

"You're asking me?" That she valued his opinion still surprised him.

Victoria met his gaze square on. "Of course. I want the support of the family in this decision."

"All I have to go on is the outcome from your back surgery. When I see how much better you are now than before, I want to say go for the hip surgery. But I didn't experience the pain before or after the surgery. In the end, Tori, you are really the only one who can make the decision. I'll support whatever you decide."

Victoria picked up a second slice of pizza. "So Mom tells me you ran into your old girlfriend."

Eric gave a shake of his head at the rapid change of subject. He swallowed the bite of pizza he'd taken and took a drink of his soda. "Yes. Talk about a strange twist of fate."

"Not fate," Victoria informed him. "God."

"What?"

Victoria cocked her head to one side. "You honestly think it was only a coincidence that you and Ana...Staci ran into each other?"

Eric had thought it was strange. Weird. Lucky. He hadn't really thought that maybe God had arranged it all. Was that possible? In New York, he'd had some time to think about the whole situation, and he'd come to a couple of realizations.

First, he owed Staci an apology. The man he'd been six years ago was a person he wasn't proud of. That man had been prideful, determined to get what he wanted. And what he'd wanted was Ana. He'd treated her badly—not in a physically abusive way—but he'd controlled the relationship from the start. He'd manipulated her into what he wanted her to be.

She'd been so young—twenty to his twenty-six—and so naïve that it had been relatively easy. So easy that he hadn't even realized what he was doing until well after things between them had ended. He knew now it had come from a place of fear. He hadn't known how to be in a relationship—not a real loving one—so he'd done his best to make sure he was never vulnerable to her by controlling all aspects of their interactions.

Along with that apology, Eric had decided to give her what she wanted. She'd made it clear she wanted him out of her life. He overruled her because he wanted answers. Once again putting his wants and needs ahead of hers. It was time for that to change. He'd go see her on Sunday and let her know that this time he really was going to leave her alone.

"Knock, knock." Victoria tapped the back of his hand with her knuckles. "What are you thinking?"

"That I've found Staci in order to try to make things right but nothing more. It's what she wants."

"Do you think she's prayed about it?" Victoria asked.

"What?"

"Do you think she's prayed about wanting you out of her life?"

"I haven't a clue," Eric admitted, intrigued by Victoria's observation.

"Then maybe you should ask her that the next time you see her."

Eric smiled at his sister whose faith was so much stronger than his own. "I just might do that."

The empty suitcase remained where she'd put it almost a week ago. Clothes still sat in organized piles, taken from and added to as needed. Unfortunately, she'd needed a few more things in the past couple of days. The flu had done a number on her little girl. Starting Friday night, it had been constant upchucking and diarrhea. Her washing machine had gotten a work-out.

Thankfully, things had slowed through the night and the last stomach upset had been just before midnight. Sarah had finally fallen asleep around one o'clock, woken around seven and spent the morning watching television. Staci had managed to give her bits of cracker and ginger ale every twenty minutes or so. She'd been so relieved that Sarah had kept it down. Hopefully, they'd turned the corner.

She'd kept her home from church though Sarah had begged to go see Miriam and her friends in Sunday school. Staci felt guilty that she'd been glad for an excuse to stay home. Knowing that Eric had the name of her church made it a place that was no longer safe. Sooner or later she'd go back, but it had been too soon.

Staci finished folding the sheets she'd had to wash after the last bout of sickness. Sarah had gone down to sleep just fifteen minutes ago. Hopefully, she'd sleep for several hours. Staci needed a little downtime herself. Her heart went into overdrive whenever Sarah was ill.

She carried the folded sheets to the hall closet and put them on a shelf. As she closed the closet, the doorbell rang. Though a sound machine in Sarah's room masked most of the noise, Staci didn't want to take the chance that the doorbell might wake her. She ran down the stairs, reaching the door just as the bell rang again. She jerked it open.

She froze when her gaze collided with hard dark one.

"I want to see my daughter."

Chapter Five

STACI gripped the edge of the door so tightly pain shot through her palm. Panic exploded within her along with regret that she hadn't taken Sarah and run when she'd had the chance. She should have known, but she'd been so reluctant to rip Sarah away from all she'd known. Now her world was going to change anyway, and there was nothing Staci could do to stop it.

"I want to see my daughter."

Although he didn't step any closer, his presence pressed at Staci in a palpable way. Sparks of anger flecked his intense gaze. Staci had seen it before—his anger—but it had never been directed at her. In their two years together, Staci had always done what he'd wanted, so he'd never vented his anger in her direction.

She took a deep breath. "Eric? What are you doing here?"

His eyes narrowed and she saw his jaw tense. "Let's not play games. I know you have a daughter, and I know she's mine."

Staci tried to mentally flip through all possible responses. Denial didn't seem like an option—not to mention, it would be a lie. How she handled things now could make a big difference in how it all played out. "You'd better come in. But please, keep your voice down. She's sleeping."

Eric didn't look at her as he stepped past her into the hallway. Just seeing him there—in her home—sent her already-fragile emotions into overdrive. She closed the door behind him then led the way into the living room. He made a beeline for the pictures on the mantel over the fireplace. Staci stood quietly, watching as Eric took in the chronicle of Sarah's life. Her most recent picture had been added just last week. The one where her little size was most obvious. That was the one he picked up.

He turned back toward her, his gaze still fastened on the picture. "Her name is Sarah?"

"Yes." Staci crossed her arms. "Who told you?"

Eric looked up. "Your friend inadvertently let it slip at church this morning. I guess she didn't realize it was supposed to be a secret."

"I never told her to keep it a secret," Staci admitted. "I never realized it would be…necessary."

Eric took a step toward her, the picture pressed to the breast of his jacket. "And why wasn't it necessary?"

Staci gripped the sleeves of her sweater. "You made it clear from the beginning of our relationship that there would be no marriage. No kids."

"That night—that last night before I left for Africa—you knew, didn't you?"

Staci shook her head. "I didn't find out until a few weeks later. By then I'd already left LA."

Eric turned away. "You should have told me."

"Really?" Staci took a step toward him, embolden by the anger that flared to life within her. "I should have told you so that you could do what? Marry me? We already know that wasn't going to happen. More than likely you would have told me to get rid of it." Though Eric had his back to her, she saw his shoulders jerk at her words. "You can't deny it. You would have told me to do what I had to do to rid our lives of the inconvenience of a child."

Eric set the picture back on the mantel. He shoved his hands into his pockets. When he turned back to face her, he looked like he'd aged ten years. "You're right. I probably would have. I guess we have God to thank for giving you the wisdom to not tell me. I wish I could say that I would have done the right thing—married you, taken responsibility for the child—but we both know that would be a lie. I was a very different person back then, A...Staci. Believe me when I say that I won't be making the same mistake twice."

"So you just plan to walk into her life and take over? It's what you've always done best, isn't it?" Tremors grabbed at Staci's legs, and she had to gather every ounce of her strength to keep from crumpling to the floor. She had wanted a father for Sarah, but she'd also wanted a husband for herself. Someone who would love them both. Who would love her like she'd never been loved in her whole life. Unconditionally, passionately and without reserve.

Eric wasn't offering that. At least, not to her. Pain gripped her heart with such intensity she nearly cried out. Was this the first step to losing her daughter to him?

"She's not like other children," Staci blurted out. If any part of the old Eric existed, he'd balk at claiming a child that was anything less than perfect.

Eric nodded. "Your friend mentioned that she was born with a type of dwarfism."

Staci jerked back. He knew and yet he was still here? "And that doesn't bother you?"

"It would have bothered the man I was when I was with you. For too many years I denied myself a relationship with my sister because of her dwarfism. I won't make the same mistake with my daughter."

Staci's brow creased. "Your sister has what Sarah has?"

"I don't know. Your friend didn't know the exact type of dwarfism Sarah has."

"Pseudoachondroplasia. It means—"

"I know what it means," Eric said. "When I finally made things right with Victoria, I found out all I could about dwarfism and her diagnosis." He paused. "Part of the reason I didn't want to have children was because of Tori. Because of my fear of having a child like her."

As Staci stared at Eric, she wondered what she'd ever seen in the man. No doubt it was having her first taste of male attention that had started it. The fact that he was good-looking and charming had helped. And he'd treated her well—or so she'd thought at the time. She was so used to having someone organize and run her life she hadn't objected when Eric had done it, too. Now, however, she'd balk if someone told her how she should do things. The woman she was now would never have fallen for the man Eric had been six years ago.

The question was…what kind of man was he today?

Staci had no words. She stood in the room with the man who had been her world at one time—yet he was a stranger to her now. It left her wondering if there was any way they could work things out as Sarah's parents. Would they be able to come to any agreements when neither of them knew the other anymore? She could see the potential for pitfalls all over the place—starting with the expectations of how the other would react based on past experiences. Staci had a feeling that misunderstandings were going to be the name of the game.

"The doctor told me it wasn't hereditary," Sarah said. "He said that if neither of us were affected, the chances were high it came from a gene mutation. There can't be any connection between what your sister has and what Sarah has."

"I guess it's just a very strange coincidence. Kind of like us meeting up at the camp again." Eric turned his gaze back to the pictures on the fireplace mantle. "Can I see her?"

"She's napping, Eric. She's had the flu for the past two days, so she's exhausted." Staci lifted her chin. "I'm not going to wake her."

Eric nodded. "I understand." He walked past her to the doorway. The front door opened with a gust of cold air. He turned back and reached out to grasp her arm.

Even through the thickness of her sweater, her body responded to his touch. Her breath whooshed out of her lungs—not out of fear, but because of things she'd rather forget.

"Don't run, Anastacia," Eric said to her, his gaze intense. He bent his head down to her. "I let my search for you lapse, but I would never stop searching for my daughter. Never."

Staci met his gaze without flinching. She would do what was best for Sarah. Since she'd been her mother for five years, Staci felt confident she was the only person qualified to determine that.

Eric released her arm and with a nod of his head, left the house, closing the door behind him. Staci reached out and turned the lock. She braced her hands on the door and took several deep breaths.

Her first instinct was to do everything he wanted when it came to Sarah, thinking that if she cooperated with Eric from now on, no more surprises would pop up. But there was a huge part of her that balked at the idea of once again putting aside her own feelings and opinions in deference to him. That's how it had once been. She couldn't let it go that way again.

But at all costs, she wanted to avoid pushing him to the point where he'd file for joint custody. She didn't know him well enough now to be certain that he could be the father Sarah needed.

Staci had a feeling the tug of war concerning what she should do was just beginning.

As Eric approached the on-ramp to I-694, he slowed for a moment. His apartment was the opposite direction from his parents at this juncture. Part of him wanted to go tell his family all he'd learned today. They had another grandchild. A niece to go with the nephew already in the family. But what could he tell them about her? Sure he could give a basic overview. She was beautiful and like her aunt. He didn't know what food she liked to eat. Or her favorite color. Not even her favorite show on television. All things a father should know.

Eric turned in the direction of his home. He needed some time to let this sink in. Anger. Regret. Disappointment. They all coursed through his veins in varying degrees. All of it was directed at himself. Not at Staci. She'd done what she thought was right for her and for their unborn child. There was no doubt in Eric's mind that Sarah would be a far different child had she been raised in the environment that he and Staci had lived in. If she'd even been allowed to live.

He had no one to blame but himself for the man he'd become as he'd left his teen years behind. Oh, he'd felt justified in blaming his father, but there were points along the way where he could have made different choices.

Eric pulled his car into the underground garage and turned off the engine. He gathered up his Bible and the bulletin from the church service that morning. Once inside the condo, he put them on the counter and turned his cell phone back on. He'd switched it off when he'd gone to see Staci to make sure they had no interruptions.

There were no messages on the cell, so he set it on top of his Bible. He stood for a moment in the kitchen, uncertain of what to do next. What *did* one do when they found out for the first time that they had a daughter? A five-year-old daughter?

His world had been blown out of orbit. Control and order had been wrenched from his grasp. He felt like a boat adrift on a huge ocean with no sign of the shore in sight. It was an unfamiliar feeling, one he didn't like.

Eric peeled off his jacket and dropped it over the back of a chair. He loosened his tie and headed for his bedroom. In ten minutes, he was in the gym he'd set up in his spare room, muscles burning as he pumped more weight than usual. He'd worked out many a problem in his life while pumping iron.

Unfortunately, it didn't seem to be working as well this time.

"So you're telling me that you want to leave the company?" Marcus Black asked, his hands resting on the desk in front of him, fingers intertwined.

"Not *want*, Marcus. I *need* to leave BlackThorpe."

"What's wrong with your job?"

Eric looked across the desk at the man he admired and had enjoyed working for. "Only one thing. The pressure I'm getting to take a long-term overseas assignment."

Marcus leaned back in his chair, a frown on his face. "That was part of your contract, right? No overseas assignments?"

"Yes, that was in the contract."

"So you're saying that the only reason you're leaving is because of that?"

Eric nodded. "I don't want to leave Blackthorpe. I just feel that my requests to not be pressured into taking them have been brushed aside."

"You've talked with someone about this already?"

"Of course." Eric hoped he didn't sound as indignant as he felt. "I wouldn't be making a move like this if I hadn't exhausted my efforts here. I spoke to John Timmons several times about it. Mentioned that my contract precluded assignments like the one to Africa."

"Well, your resignation letter was the first I'd heard of it." Marcus's brow creased over his intense blue eyes as he leaned forward. "Let's chat here, Eric."

Staci got up Monday morning, determined to keep her usual schedule. After Sarah picked out her outfit, she helped the little girl get dressed. Thankfully, she'd eaten a huge breakfast, which showed more than anything that she was doing one hundred percent better than just twenty-four hours earlier.

Surprisingly, there had been no early morning call from Eric. She hadn't given him her number but so far he'd managed to figure out everything else in her life. Getting a phone number should be a snap for him.

"Going to the 'tudio, Mama?" Sarah asked.

"Yep. Did you get your videos?"

Sarah lifted the bag from the floor next to her. Staci bundled them both up and headed out for the car. The sun was shining, but the air held a bite to it. A typical January morning in Minnesota.

The drive only took ten minutes. Though she could have had her studio in the home, she decided to lease a space instead. Choosing a location close to the house had been the compromise. She pulled to a stop in front of the strip mall. Sarah darted ahead and waited for her at the door.

Once inside the studio, Staci put the lunch she brought into the small fridge. Sarah knew her routine and settled into the tiny playroom

Staci had set up. Because she had no immediate lesson, she left the door between the piano room and the playroom open as she took the time to practice herself.

As in years past, her music was her release. Into the notes, she poured her confusion, her pain, and hurt. For the first time in several years, turmoil ruled her world again. She didn't like it. Not at all. She was angry at Eric. Six years ago she'd been hurt when he'd not done what she'd hoped. Today...today she was just plain mad.

Why couldn't he have left her alone?

He had always said the last place he'd ever live was Minneapolis. She'd counted on that when she'd looked for a place to settle after leaving California. Why was he here?

Eric headed for Philip's as soon as his meeting with Marcus was over.

"Is Philip available?" Eric asked the secretary behind the desk in the main area of Philip's suite of offices.

"If you'll give me your name, I'll check." The woman stood and looked at him expectantly.

"Eric McKinley. I spoke with him last week."

"Have a seat." The secretary waved toward the chairs against the plate glass window. "I'll be right back."

Eric didn't sit down but shoved his hands into his pockets and stood staring out the window. Gray clouds were gathering on the western horizon. Though the day had started out sunny, it was turning dreary. Things sure could change in a hurry. Kind of like his life. He never could have predicted the outcome of his meeting with Marcus.

"Mr. McKinley?"

Eric swung around to see the secretary had returned.

"Philip will see you now."

"Thank you," Eric said and followed her down the hallway.

Philip stood as Eric walked into the office. "Hey, Eric. I didn't expect to see you so soon. Have a seat."

Eric settled into the chair across from Philip. "Sorry for barging in unexpectedly. I just came from a meeting with Marcus Black."

"And how did that go?" Philip sat down and leaned back in his chair. "I've heard good things about Marcus."

"I haven't had too many personal dealings with him...being a lower man in the company."

"How did you manage to get the meeting today?"

"I handed him my resignation since my immediate supervisor wasn't in. Apparently John Timmons, my boss, hadn't passed on my objections to the assignments I was being pressured to take. When I told Marcus about that, he said it was no problem since my contract specifically spelled out about the long-term assignments. Apparently, my other skills and experience were worth far more to them on this side of the ocean."

"Why was Timmons putting so much pressure on you to go?"

"Probably because he feared what has ended up happening."

"And what's that?"

"I now have John Timmons' job, and I believe he'll be on his way to Africa shortly."

"So I guess that means you won't be coming to work here," Philip stated matter-of-factly.

"I'm afraid not. But you'll never know how much I appreciate your willingness to give me a job."

"Our loss is their gain, that's for sure. Maybe we'll just utilize BlackThorpe for security issues rather than having our own in-house person for the time being."

"I would be happy to work with you on that. Especially with regards to Africa. That continent is my specialty, and if I can give helpful information to you or your workers, I'm definitely up for that." Eric stood and held out his hand. "Well, I don't want to take any more of your time. I have a couple more errands to run this afternoon."

Gripping Eric's hand in a firm shake, Philip said, "I hope we'll see you around."

"You can count on it." Eric grinned. "Just ask Staci—I'm like a bad penny, always turning up."

Philip walked with him to the foyer are where Eric said goodbye and entered the elevator that would take him to the main floor. As he pushed open the front door of the building, a gust of bone-chilling wind buffeted him. Eric pulled the edges of his jacket together and headed for his vehicle. It wasn't until he was in the protection of the car that he realized he'd forgotten to ask Philip for Staci's number.

Now he had no choice but to go to Staci's house and see if she was home. And if she wasn't, he planned to sit in her driveway until she came back.

Chapter Six

STACI saw his vehicle the moment she turned into her cul-de-sac. She'd never actually seen his car, but there was no doubt in her mind that the black truck in her driveway belonged to Eric. The thought crossed her mind to turn and run, but it wasn't like she could just drive past the house and keep on going. Staci had a feeling that said black vehicle would be on the tail of her smaller SUV before she even made the turn in the cul-de-sac.

There was no sense in running.

She couldn't say why it irked her that he'd picked the right side of the double driveway to park on. It was like he knew which side she'd need free to pull into her spot. When she hit the button of the garage opener, the door slid open to give her a clear shot to her normal parking spot.

Staci guided her car inside and killed the engine. Her finger poised over the button on the opener. One push and a steel door would separate her from Eric. She hesitated then closed her hand into a fist and lowered it. Before she could pull the handle to open the door, it opened from the outside. Staci looked up and saw Eric leaning with a forearm against the roof of the car.

She swung her legs out of the car and stood, forcing him to take a step back. "I didn't expect you here today."

Eric shrugged, his gaze going to the tinted back windows of the SUV. "I didn't have a number to reach you so I was left with coming here."

"I figured if you'd tracked down my house you could get my phone number, too. Last I checked, Denise and Philip both had it."

Eric arched a brow. "It didn't seem you were all too keen to give me the number at the retreat."

"You were right about that." Staci leaned in and got her purse.

"I want to see Sarah."

"She's sleeping in her car seat." Staci held out her keys. "Why don't you open the door, and I'll bring her in."

"You have an alarm system?" Eric asked as she dropped her keys into the palm of his hand, careful not to touch him.

Staci nodded. "My birthday."

Eric hesitated, his gaze leaving hers for a moment.

Trying to ignore the shaft of pain that shot through her, Staci gave him the number. Every encounter with him cast their previous relationship in a worse light. He'd remembered her birthday the two years they were together. But it obviously hadn't been a date that had stuck with him in the past six years. She hated that she remembered his, that not a year had passed when she hadn't thought of him on August eighth and wondered how he was doing.

Staci waited until Eric unlocked the door before she opened the back door of the SUV. Sarah's eyes opened as Staci unlatched the straps on the car seat. Her big brown eyes gazed at Staci sleepily. "Home, Mama?"

"Yes, sweetheart, we're home." Staci finished with the straps and helped her from the car seat. "We have a visitor."

"Really?" Sarah grinned. "Miss Miriam?"

"No. A friend I had a long time ago. He's come to see us."

"Will he like me?"

"Yes. He will." Hoping she was right, Staci pushed the button to close the garage door, gathered up their bags and held out her hand for Sarah. The little girl's fingers interlaced hers and together they walked to the door leading to the kitchen entrance. Her shortened legs stretched to climb the steps to the kitchen. They found Eric seated on one of the stools at the counter, facing the doorway.

Staci watched as his gazed zeroed in on Sarah. She watched for the telltale signs of shock, rejection. One such look and Eric would be out the door, and she'd be on her way to a new location.

Instead, she saw his expression soften as he watched Sarah take off her jacket. Eric moved from the stool to a lower chair at the table. Staci slipped off her own coat and hung them both on the hooks near the kitchen entrance.

"Sarah, this is Eric." Staci moved closer to where Sarah stood staring at Eric. She rested her hand lightly on Sarah's shoulder. "Eric, this is Sarah."

Eric leaned forward, bracing his elbows on his knees. "Hi, Sarah."

"Hi," Sarah replied, her head tilted to the side. Sarah loved people, but she'd learned to take it slow before assuming they loved her back.

Convinced that he wouldn't hurt her, Staci hung back. She settled on one of the stools, hooking her heel on the lower rung. And for the first time, Staci watched her daughter interact with her father. She closed her eyes then opened them, blinking a couple of times. This was the moment she'd never even allowed herself to imagine.

Eric watched the little girl who regarded him so seriously. Though clearly her dwarfism wasn't in any way connected to Victoria's, the resemblance to his sister was clear in the short stature. But more telling were the bits of himself he saw in her. The bits of Staci. She was perfect. Though the world might question his perception, say it was tainted by his fatherly view of her, he knew it was true.

It took all his inner strength not to reach out and pull her close. To wrap his arms around this precious child for the first time in her short life. "So, you girls hungry?"

Sarah's eyes grew wide. "Are we going out?"

Eric glanced over Sarah's head and saw Staci smile. It hit him in the gut as he realized it was the first time in six years that he'd seen that beautiful expression on her face.

"She loves to eat in restaurants."

"Is that all restaurants or just the ones with golden arches?"

"Well, the golden arch supper club is one of her favorites, but she'll eat pretty much anywhere."

"Since I want to make a good first impression, and I haven't been to said restaurant in quite some time, I think we'll go to…McDonald's!"

"Yay!" Sarah turned around to face her mother. "Can we go, Mama?"

Staci approached her and laid a hand on her dark curls. "Yes, we can." She looked at Eric. "Let me just freshen us both up."

Eric nodded and watched as they left him alone in the kitchen. He stood and walked into the living room, in search of the pictures he'd seen on his first visit to Staci's home. This time he zeroed in on the pictures of Sarah in her younger years. That first time, he'd just wanted to see what she looked like now. He could have walked right past her on the street and not known who she was. He had needed to know what she looked like, needed to know that he would recognize her from that moment on.

With a finger, he caressed each image of his daughter. Emotions coursed through him. Anger was most predominant but also most unfairly directed at Staci. He closed his eyes and turned that emotion back where it belonged—on himself. He had no one else to blame for why Staci had left six years ago.

"Ready to go?" Staci's voice drew him from the dark mood that had taken over him. He took a deep breath and practiced a smile before turning to face the two of them.

"I'm ready if you are."

Even with her dark hair and eyes, Sarah looked so much like Staci. There was no doubt they were mother and daughter. Her type of dwarfism manifested itself in her body, but her facial features were unaffected. There didn't seem to be as much of him in his daughter— just his coloring.

He wondered if there was any room in the family relationship between Sarah and Staci for him. Until that moment, he didn't realize how desperately he wanted to be part of that family unit. To be a father.

"We'll take my truck," Eric said as he crossed the room to where they stood.

"I think it would be best if we take separate cars," Staci said.

"Why?"

"Sarah's car seat is installed in my car. We can't take it out. And I'm pretty sure you don't have one in your truck."

Eric couldn't believe he hadn't thought of that. He obviously had a lot to learn about kids and their needs. "Okay. I'll follow you to the restaurant."

Not surprised that she hadn't offered him the opportunity to ride with them in her car, he backed his truck out of the driveway and waited for Staci to pull ahead of him. Eric followed hard on her bumper, determined not to get left behind. Now that he'd found Staci and Sarah, he'd do everything in his power to make sure they never disappeared again. The thought chilled him.

Staci headed to the closest McDonald's with a play area, fielding questions from Sarah as she drove. When she came to a stop in the parking lot of the restaurant, Eric's truck pulled in next to hers. Before opening her door, she took a deep breath, held it then exhaled.

"Going in, Mama?" Sarah asked from the back seat.

"Yes, sweetheart." Staci pushed open her door and met Eric as he came around the front of his truck. She opened the back door and unlatched the car seat. "Out we go." She lifted Sarah onto the pavement of the parking lot.

The little girl looked up at Eric. "You're tall."

"Yep. Just tall enough for my feet to reach the ground."

Sarah looked down at her feet then back up at Eric. "Mine reach the ground, too."

"Then you're just the right height for you."

Staci felt her heart soften a little toward Eric. Just a little. This was a side she had never seen before. Was it a common side now? Or one he pulled out when he wanted something? She knew from past experience that Eric wasn't above utilizing whatever was necessary to get what he wanted. And he'd made it pretty clear that what he wanted now was a relationship with his daughter.

"C'mon," Staci said, holding her hand out to Sarah. "We don't want them to run out of burgers before we get ours."

"Nuggets, Mama, not burgers."

"Right...nuggets."

Eric held the door open for them. Staci took Sarah into the area enclosed for the kids.

"What should I order for you two?" Eric asked as he shrugged out of his jacket and laid it across the metal back of one of the chairs.

Staci told him what they usually ordered. "Can you remember that? Or should I go get the food?"

Eric smiled at her, his brown eyes soft. "I think I can handle it."

Staci tried to ignore the flutter in her stomach. That smile of his had always done things to her. It wasn't fair that after six years apart he could still affect her in this way. She turned to help Sarah take her jacket off. "You can go play for a few minutes before we eat, okay?"

Sarah nodded.

"Just remember to be nice and don't jump off the structure, okay?"

Because it wasn't quite five o'clock, the play area was fairly deserted. Staci was glad for that. There was less chance of Sarah being teased and stared at when there were fewer children around. On more than one occasion, a mother had approached Staci to tell her that Sarah was too young to play in the play area. She tried to cut them some slack since most people were uninformed about kids like Staci. Even *she* had been clueless when they'd first told her about Sarah's condition. So she tried not to judge people for their innocent ignorance. It was the intentional ignorance of some people that got her back up.

Staci propped an elbow on the table and rested her chin on her fist. She watched as Sarah scampered up the enclosed part of the plastic structure. Little did her daughter know how much her life was about to change. Staci knew she couldn't deny Eric what he wanted. Not when it was what Sarah had been wanting, too. That father-daughter relationship.

"A penny for your thoughts."

Staci swiveled around to see Eric putting a tray down on the small table next to where she sat. A glance at the tray revealed that he'd managed to get their order right. "You don't want to know them."

His eyebrows rose at her response, but he didn't comment on it as he began to unload the tray. "Where's Sarah?"

"She's in the structure. With winter here, she misses being able to climb and slide outside."

"Do you want me to get her to come eat?"

Staci hesitated then nodded. While he walked into the open area where the play structure was situated, she set out Sarah's Happy Meal and then her own salad.

"The slide is the funnest thing," Sarah was saying as she walked back with Eric.

"I'll have to take your word for it because I don't think I'll get to try it out for myself."

Sarah giggled. "You're too big."

"But the slide is just the right size for you."

"Yep," Sarah agreed as she slid onto the bench-style seat opposite Staci.

Eric took a seat next to the little girl. Their seating arrangement gave Staci a clear view of them as they interacted throughout the meal. It was a sight that reassured and yet frightened her at the same time. Her daughter was clearly taken with Eric, but the end of her meal signaled a return to the play structure, and nothing interfered with playtime for Sarah.

Eric swiveled to watch as she scampered back to the structure. "She's wonderful."

"Yes, she is." There was no sense denying the obvious.

"When's her birthday?" Eric still didn't look her way.

Staci told him and could almost see the wheels turning in his head as he did the calculations.

Eric looked at her, his brow creased. "Okay, I'm going to ask a question to which I don't want the obvious answer." He paused. "How did this happen? We were very…careful."

Staci didn't want to think about that aspect of their relationship. "No birth control is one hundred percent effective. Plus, I'd been sick with the flu while you'd been gone and hadn't exactly done a great job of taking my pills during that time." She shredded a napkin onto the tray in front of her. "I didn't really think about it when you came home that time. I guess I'd missed enough to make it possible for me to get pregnant."

She glanced up in time to see Eric's eyes glaze over as he slowly nodded. "So the fact that I didn't want to be a father didn't play a role in your decision to go?"

Staci sighed, never having imagined she'd be having this discussion with Eric. "No. The major reason for my departure was that I knew our relationship couldn't continue. It was something I realized pretty quickly after becoming a Christian. You reinforced my decision that night by reiterating your position on marriage. What else could I do?"

"Did you consider telling me about your experience?"

Staci raised both eyebrows. "Are you kidding me? I'm pretty sure you told me at least once that the next time you darkened the door of a church would be at your funeral."

"Yes, I did say that." He let out a sigh. "You're right. It wouldn't have made a difference."

"In fact, it would have made things worse."

Staci saw Eric's gaze go past her shoulder and turned to see a small, blonde woman approaching them. She recognized her instantly as the nurse who had helped with Sarah when she'd been hospitalized in November. Staci started to greet her until she realized that the woman's attention was actually focused on Eric.

"Hi, Mel," Eric said as the woman stopped next to their table. "I didn't imagine you'd be in a place like this."

"Yeah, my one indulgence after a long week of work." She tilted her head. "How are you doing?"

Eric shifted on his seat. "Fine. And you?"

"Tired. Just worked a double shift. I'm on my way home."

Eric gestured to Staci. "Uh, this is—"

"Sarah's mom!" Mel said with a smile. "How is she doing?"

"Much better. She's playing right now." Staci pointed to where Sarah appeared at the end of the slide, a huge smile on her face.

"That's wonderful to see. So often we only see them when they're sick or on the mend, but seeing her having fun playing is great." Mel looked back at them with a smile. "I'll let you get back to your meal. I need to get home. I'm dead on my feet."

After they said their goodbyes, Staci watched as Eric's gaze followed the woman's exit from the restaurant. "Friend?"

Eric looked back at her, his expression unreadable. He paused before saying, "Ex-girlfriend."

"Really?" Staci arched a brow. "You on good terms with all your ex-girlfriends?"

"Apparently I'm a better friend than boyfriend." He leaned back and crossed his arms.

"How long does it take to get to that point? She seemed pretty friendly toward you."

Eric rolled his eyes. "Just a week."

"Oh my." Staci tried not to grin. She wasn't even going to try to figure out why she found it so funny that her ex-boyfriend was having girlfriend troubles.

"So what's my problem?"

Staci gave her head a shake. "What?"

Eric leaned forward, his expression serious. "You dumped me. Every girl I've gone with since you has dumped me. What's up?"

"Well, I just told you what *my* reason was. I have no idea why the other girls broke up with you." Staci was finding the situation funnier by the minute. "Why don't you ask them?"

"I do." Eric's expression had turned dark. "Never mind. Listen, I want my family to meet Sarah."

The rapid change of subject shook Staci. "Um…I'd rather take it a little slower. Sarah doesn't even know that you're her father."

"Then tell her." Eric's tone brooked no argument.

Staci felt her stomach clench, the salad she'd eaten just minutes ago threatened to reappear. "It's not that easy."

"What did you tell her about her father? That I was dead?"

Staci shook her head and swallowed. "No. I told her that sometimes someone isn't ready to be a mommy or daddy. When that happens, they don't stay a part of the baby's life."

"So she thinks I just left her?"

"No, I told her that you had a very busy job that meant you lived overseas a lot."

"And she bought it?"

"Well, she's only five. All she understands is that her daddy lives far away and can't come see her."

"So why don't you want to tell her that now I live closer and I *do* want to see her?"

Staci looked over to see where Sarah was. From the instant she'd heard her name at the camp, she had known this moment would come. Why hadn't she prepared herself? She took a deep breath. "Okay, I'll tell her. But can we go slow on having her meet your family? She's only five. Can we take this a step at a time?"

Eric regarded her. "Don't run off again."

Staci felt a surge of anger. "I'm trying to do what's best for my daughter, Eric. She's dealt with a lot in her short life. I think I'm the better judge of what's best for her."

"I'm her father. She has a right to know."

Staci crumpled the napkin she held into a tight ball in her fist. "You didn't want to be a father. You made that perfectly clear to me. I did what I had to for her and for me. We've done fine for the past five years." She leaned forward, her voice dropping to a harsh whisper. "You have *no* right to march into our lives and tell me what I should and shouldn't do. In fact, you have no rights at all."

Eric's eyes narrowed. "That's easily rectified."

Staci's breath caught in her lungs. She'd pushed him too far. Exactly what she'd vowed not to do.

"Mama?"

Staci looked over to see Sarah had approached the table. How much had she heard?

"Hi, sweetheart. Done playing?"

Sarah nodded. "But I want ice cream."

"We'll get you a sundae to go, okay?" Staci stood. "It's time to head for home."

Eric got to his feet as well. "This discussion isn't over. We'll do it your way for now, but drag your feet too long—especially with regards to my family—and I'll take things into my own hands."

Staci placed a hand over one of Sarah's ears and pressed the little girl's head against her leg. "Don't threaten me, Eric," Staci hissed. "I'm not the same doormat of a girl I was six years ago. I fight for what I think is right."

Eric's eyes narrowed briefly before he dropped down to Sarah's level. Staci moved her hand from her daughter's head.

"I'll see you again, cutie-pie." He touched her daughter's cheek. "Take care of yourself."

The look Eric gave her as he turned to leave would have crushed her six years ago. But she was stronger now. Wasn't she? If so, why were her legs shaking? Why did she feel like she was going to be sick?

"Ice cream, Mama?" Sarah tugged at her coat.

"Yes, sweetheart. Let's get you that ice cream." Staci pulled herself together. For the sake of Sarah, she had to stay in control. Of herself and the situation.

Chapter Seven

ERIC pulled out of the parking lot, anger pumping through his blood. The last time he'd been this angry at Staci had been when he'd come home after eight weeks in Africa to find her gone. He gripped his wheel, cranked it right and pulled onto the street next to the restaurant. His plan to head for home was averted when he turned into a nearby parking lot and came to a stop in a spot that gave him a view of the lot he'd just left.

It wasn't long before Staci came out with Sarah. The little girl held a cup in her hand which Eric assumed was the promised sundae. His heart clenched as he watched Staci lift their daughter into her vehicle.

He thumped the steering wheel with a closed fist. Man, he'd messed up royally. This latest situation showed him that he needed to rethink his game plan. He'd been using his previous experience with Staci to decide how to handle her now. As she'd pointed out to him, she was a very different woman now than she'd been six years ago.

And frankly, he was different now, too. He should *not* have acted the way he did. But he had, and now he owed Staci an apology. Another one.

Her SUV left McDonald's, heading back in the direction they'd come earlier. He wanted to follow her and apologize right then, but he decided to wait a little while. Hopefully until Sarah was asleep. This conversation needed to be held without the distraction of the little girl—no matter how wonderful she was.

Eric sat in the parking lot a little while longer, praying and gathering his thoughts. When he felt more calm, he turned his car in the direction of the nearest department store.

Staci checked in on Sarah one last time to make sure she was asleep. The little girl had been hyper after the trip to McDonald's but had settled down during her bath and bed preparations. Staci had managed to resist the pleas for more than one story. She'd tucked her in and kissed her goodnight before going to her own room to change.

Feeling more relaxed in a pair of flannel drawstring pajama pants and a long-sleeved thermal top, Staci went back downstairs to get a cup of hot chocolate. As she waited for the water to boil, she closed her eyes and took several deep breaths. While going through the bedtime routine with Sarah, she'd been able to put thoughts of Eric aside. But now that silence had descended throughout the house, Staci found that last horrid conversation she'd had with him replaying over and over in her mind.

She poured water into the mug, surprised to find her hand shaking. The spoon clinked against the sides of the mug as she stirred the water and cocoa. She tapped the spoon and laid it in the sink. Gripping the mug between both hands, Staci took a sip then walked into the living room. She flicked on the switch that started the gas fireplace and settled into the chair nearest the warmth. She drew her legs up and stared at the flickering flames.

When she'd stood up to Eric earlier, she'd felt so strong. So capable. But weakness had quickly set in. Even now her stomach trembled, and she began to second guess everything she'd said and done. What if she'd pushed him too far? What if he decided to pursue joint custody because of what she'd said tonight? She'd meant every word, but she could have said it in a more diplomatic way.

She didn't want this to escalate things, but if it did, she had no one to blame but herself. Staci knocked her knuckles against her forehead. "Stupid. Stupid. Stupid."

She set the mug on the small table next to the chair and clasped her hands together. A chill gripped her in spite of the warmth flooding the room from the fireplace. Staci pulled the fleece throw from the back of the chair and wrapped it around her shoulders. Their future hung in the balance and the man holding the scales was someone she didn't know anymore.

The man Eric had been six years ago hadn't been interested in being a husband or a father. Now he was back—different—and armed with enough information and power to turn their whole world upside down.

This was so unfair! How dare he march back into their lives and throw everything into upheaval. Just because he'd changed his life around. Just because now he'd decided he wanted to be a father. What right did it give him to do this to her and Sarah?

Staci looked upward. "Why did You allow this to happen? After all we've been through, why this?"

The doorbell rang, interrupting her internal turmoil. She debated just ignoring it, but when it rang again, she got up, still clutching the fleece throw around her shoulders. In the darkened hallway, she flicked the switch to illuminate the front porch. She went up on tiptoe to stare through the glass window near the top of the door.

Her heart skipped a beat when she saw Eric standing on the porch. She lowered herself, hands pressed to the wood of the door. The doorbell rang again. There was no ignoring it. He would know she was there after the porch light came on.

Taking a deep breath, Staci gripped the knob and twisted. A cold blast of air rushed in, eating through the flannel of her pants and socks. She stepped into the gap of the open door and stared at Eric.

"Can I come in for just a moment? I promise I won't stay long."

Staci debated then stepped back, opening the door enough for Eric to step into the hallway. She closed the door behind him and flicked on the hall light.

Silence hung heavy between them for what felt like an eternity before Eric cleared his throat. He shifted his weight from one foot to the other. "Listen, I'm sorry about earlier."

Surprise shot through Staci. In all their time together, he'd never apologized to her. Never. "Um...okay. I'm sorry, too."

"We need to talk soon, but I'm hoping that our next conversation won't go as badly." Eric held something out to her. "Here. I remembered that these were your favorite."

Staci stared down at the box of chocolates in Eric's hand. They were indeed a favorite of hers. One that she hadn't indulged in all that frequently since the extra pounds she'd gained with Sarah had never quite slid off. She released her tight grip on the throw and grasped the box of chocolates. Eric didn't let go of the box immediately, and she looked up to find him staring intently at her.

Warmth flooded her, making the throw suddenly unnecessary.

"I really am sorry," he said again, his expression seeming to support his words.

Staci didn't know what to say. But in the end, she didn't have to say anything. Eric released the box and opened the door. One more blast of cold air and he was gone.

Staci stood in the hallway staring in shock at the closed door, wondering again about the man Eric had become. He'd given her plenty of boxes of this chocolate in the past, but never before had it been for an apology.

She took the box back into the family room and settled back down in the chair she'd vacated earlier. The throw slipped off her shoulders as she sat there. The cellophane covering the box was sticky beneath her fingers as she remembered other boxes of chocolate. Ones she had never allowed herself to fully enjoy. When her finger snagged on a piece of paper taped to the top, she pulled it free and looked at it. It was Eric's business card. Turning it over, she saw that on the back he'd scrawled his cell and home phone numbers along with a message.

We need to talk. Call me when you're ready.

Her breath rushed out in a whoosh. The ball was back in her court. In addition to the candy, he'd given her back the control she so wanted.

Would this chocolate taste sweeter for how it was given? She scratched the plastic with a nail, ripping it open. Lifting the lid, Staci took one out and stuck it in her mouth. She put the lid back on and set the box next to the mug of hot chocolate so she wouldn't be tempted to take another. She pulled her legs up and wrapped her arms around them, savoring the taste of chocolate melting on her tongue.

She slid her fingers over the thickness of the card feeling the raised print of his business information. Though she was glad for this latest twist of events, Staci couldn't help but wonder how long it would be before Eric tried to wrest control back again. And then what would happen to her fragile world?

Suddenly, the chocolate didn't taste as sweet as it had moments ago. Staci picked up the mug of now lukewarm hot chocolate and washed the smooth taste of expensive chocolate out of her mouth.

∞

Eric stood from behind his desk and stretched. He walked to the window and stared out his tenth-floor window east toward the Mississippi River. The sun reflected brightly off the water, bringing with it rising temperatures. No doubt a lot of the snow would be gone because of the unseasonably warm day.

It had been two days since he'd given the chocolates to Staci along with his business card. She had a way to contact him, but short of camping out on her doorstep, he still had no way to get hold of her. He'd wanted to be patient with her. He'd wanted to let her take the lead in this. But this was ridiculous.

Two days! Couldn't she have made up her mind about whatever it was she wanted to do by now? He may have changed, but waiting around forever was still not something he was good at. Surely she realized that. And if she didn't, it wouldn't be long until she did. Eric would give her until the end of business today to call him. If he didn't hear from her, she'd find him once again on her doorstep.

Eric turned from the window and returned to his desk. He had more work since stepping into his new position. In addition to his previous projects, he now had administrative duties that didn't exactly excite him, but it was a small price to pay for being able to stay on this side of the world. Especially since he'd found out about Sarah.

Just after noon his phone rang. Keeping his gaze on the file he'd been perusing, he pressed the receiver to his ear. "McKinley."

"Eric? It's Staci."

Eric straightened, his attention immediately drawn from the file. "Staci? I wondered when I'd hear from you." There was a beat of silence on the other end, and Eric wished for a moment he could take his words back. "Is everything okay?"

"Everything's fine. I just wanted to let you know I told Sarah that you are her…father."

"Really?" Eric's breath caught in his lungs. "I don't know what to say."

"You don't have to say anything. I just wanted you to know."

Moisture pricked at Eric's eyes. For some reason, Sarah knowing the truth made it so much more…real. "Thank you, Staci. I know this isn't easy for you."

"She has the right to know. And she so badly wants a father."

Eric felt the weight of responsibility settle on his shoulders. He was no longer just a father in name. Things were going to change. "Can I come by and see her?"

Another beat of silence. "Sure. Why don't you come for supper? We're cooking Sarah's favorite."

Though shocked at Staci's invitation, he was not about to turn it down. "That would be nice. What time?"

"We usually eat at five-thirty, but you can come anytime."

Eric agreed and thanked Staci again. As he hung up the phone, Eric looked out the window in sudden appreciation of the sunlight.

Staci waited for the water to boil, wondering if Eric liked macaroni and cheese. He hadn't even asked what Sarah's favorite food was. She tapped the spoon on the edge of the pot and laid it in the spoon rest. In deference to his presence, she'd also baked a couple of chicken breasts and made a salad.

When the doorbell rang, she heard Sarah's footsteps racing toward the door.

"Sarah! Wait!" Staci stepped out in the hallway just as Sarah reached for the door knob. "You know the rule."

Sarah turned, her brow furrowed in a frown. "But it's my *daddy!*"

"We don't know for sure. Always let mommy check before you answer the door."

"'kay." The little girl planted her hands on her hips. "Check!"

With an exasperated smile, Staci went up on tiptoes to look out the window in the door. She gave a nod to Sarah when she spotted Eric's familiar face.

Staci barely had time to step away from the door before Sarah yanked it open.

"Daddy!" Sarah shrieked and threw herself at Eric.

Staci gripped the door knob and watched as Eric bent down to scoop Sarah into his embrace. She blinked as tears stung her eyes. For the first time in all the years she'd known Eric, she was seeing love on his face. But it wasn't for her…never had been for her.

Eric glanced up from his embrace of Sarah. Staci was staring at them with a shattered look on her face. Their gazes met, and in a heartbeat her expression smoothed out. What had been going through her mind to produce such an expression? He straightened as she waved them inside.

"C'mon in." She stepped back and opened the door all the way so they could come into the hallway. "Why don't you two go into the living room while I finish up dinner? Sarah, remember your picture books? You could show them to Er…your daddy."

"In there," Sarah said, pointing toward the entrance to another room.

As he carried her into the living room, he glanced over his shoulder in time to see Staci pass by on her way to the kitchen. She didn't even look in their direction. As he set Sarah down, he had to remind himself that this was likely very difficult for Staci. He needed to cut her some slack.

"Look, Daddy, look." Sarah pulled again on his hand. Eric turned his attention to her and the book she held out to him. "All about me."

Eric took the book and lifted Sarah onto his knee. "Okay, tell me all about you."

The books were a wonderful chronicle of Sarah's life. Eric could see the love Staci had poured into them. They'd made it through two books before Staci called them for supper.

"We'll look at the rest later," Eric told Sarah. "Your mom's calling us to eat."

The little girl slid off his lap and headed out of the living room. Not familiar with the layout of the house, Eric followed behind her.

"Wash up, sweetie," Staci said as she put a bowl and platter on the table.

Sarah slid a step-stool up to the sink and climbed to the top. Eric watched as she went through the motions of washing her hands. It was intriguing to see how easily she made her way around her world. Obviously, Staci had done what she could to help her daughter adapt to a world that was not friendly to someone her size.

"I hope you don't mind mac and cheese," Staci said from behind him. "It's a once a week treat for her. Not exactly adult fare."

"No problem." Eric turned, taking in her appearance for the first time. She wore a very casual outfit of jeans and a sweater, and her hair was pulled back in a ponytail and her skin appeared relatively free of makeup. The difference between Staci and Ana was startling. Even when they'd been home in their condo, she'd never dressed too casually. Usually, she had worn a dress, but if she did wear pants, they'd been pressed slacks with a sweater or blouse. Hair and makeup had always been done as well. It was quite a contrast, and one he found more attractive than he might have thought he would.

"You can sit on that side." Staci pointed to the side of the table that had two place settings. A booster seat was on the outer chair. Eric slid past it and settled onto the chair next to the window.

Staci helped Sarah into her booster then took a seat across from them.

"Can I pray, Mama?" Sarah asked.

"Certainly, sweetheart."

Eric listened in awe as his daughter said grace. The moment seemed almost surreal to him. He'd never have imagined he'd be sitting at a kitchen table with Staci listening to their daughter pray. It was absolutely amazing!

Neither he nor Staci said much throughout the meal. They didn't really have the opportunity as Sarah seemed determined to fill him in on all the things he'd missed in her life so far.

When they finished their meal, Staci said, "Go ahead and finish the albums. I'll bring dessert in."

Staci scraped the plates before putting them in the dishwasher. She didn't rush. They would still be perusing pictures for a while. She needed a bit of breathing room. The evening was taxing her in ways she hadn't imagined it would. It had taken everything within her to keep from slipping into the "happy family" mode, to imagine what it would be like if he didn't just want to take on the role of Sarah's daddy but of her husband, too.

But she couldn't let herself imagine what it would be like if he didn't just love Sarah but that he loved her, too. It was what she had longed for from him the two years they were together, but he'd never given that to her. They'd connected on a physical level very well. Emotionally, however…it was only through her music that they'd come close to sharing a deeper connection. But love? No, that hadn't been part of their relationship.

It would never work, Staci reminded herself as she wiped the table. More than anything she wanted a marriage that gave Sarah a good example of what a Christian marriage was all about. Distaste lingered whenever she thought of her parents' marriage. Having run into some good relationships and marriages after joining her church, she'd realized exactly how wrong her parents' marriage was. No respect between them. No love. And definitely no commitment. Oh, they had both been committed to the fame they hoped to achieve through their daughter. But that was *all* they had in common.

Staci never, ever wanted a marriage like that. She wanted one filled with love, laughter, and respect. And though she was uncertain of the laughter and respect with Eric, she could say without a doubt that love wouldn't be part of any marriage they had.

Six years ago he'd made no secret of his attraction for her, and love had actually been mentioned plenty.

I love the way you look in that dress.

I love the smell of your perfume.

I love your body.

Oh yes, he'd loved lots of things *about* her, he just hadn't loved *her.* And if he hadn't loved her when he thought her perfect, he certainly wouldn't love her now when she was pretty much the opposite of everything she'd been six years ago. In appearance and personality.

Staci slipped five cookies onto a small plate. She poured a glass of milk for Sarah and a cup of black vanilla hazelnut coffee for Eric. She piled all of it on a tray and walked through to the living room.

Eric sat on the floor with his back against the couch and his legs stretched out beneath the coffee table. Sarah knelt beside him, pointing out things in the last album. They both looked up when she walked in.

"Dessert for you two." Staci put the milk in front of Sarah and handed the coffee to Eric. Sarah immediately took one of the cookies when Staci put the plate on the coffee table.

"My favorite," Sarah informed him with a grin.

"They look delicious." Eric took one and bit into it. "I agree. They're very good."

"Half an hour until bedtime," Staci said then left them alone again.

She wasn't part of this relationship. Back in the kitchen, she pressed one hand to her heart and gripped the edge of the counter with the other. This was too hard. If only she could rewind a few days, maybe even a few weeks. She'd do things so differently.

But then she thought of her daughter, crouched beside her father, sharing her life with him. Staci rubbed her forehead. No matter the pain she was feeling, she knew she wouldn't take away what Sarah was enjoying now. The joy on her little face made the pain ease...just a bit.

When bedtime came, Staci relinquished part of her role in the routine to Eric. After helping to get her changed and washed up, Staci stood just outside the door, listening as Sarah talked her father into reading two stories instead of her usual one. Staci would have called him a softie, except she had caved on many occasions herself. When Sarah pushed for a third story, Staci turned and walked down the stairs to the kitchen.

Eric would be leaving soon and then—and only then—would she allow herself to fall apart. She took the time to write down her home and cell numbers on a small piece of paper for Eric. He would be down in a few minutes, and she wanted to return the favor of the numbers he'd given her.

"Staci?"

She took a deep breath and turned. "She asleep?"

"Out like a light." Eric moved closer. "One minute talking, the next asleep."

Staci crossed her arms. "Yeah. She has two speeds. Fast and stop."

Eric leaned a hip against the counter, hands in the front pockets of his jeans. "You've done such a good job with her."

"I've done the best I could. Kinda going into it blindly since the only example of mothering I'd had was one I never wanted to follow."

"Well, even though I've never met your mom, I think it's safe to say you've succeeded in not being like her."

Staci nodded. He was right. No matter what else, Sarah knew she was loved, something Staci had never experienced until Sarah was born. That unconditional, so-intense-it-hurts love. It was only from Sarah that she heard the words she'd longed for so many years to hear.

I love you, Mama!

Tears threatened to spill over, so Staci blinked and cleared her throat. "I suppose you want to set up a meeting with your family now."

"Yes, they'll want to meet her."

"Have you told them yet?"

"No, I wanted to make sure this was really happening."

"Just give me a call and let me know when the meeting is."

"I don't have your number," Eric reminded her.

"I wrote it down for you." Staci had to reach past Eric to retrieve the paper.

She glanced up at him and as their gazes met, she was flung back in time.

Did he close the distance between them? Or did she?

In the end, it didn't matter. His head lowered toward her as she lifted hers. Their lips met and waves of memories swamped her. She felt his hands at her hips as her fingers splayed across his chest. It was like coming home. Curling up with a favorite book. Tugging on a favorite t-shirt.

Everything she'd tried so hard to forget pushed past her barriers. His touch. His scent. His taste. When the kiss deepened, she clutched at his sweater, the edges of the paper she held cutting into her palm. His hands slid to her lower back, pulling her close.

Six years were gone.

In the time it took for their lips to touch, to feel the familiar press of his body against hers, their time apart vanished.

And then it was over.

He moved back. Put her away from him. Without a word, he retrieved the crumpled paper from her hand and left the kitchen.

Pain swamped Staci. It had hurt when she'd left him, but having him leave her without even saying anything—that hurt ten times more. It just reinforced what she already knew.

That physical connection was still there—as strong as ever—but love was not part of their relationship. Never had been. Never would be.

Chapter Eight

ERIC swung the truck around the cul-de-sac and headed out onto the main road. He drove two blocks before pulling over to the side of the road and turning off the headlights.

Could things have gone more wrong? He dragged a hand through his hair, not surprised to find it shaking. Of all the ways the evening could have ended, that hadn't even been on the list. Not that it hadn't been enjoyable. It had been. But that was the problem.

They couldn't go back to that part of their relationship. Six years ago, it had been the best of what they'd had. Now it would only be the worst.

Eric rapped his forehead with his knuckles. How was it that no matter which way he tried to go in this...relationship with Staci, it was the wrong way? And no doubt his next move would be wrong from Staci's perspective, too, but with each bad encounter, the chances of her bolting went up. He couldn't allow that to happen, which meant he had to pursue joint custody. If he made it so it was a felony for her to leave with Sarah, maybe she'd think twice about taking off again.

It was either that or marriage. But somehow he didn't think the marriage idea would go over all too well with Staci.

And now he owed her *another* apology. But there needed to be a plain understanding between them that what had happened at her house could never happen again.

He thought of that verse in Philippians….*whatever things are pure, whatever things are lovely, whatever things are of good report, if there is any virtue and if there is anything praiseworthy—meditate on these things.* What had passed between them tonight was not promoting pure, lovely nor virtuous thoughts in his mind. In fact, it was bringing up memories and physical feelings he couldn't allow himself to dwell on—and yet he kept playing them over and over again. He needed to rein in his thoughts and focus on pure things. It would take effort, but he could do it—this time—but if it happened again—if it kept happening—he would be fighting a losing battle.

Eric took a deep breath and blew it out, fogging the windshield briefly. He needed to put it behind him and move forward. Next on his list was to tell his family about Sarah. He'd held off for as long as possible, wanting to make sure that Staci would really let him claim the role of father before telling his parents and siblings.

He glanced at the illuminated clock on his dashboard. There was still enough time to go to his parents' place.

One more deep breath and he put the car into gear and headed for their house.

Staci woke feeling wrung out. It had taken far too long to fall asleep after her time with Eric. And then falling asleep had led to dreams or nightmares, depending on how she chose to look at the situation. What scared her most was that after their…interaction, Staci was almost willing to overlook the bad parts of their relationship and think about the possibility of being with him again.

She sat up, the blanket pooling in her lap. Rubbing her eyes, Staci swung her feet over the edge of the bed. There was nothing she'd like more than to stay in bed all day, but duty called. Both her duty as a mother and as a piano teacher. She couldn't bail on them, no matter how much she wanted to hide from reality.

Though exhaustion tugged at her, Staci went through her day, trying hard to keep her mind occupied with things other than Eric. It was with a sigh of relief that she closed the door behind her last student. She leaned against the door for a moment.

"Ready to go, Mama?"

Staci turned to find Sarah behind her, already dressed. "In a hurry?"

"Isn't Daddy coming for supper again?"

"I don't think so, sweetheart." Staci moved to pull her coat off the hook.

"But why not?" Sarah's brows drew together as her lips turned downward. "I want him to come for supper again."

"I know but not tonight." Staci bent down to button Sarah's jacket.

The scowl on Sarah's face was so intense it was almost funny. "Then can we go to McDonald's?"

Staci laughed, glad to be dealing with Sarah's problems instead of her own. "Okay, we'll go to McDonald's, but that's the last time we go this week. And you'll have to eat some of my salad. Deal?"

Sarah wrinkled her nose. "Okay. Deal."

After a quick stop at the fast food restaurant, they arrived home just after six. Staci checked her messages, a bit surprised to find nothing from Eric. She figured he'd be phoning to make arrangements to get together with his family.

"Can I color a picture for Daddy?" Sarah asked after she was showered and changed into pajamas.

"Sure." Staci pulled down the box of crayons, markers, and paper.

While Sarah colored at the breakfast nook, Staci started to make a batch of cookies. Between Sarah's chatter and the need to focus on the recipe, Staci found she was able to keep from thinking too much about Eric.

By eight o'clock, however, the house was quiet. Staci turned on the monitor to Sarah's room then went to the piano in the living room. It wasn't like the grand piano she had at her studio, but it played well enough and she needed the solace of her music tonight. It was the only thing guaranteed to occupy her mind completely.

Normally she avoided the classics—they were what her parents had demanded she play. It had been their dream that she play with the best orchestras across Europe and North America. But tonight, they called to her.

She rested her fingers on the coolness of the ivories and paused. She rubbed the smoothness, trying to pull the music from deep within her. Eyes closed, she pressed just one key. Then another. Soon it came, and the tension seemed to flow from her shoulders down to her fingertips and out onto the keys.

Music crashed as she launched into one of the more demanding pieces she'd memorized so long ago. All her fear, anger and uncertainty played itself out in her music. Then came a softer piece and with it, tears for love and heartache. As she played the last chords, Staci sat slumped on the bench. Spent.

As usually happened when she played, the tension had eased, and Staci felt more at peace. She lowered the keyboard cover and scooted the bench back. After turning off the lights in the living room, Staci went to the kitchen and poured water into a mug and stuck it in the microwave to heat it up.

When the doorbell went, Staci turned and stared at the entrance to the hallway. The last time her doorbell had rung at this time of night it had ended up being Eric. Something told her that was the case again tonight.

She heard the microwave ding as she headed down the hallway to the front door. A glance out the window proved her suspicions correct. Eric stood on her front porch, hands in the pockets of his jacket, head bent.

Did the man not believe in a phone? She'd given him her numbers. Could he not use them?

She switched on the porch light and swung open the door. "Sarah's asleep."

Eric nodded. "I figured she might be. Can I come in for a minute?"

Staci hesitated then stepped back.

"First, I told my family about Sarah. They want to meet her."

Staci had figured that would happen sooner rather than later. "When?"

"Sunday dinner after church. Would that work?" Eric's expression was serious. His brown eyes were nearly black with intensity.

"That would be fine. If you come to our church, you could take her right from the service."

Eric's brow furrowed. "I'm not just taking Sarah. They want you to come, too."

Staci couldn't identify the frisson of emotions that shot through her. Was it fear? Apprehension? Anticipation? She crossed her arms. "I don't know that that's a good idea."

"Staci, we have to figure out a way to work this out together. This can't be me and Sarah and you and Sarah. You are part of who Sarah is. My family wants to get to know you."

"Are they angry with me?" Staci asked.

"Angry?" Eric looked surprised. "Why would they be angry with you?"

"Because I kept Sarah away from them all these years."

Eric gave a shake of his head. "I don't think you have to worry about that. They know that the blame for that lies firmly on me." He gave her a persuasive look. "Please. For my parents' sake. Besides, it will probably be easier for Sarah to have you there."

"Okay. We'll come."

Eric hesitated then said. "We need to talk about last night."

Staci swallowed. "I'd rather not."

He sighed and closed his eyes for a moment. "Listen, Staci, all I want to say is that we need to make sure that doesn't happen again."

It felt like a knife through her heart, but it wasn't totally unexpected. And he wasn't wrong. Unable to make her vocal cords work, Staci just nodded. She reached past Eric to open the door.

"I'm sorry," Eric said as he stepped onto the porch.

As she closed the door behind him, Staci wondered exactly what he was sorry for. She had a list of things she wished he'd apologize for, but she figured whatever it was he was sorry for didn't appear on that list. *He* probably didn't even know what he was apologizing for.

Staci locked the door, turned off the porch light and returned to the kitchen. She heated up her water again and stood there stirring in the hot chocolate powder. It surprised her that she wasn't completely falling apart.

The man who still tugged at her heartstrings had told her there'd never be anything between them. He'd dismissed their kiss as nothing.

But he still understood that she was significant in her daughter's life. Right now, that was the most important thing.

⌒⌒

Sunday morning, Staci dressed herself with as much care as she did Sarah. She felt like a huge test loomed before her. Would they think her a worthy mother for their grandchild?

"You look pretty, Mama," Sarah said from her perch on the bed.

Staci smoothed her hands over the lavender sweater set and black pants she wore. It had taken her forever to decide on the outfit. She wanted something that she felt good in to give her confidence. Hopefully, this outfit would do the trick because her nerves were getting the better of her.

"Ready to go?" Staci lifted Sarah from the bed. The little girl wore her favorite dress. A long, full-skirted purple velvet dress with a white lace collar. It was a little formal for church and a dinner, but Staci wanted Sarah to wear something she felt good in as well. And it appeared to be working as Sarah gave a little twirl as she skipped to the doorway.

Knowing that the temperature had dropped through the night, Staci bundled Sarah into the long coat and high boots she had for her. Staci pulled on her own coat and boots before going to the garage to head for church.

Once there, Sarah darted off to find her class which Miriam taught. After Sarah was settled in her class, Staci made her way to the sanctuary where the main adult Sunday school was held. She slipped into the first empty row behind the group meeting for the class.

One of the church's assistant pastors led the group and started them off with prayer. Mid-prayer, Staci felt movement on the pew beside her. Cracking an eye open, she glanced sideways, surprised to see Eric seated next to her, head bent. Once again, the surreal feeling of the moment struck her—sitting in a church with Eric next to her.

"I had a car seat installed for Sarah. Do you want to have a look at it?" Eric asked Staci after the service. "I'd like to be able to take her in my vehicle on occasion."

"Sure. Let me pick Sarah up from her class and we can go."

He followed her down the hallway to the door of the room where Sarah waited. She greeted her dad enthusiastically and insisted on introducing him to her teacher. He didn't miss the startled look that she shot Staci then him.

"We've got to go, sweetie," Staci said as she took Sarah's hand. "We have to be somewhere for lunch."

Sarah seemed reluctant to leave her friends but followed her mother to a nearby coat rack. Staci slid a small coat off a hanger and handed it to Eric.

"Do you mind if we take my truck to my parents' place? It would be easier than you having to follow me." Eric bent down to slip the coat on Sarah and then buttoned it. "We can drop your car by your place and go from there."

The little girl gave him a smile that squeezed his heart. He glanced up and saw Staci watching them, her expression serious.

He straightened, keeping a hand on Sarah's shoulder. "So, do we just take one vehicle?"

Her gaze went from Sarah to him. "Okay. That's probably easiest."

"Then let's check out that car seat." Eric held out a hand to Sarah, and they walked out of the church together with Staci right behind them.

They were at his parents' place within the hour after a drive that had been anything but quiet. As usual, Sarah had plenty to say about everything they saw as Eric drove. Of course, that was after she filled them in on all she'd done in her class that morning. Staci responded when comments were made directly to her, but otherwise she sat with her head turned toward the passenger side window.

Eric would have given his left leg—and maybe his right one, too—in exchange for something that would let him read her mind. Her expression gave absolutely nothing away. She'd been schooled at a young age to never let any emotion show. And she was as good at it now as she had been six years ago. He'd never known what she was thinking. Of course, he hadn't taken the time to investigate further. He had seen what he wanted to see. She'd seemed happy, except for that last night when she'd quietly asked about marriage. Clearly, she had depth that he'd never imagined—never explored. He'd had his chance and lost it. Getting close to her now was like trying to cross a moat filled with alligators. Her defenses were well and truly in place, and he didn't foresee them coming down anytime soon.

"You okay?" Eric asked as he pulled into the driveway of his parents' home.

Staci shot him an unreadable look. "I'm fine."

"You don't look fine," Eric pushed.

She shrugged. "You didn't talk much about your family."

Eric nodded. "That's true. At the time, I was estranged from them, and I can guarantee that I wouldn't have had anything good to say because of that. It's probably better I didn't talk to you about them back then." He paused. "They're great people, Staci. Just give them a chance."

"Can we go in now, Mama?" Sarah was definitely more eager than her mother for this event to take place.

He heard the snap of Staci's seatbelt releasing and undid his own. "I'll get Sarah out."

There was a rush of cold air as the passenger door swung open. He opened his own door and then got Sarah from the back seat. Staci stood waiting for them at the hood of the truck. Eric took Sarah's hand and laid a hand on Staci's back to guide her to the front door.

The door swung open before they even got there, revealing the welcoming faces of his parents.

Staci picked at the food on her plate. Not that it wasn't good. In fact, it was quite delicious—what she'd managed to eat anyway. Eric's family had been friendly and obviously curious. She could see that they doted on Eric and now they doted on Sarah. The little princess was soaking up the attention like a sponge in water.

Sarah had long ago abandoned her plate of food and was now playing with the new toys given to her by her grandparents and aunts. If it hadn't been *how* these people had come into her daughter's life, she'd be delighted at their presence. Seeing Sarah with her grandparents made her realize just how much she'd been missing by not having family around. They'd welcomed her with open arms and shared the same unconditional love for Sarah that Staci did.

"Feeling a bit overwhelmed?"

Staci looked over and saw Victoria standing near the edge of the sofa, a plate of food in her hand. With a little effort, the small woman settled on the couch beside her. "I know it's a lot to take in all at once. We're pretty harmless. I promise. Well, most of us."

Victoria's gaze went to where her older sister sat before looking back to Staci.

"It's just been Sarah and I for so long that this is all pretty new. To me at least." Staci gave Victoria a wry grin. "Sarah seems to have taken to it quite well."

"She's a wonderful girl." Victoria lowered her plate onto her lap. "You've done a great job with her."

"I've tried my best."

"She is living the childhood I wish I'd had." The wistfulness in Victoria's voice surprised her.

"I thought...I thought your family were Christians."

Victoria gave her a sad smile. "They were. They are." She paused. "Did Eric not talk about his past?"

Staci shook her head. "No, he didn't tell me much of anything. When we were together before, he just said he wasn't in contact with his family anymore. I never pressed for answers."

Victoria looked around before she spoke, her voice low. "My parents were missionaries in Africa. Eric was nine years old when my dad had an affair with a single woman missionary there. The family was forced to leave the mission field and eventually they left the mission as well. My mom didn't realize she was pregnant with me until they got back to the States. I was born seven months later.

"Eric was angry at everyone back then. The mission, our mom, our dad…especially Dad." The young woman looked down at her plate. "And God…he was very mad at God. When they diagnosed my condition, Eric viewed it as yet another horrible thing in his life. He couldn't figure out why God was letting all the bad stuff happen to us."

A whole lot of pieces fell into place in the puzzle of her and Eric's relationship regarding his reluctance to get married, to have children. Too bad it was too little, too late. Did he still carry a lot of the same prejudices even though he'd turned his life around? Clearly, from his father's example, being a Christian didn't exempt a person from temptation and sin.

"The tension in my early years meant that I didn't get a whole lot of attention. At least not the positive kind. The only time I seemed to have their undivided attention was when I got sick or hurt. My mom did her best to make me tough."

"Tough?"

"Yes. She knew my life wouldn't be easy as a little person, so I think she felt it was best that I be strong, able to withstand teasing and bullying." Victoria paused. "I never felt very safe as a child. She did what she thought was best. Sarah is so fortunate to have you."

"I've tried to protect her from places where I know she'll suffer teasing, but I also try to encourage her to be around people and to be herself."

"Whatever you're doing looks like it's working."

"She will be going to kindergarten in the fall. That's making me nervous. Sometimes I worry that I'm being too overprotective."

"Better to err on the side of caution," Victoria told her. "At least from my perspective. She seems stronger and more well-adjusted than I was."

"You seem fine now."

Victoria laughed. "Are any of us truly fine?"

"True. But your relationship with your family appears good," Staci pointed out.

"It is good. It's better than it was for sure. Eric may have left us physically when he turned eighteen, but we all left the family emotionally at different points in our lives. Brooke, for example, hasn't ever forgiven our dad and has been determined to live her life the way she wants since she left home."

"Is her son's father still around?" Staci asked.

Victoria shook her head. "We don't even know who he is. She was pretty tight-lipped with that information. All I know is that he just helped reinforce Brooke's impression that all men suck."

Staci looked over to where Brooke sat talking with her mother. Her dark auburn hair hung in loose curls over her shoulders. She wore a peasant style blouse and a long skirt, giving her a bit of a hippy look. All she needed was a ring of flowers around her head.

"So don't think we've got it all figured out. We've got a long ways to go but having Eric home again has helped tremendously to bring us back together." Victoria waved her hand at the gathering of people in the living room of her parents' home. "It isn't easy, but I keep praying we'll come to full healing in our family."

Even with the rift in their family, Victoria and Eric had something she'd never have. She felt a pang of wistfulness. Barring a miracle, she would never see her family in similar circumstances. "You're still very blessed. You have love."

"Yes, I am. We all are." Victoria reached out and gripped her hand. "Be a part of our family, Staci. We're not perfect—never will be—but we'll love and accept you and Sarah if you let us."

Staci hesitated. How could she be part of this family? It didn't appear that Eric was making room in his life for her. For Sarah, yes, he'd opened his life wide open, but there was no indication of any role for her. She knew that he was including her in things now, but Staci was pretty sure that was to help Sarah adjust to the new people in her life. And what about when he got his next girlfriend? That would be terribly awkward. And heartbreaking.

But she liked Victoria—and the rest of the family, too. After being on her own for so long, this warm, loving family pulled at her.

"Sorry." Victoria gave her an apologetic look. "I don't mean to push you. Just know that you're always welcome at family functions."

Chapter Nine

ERIC snapped Sarah into her seat and climbed behind the wheel. Staci sat in the passenger seat looking much more relaxed than when they'd arrived. "Made it through unscathed?"

Staci nodded. "You have a lovely family. Victoria is wonderful and such a good example for Sarah."

"They did seem to get on pretty well."

When there was no chatter from the back seat, Eric looked in his rearview mirror and saw that Sarah was fast asleep. "She's down for the count."

Staci turned and looked at Sarah. "Not too surprising. After the excitement of the afternoon, I figured she'd conk out."

"There's so much about her I don't know." Eric kept glancing back at Sarah. In sleep, she looked so peaceful and angelic.

The silence that filled the cab of the truck as he drove was suffocating. Eric searched for words, but conversation hadn't ever been a big thing for them. Back then, they'd managed to get by on small talk about things going on in their lives or the lives of their friends. Without that, he didn't know where to begin, so by default he landed on the only thing they had in common anymore.

"Can I spend some time with Sarah this week?"

"Yes. Certainly. Just let me know what works for you."

"Thank you for making this easy for me."

He glanced over in time to see Staci shrug. "I'm trying to do what's best for Sarah."

As they pulled to a stop in Staci's driveway, Eric swallowed, unsure of the best way to broach this next subject. Straight on, most likely. "Listen, Staci, I'd like to talk about a joint custody arrangement."

If the silence had been suffocating before, it was even worse now.

"Why? I'm letting you spend time with her." Staci's voice was tight. "It's not like I'm getting in the way of your relationship."

"That's true, and I appreciate it." Eric gripped the steering wheel. "But I want to be able to have a say in her upbringing. And if the worst should happen to you, God forbid, I don't want to have to deal with a custody battle in order to take care of my daughter."

Silence.

"I'm not trying to take her away from you, Staci. Trust me."

More silence.

"I just..." Eric paused. "I just want to be her legal father."

"You don't trust me," Staci stated flatly.

Eric swung to face her. "What?"

"You think I'm going to run with her again."

The thought had crossed his mind, but he'd tried not to dwell on that reasoning. "No, that's not what I think. I don't blame you for what you did six years ago. I wasn't ready to be a father. I didn't deserve to be a father. I'm different now. Give me this chance."

Staci gave him a frustrated look. "I don't have a choice, do I?"

Eric sighed. "I don't want this to be a battle. I just want to take responsibility for her. I want to have a say in her life. And I will pay child support for her as well."

Without responding, Staci pushed open her door, letting in a gust of cold air. She shut the door and came around just as Eric got out.

"I'll carry her in," he said.

Staci nodded and headed for the front door. By the time Eric got there, she had it unlocked and open. "I'll take her from here."

Deciding not to push his luck, Eric transferred the sleeping girl into her mother's arms. He ran a hand over her soft curls and bent to press a kiss on her forehead. As he straightened, his gaze met Staci's. "I don't want to be your enemy, Staci. I just want to be her father."

Staci blinked once before turning away. Eric reached out and pulled the door closed after she'd walked into the hallway. He stood for a moment with his hand on the doorknob, wishing for all the world that he was on the inside of this little family instead of out in the cold.

He got into the truck and backed out of the driveway. The day had certainly had its high and low points. Seeing Sarah interact with his family—especially Victoria—had been a thrill. Staci had even seemed to fit in well.

His cell phone rang as he headed down East River Road. He put his earpiece in and answered the call.

"Hey, big brother!" Victoria's voice sounded happy and excited in his ear.

"Hey, Tori." Eric wished he felt has a good as she sounded.

"So, that went really well, didn't it? I just adore Sarah, and Staci is a real sweetheart, too." Victoria paused. "So are you going to propose?"

Propose? "Uh. I'm not sure about that."

"Why not?" Only Victoria could make it sound like his uncertainty was the stupidest thing on earth.

"There are a lot of extenuating circumstances here." Eric braked for a red light. "There's lots you don't know about what went on six years ago."

"Did you beat her?"

"What?" Eric jerked back. "Of course not."

"Did you cheat on her?"

"No, Tori. Our relationship was just not the most healthy thing for either of us."

"But you've changed. Hasn't she?"

"Yes. But just means that we're basically strangers to each other. We can't even claim friendship at the moment."

"Well, you're going to have to work on that for Sarah's sake. She deserves parents who at least get along if they're not going to be married."

"You're right. I'm not arguing about that. I just don't think that marriage is the best idea."

"But you're not ruling it out?"

Eric laughed. "You are like a dog with a bone."

"So?"

"You're not going to let this go, are you?"

"Nope."

"Fine. I'm not ruling anything out—not even marriage. Finding Staci the way I did after having given up on ever finding her has shown me that God works in mysterious ways—as you pointed out the other day. I'm not gonna say no, but I'm also not gonna say yes."

Victoria sighed...loudly. "You know, you're a pain in the behind sometimes."

"Sometimes? I guess I'm not doing my job as annoying big brother too well."

They shared a laugh before Eric ended the call. He pulled into the underground parking lot of his apartment building and had a sudden urge to buy a home. Sarah needed a place to play, to run. His apartment didn't have what a young girl needed. And though he was only hoping for joint legal custody, it was his desire to have joint physical custody at some point, too. Not now though. She was still young enough to be better off with her mother.

But some day...

Eric tried to remain optimistic as he punched the button for his floor. However, the earlier scene with Staci didn't bode well for that future without a fight.

Staci knelt beside Sarah's bed. With gentle fingers, she brushed back the feathering of bangs across her forehead. She was still trying to recover from the bomb Eric had dropped. It shouldn't have surprised her. She had realized it was a possibility—just not that it would happen so soon.

Lord, I don't want to lose Sarah. Please let me keep my baby girl.

It wasn't fair. Even he had said that six years ago he wouldn't have wanted the baby. She had faced the news of the pregnancy alone. Every decision she'd made since then she'd made on her own. She had cared for Sarah by herself. She'd been the one listening as the doctor gave her the news of Sarah's health issues. She'd been the one up at night with a teething baby. All of it out of love for this little girl that in all likelihood he would have encouraged her to "get rid of" if he'd been around when she'd received the news. And now he was marching back into her life like he had every right to be Sarah's father.

It just wasn't fair.

Staci slid down to sit on the floor. She laid her head on the pillow next to Sarah's and closed her eyes. Her hand lightly gripped the little girl's. This was her precious baby. The child she had never even dreamed of having but who had become her whole world. She couldn't—she wouldn't—let anyone take her away.

Eric grinned when he spotted Sarah peeking through the large glass window of the living room of the house. He hoped that Staci didn't kick him out. Arriving without calling first probably wasn't his best idea, but he'd just found himself turning onto the cul-de-sac on his way home from work.

"Daddy!" The door flung wide open, and Sarah launched herself into his arms.

"Sarah!" Staci came flying down the hallway, a cordless phone in one hand. "I've told you *not* to open the door unless I'm here with you."

"It's Daddy," Sarah pointed out indignantly.

Staci sighed. "I can see that." She glared at Eric. "You explain to her. I have to finish this call."

She spun around and marched back down the hallway toward the kitchen. Eric stepped into the house and closed the door. "Your mom's right, Sarah. Don't ever open the door without her here with you."

They walked into the living room. "But I *saw* it was you." Sarah pointed to the large front window. "I was looking out the window and saw you."

And how was he supposed to handle this? "Uh...Okay, but you still need to wait for your mom next time, okay? Even if you know for sure it's me. Promise?"

Sarah's lower lip poked out a bit as she gave a little toss of her head. "Promise."

Eric pulled her close and hugged her. "Mommy and I only ask this of you because we love you and don't want anything to happen to you."

Staci came into the room, phone still in hand. She stared at him, her brow furrowed. "Did I forget you were coming over?"

Eric stooped to place Sarah on her feet on the floor. "No, I sort of just stopped by."

"Oh. Is something wrong?"

Eric shook his head. "Just wanted to see Sarah." He pointed to the phone. "Problem?"

Staci sighed. "You could say that." She tipped her head to the side and wrinkled her nose. "And it's your fault."

"My fault?" Eric placed his hands on his hips.

"Yes." Staci flopped down on the couch and let out a long sigh. "You were the one who insisted on the contract."

"Contract?" Eric felt like he was wandering through a field of land mines, fearful of saying the wrong thing. "I have *no* idea what you're talking about."

"Stubborn Heart. Remember that group? I played on their first album."

Eric settled down in the chair across from her. "Ah, I remember now. Is that the contract I encouraged you to sign with them to play on two additional recordings?"

"That's the one." Staci laid the phone on the end table. "That was my agent. They're calling me in for the third recording."

"You did the other one?"

"Yes. Two years ago I went to New York to record with them."

"What did you do with Sarah?"

"Miriam went with me. She cared for Sarah while I was in the studio."

Eric leaned forward. "Where do they need you to go now?"

"Los Angeles. And they're doing it on short notice. They were originally planning on doing it a couple of months from now. Instead, I need to be there tomorrow night."

"What are you going to do about Sarah?"

Staci paused, eyes down, her fingers plucking the fabric of her pants. "I was wondering if you could stay with her for a few days."

Eric mentally flipped through his schedule. "I should be able to. Victoria can help me out, too."

"Doesn't she work?"

"Yep, but she has her own company so she can adjust her schedule."

"What type of company?"

"TASC."

"Task?"

"The Accessibility Solutions Company. She and a friend started it up to provide products to others with dwarfism. Products to help them with being little people in a big person world."

"That's very interesting. Is there that large a market for products like that?"

"Large enough. They've since expanded into other areas where people need specialized products for accessibility as well."

"Are you sure she can help? Miriam could help you, too."

"I think this would be the perfect time for me and Sarah to bond." Eric hesitated. "Are you okay with it?"

Staci looked at him, and he could see the hesitancy in her gaze. "Not sure. If I hadn't gone to the retreat and seen that she was fine for a couple of days without me, I probably wouldn't be okay. But…you'll take good care of her, right?"

Eric knew she didn't want the standard "of course" response. "Yes, I'll take good care of her. I'll do the best I can. And you know I never do anything halfway."

Staci blinked. "Yes. Yes, I know that."

"Mama? Snack?"

Staci looked down at Sarah, staring at her for a moment. "Uh, sure." She looked back at Eric. "Have you had supper?"

"I grabbed a muffin around three."

Staci pushed herself up off the couch. "Come into the kitchen, and I'll fix you both something."

With his stomach growling, Eric was not going to refuse food. He took Sarah's hand and followed Staci down the hallway to the kitchen.

Sarah darted ahead of him to the table where she scrambled onto her booster seat.

"Sandwich okay?" Staci asked as she placed a scoop of ice cream into a bowl and set a cookie alongside it.

"Ice cream sandwich?" Eric asked with a smile.

"No, this is for your ice cream loving daughter." Staci put it in front of Sarah. "You'll get a regular one."

Eric watched as Staci pulled out some bread and began to work on his dinner. She didn't even ask what he wanted, just built what he knew would be a delicious sandwich from the looks of it. He found it funny how six years hadn't removed his preferences from her memory. She left off the mayo but put extra mustard on the ham. Two slices of tomato, two pickles, and no lettuce.

She added some chips to the plate and filled a glass with milk. Warmth spread through Eric. He found that he liked that she still knew him so well. Yet it was weird that she knew things like how he liked his sandwich but didn't know how he felt about life in general now. Did she even want to?

He was a bit chagrined that he couldn't say the same thing about his memories of her. He had remembered her favorite chocolates but had forgotten her birthday. Actually, he hadn't really forgotten it. She'd just taken him off-guard when she'd said it was her alarm code. Which reminded him, he needed to talk to her about changing that. Given his work was in security, he couldn't very well let her use something so easily cracked as her birthday to secure her home.

"Thanks." Eric bent his head to say grace for the food. His first bite was everything he'd hoped. "Delicious."

Staci sat down across from him with her own bowl of ice cream. "Sorry it's nothing fancier."

"Hey, I'll take taste and substance over fancy any day. And it's made just the way I like it." Their gazes locked for a moment before Staci looked down at her ice cream.

The silence between them would have been deafening had it not been for Sarah's presence. Between bites of ice cream, she told him about her day, most of which she'd spent with Miriam.

"Do you have the music for the recording session?" Eric asked Staci when Sarah paused for a breath.

"Yes, they've been sending it as they've chosen the songs."

"How many do you have to record?"

"I have music for ten songs, but they've already nixed my playing on three of those."

"And you don't need more time to practice?"

Staci shrugged. "Since we've worked together before, we usually mesh pretty quickly when it comes time to record. I have no reason to believe that this time will be any different."

Eric finished his sandwich and drained his glass of milk. Before Staci could clear them, he took them both to the sink. "I'm going to give Victoria a quick call just to confirm that she'll be available to help this week."

Staci nodded. "And I'll phone Miriam. Between the two of them, you should have all the help you need. If not, I know Miriam wouldn't balk at another trip out of town with Sarah and me. She enjoys traveling."

"I prefer the other option, personally, but we need to do what works best for Sarah." Eric pulled his cell phone from the holder on the waistband of his pants. "I'll be back in a second."

He walked back to the living room, tapping Victoria's contact information as he went. "Hey, sis, you busy the next few days?"

"No more than usual. What's up?"

"Staci has to go out of town on business for the rest of the week. Normally she'd take Sarah along, but she's giving me a chance to spend some time with her."

"She's going to stay with you?"

"No." Eric walked to the mantel to the look at the pictures there once again. "I'm going to stay here at her place. I just need some help during the day since I can't take the whole week off."

"That's no problem. I don't have any appointments scheduled this week. Most of the stuff I do have is just over the phone and via email. I can do it as well from Staci's as I can from the office."

"Thanks, Tori, I'll owe you one."

"Now, Eric, you know you owe me more than just one."

Eric laughed. "True enough."

"What time does her flight leave?"

"I'm not sure. I'll give you a call and let you know."

Victoria paused then said, "I'm so excited about this, Eric. Getting to spend time with someone who's like me. In this family, it's been hard being the odd-man out. Now there's two of us."

"And Sarah will be fortunate to have you as an example of all that a little person can do."

"You're gonna make me cry."

Eric chuckled. "Well, since I don't want to owe you even more, I'll let you go before you get too weepy."

When Eric returned to the kitchen, Staci had a laptop open on the counter in front of her. He took the empty bowls from the table and placed them with his dishes in the sink. He looked over her shoulder and saw she was on an airline page.

"Was it okay with Miriam?"

Staci glanced up and nodded. "Yes. She said to just call her if you need a hand."

"Victoria was excited to help out, too." Eric hesitated. "I'll give you a ride to the airport."

"No need. I'll take a cab or my car and use the long-term parking."

"Staci." Eric fought the urge to heave a huge sigh of frustration. "Victoria will be here with Sarah. Save your money and let me take you."

"Money is not an issue," Staci commented. "You made sure of that."

Eric grinned. "Nice to know a few good things came out of our time together."

Staci's gaze shot to Sarah. "Yes."

"I'm gonna head on home now. I'll be back here after work. Victoria might arrive a little earlier. That okay?"

"That's fine."

Eric stood and held out his hand to Sarah. "Walk me to the door?"

His daughter slid her tiny hand into his and, trailed by Staci, they walked to the doorway.

As he pulled out of the driveway a few minutes later, Eric thought about how nice it would be to stay with Sarah for even a short stretch of time. To get to be a real dad for a few days.

He sure hoped he was up to it.

Chapter Ten

S **TACI** made sure Sarah was settled in her bed then her side. She lingered in the doorway for a few minutes, watching the stillness of Sarah's sleeping form. It wasn't often that the little girl was motionless. Though Staci loved to see her so full of life and energy, she also appreciated the moments of tranquility bedtime brought.

Back downstairs, she filled the sink with warm soapy water and began to wash the dishes. She could have put them in the dishwasher, but tonight she wanted the busy-work.

It also gave her time to think.

She'd told Eric she was okay with this, but…she wasn't sure. There was no doubt that Eric and Victoria and Miriam would take good— no…great—care of Sarah. She'd done just fine with Miriam during the retreat. If only Staci had done as well.

Would she survive four nights away from her little girl?

She couldn't deny that part of her was hoping that if she gave Eric opportunities like this that he'd abandon his plan for joint custody. But she'd gone ahead and made an appointment with her lawyer for the next morning. Eric had been right about needing to be able to take care of Sarah should anything happen. For her daughter's sake, she would put things into place that would protect her. If only that would be enough for Eric.

Staci hit the ground running the next morning. She could have dropped Sarah off at Miriam's and made the errands a little less complicated, but since she was going to be gone for four days, she wanted her daughter with her.

Her lawyer appointment was first at nine-thirty and went surprisingly fast. She'd phoned the day before with all the details of what she needed to have changed in her will. And along with that, she also requested they prepare the documents she needed to leave with Eric that would give him the right to deal with any medical issues that should arise in her absence.

Sarah fidgeted until the secretary took her out of the office with a promise of a snack. Once Staci had finished with the lawyer, she and Sarah headed for the grocery store. She didn't want to leave Eric without food in the house. When they'd been together, he'd cooked on occasion so she had some idea of what sort of food he would be able to use. Although Victoria might be doing the cooking and, for all Staci knew, she might be a gourmet chef. Though pity them if they tried to get Sarah to eat anything she didn't recognize.

After a quick lunch at Sarah's favorite restaurant, they headed for home.

"I'm going away for a few days," Staci told Sarah as they unpacked the groceries. "Daddy and Auntie Victoria will be coming to stay here with you. Is that okay?"

Sarah's enthusiastic nodding sent her pigtails dancing. Clearly, the little girl had no trouble with the prospect of being separated from her mother.

"I'm leaving tonight but I'll be back Saturday night." Staci pointed to the date on the calendar she'd hung on the fridge. "Just four days."

"Will you call me?" Sarah wanted to know.

"Yes, I most definitely will." Staci put the last of the groceries away. Next she needed to wash her bedding and then make up the bed in the guest room. Her plan was to have Victoria stay in her room and Eric in the guestroom. She just couldn't even think about Eric staying in her room. Sleeping in her bed.

Not interested in the chores her mother had moved on to, Sarah disappeared into the living room. Soon Staci heard the strains of the opening song of Sarah's favorite television show.

By five o'clock when the doorbell rang, Staci had everything all done. Her suitcase sat by the front door, all the beds were ready, and she'd made supper for the four of them.

Sarah beat her to the door once more but waited for Staci's nod before opening it.

Victoria stood on the porch, a duffle bag in her hand. "I'm reporting for duty."

Staci grinned and motioned for her to come in. "I'm glad you could make it on such short notice."

Victoria dropped her duffle bag on the floor and gave Sarah a hug. "Not a problem at all. I'm thrilled to be able to help out."

"Is Eric coming soon?"

"I called him just before I arrived. He said he'd be here around five-thirty."

"Okay. I just wondered because I've made supper and wanted to know if we should wait for him."

"If you're starving, I don't suppose he would be upset if we went ahead."

"No, we're fine."

Staci picked up her bag. "Here, I'll show you where you'll be staying. Are stairs a problem?"

"They're not my favorite thing, but as long as we're not racing to the top, I'll be fine."

When they were all on the second floor, Staci led the way to her room. "I figured I put you in my room. It's closest to Sarah's, and this is where she'll come if she gets up in the night."

Victoria nodded. "That sounds good." She looked around the room. "This is beautiful."

"Thanks. I decorated it myself." The muted tones of blue and burgundy gave the room a cozy feel. The fireplace opposite the wall was gas and easily turned on and off. She used it regularly throughout the winter.

"I think I'll like staying here. And you'll have to help me decorate my house when you get back."

"Come see *my* room, Auntie Victoria." Sarah tugged on her aunt's hand. "It's all Dora."

Victoria grinned. "Ah, the favorite of the under-six set."

Staci followed them down the hall feeling a bit more at ease about leaving Sarah. She was clearly excited to have her aunt there. With a shoulder propped against the doorway, she watched as Sarah showed Victoria her room. The room had special modifications in deference to Sarah's height. She wondered if Victoria's room as a little girl had had any such helps.

She heard the doorbell ring and waited for Sarah to bolt for the stairs, but she was far too interested in showing her aunt around. Staci made her way downstairs to the door and opened it.

"You're earlier than expected," she said when she saw Eric.

He arched a brow. "Is that a problem?"

Staci stepped back so he could come through the doorway. "Not at all." She looked at his empty hands. "Do you have a bag or anything?"

"I left it in the car. I'll get it later." He shrugged out of his coat and she took it from him, suddenly assailed by a familiar scent. For a moment, she wanted to bury her face in the fabric and inhale. In all these years, he still hadn't changed the cologne he wore. It was one she'd always loved, and over the years when she'd catch a whiff of it, she'd look around to make sure it hadn't been him.

"Victoria is upstairs with Sarah getting the grand tour." Staci led the way to the kitchen. "While they're busy, let me cover a few things." She handed him the envelope she'd gotten from the lawyer. "This gives you the right to make any medical decisions for Sarah while I'm gone. I realized we didn't have time for much else on short notice, but this should cover any unforeseen circumstances."

Eric held it in his hand but didn't open it, just nodded.

"I, uh, made some supper for us. Not macaroni and cheese this time." Staci struggled to figure out Eric's mood. In the past, she'd just let his moods ride. They didn't flex that much, but occasionally his moods had swung from his controlled nature. At the time, she'd stayed out of his way and never thought much about what might have provoked the mood change as long as it wasn't something she'd done. Now, however, as she thought of leaving her daughter with him, Staci found herself wondering about it.

"How was your day?" Staci opened a drawer to retrieve a couple of pot holders. "You seem…distracted."

Eric sat down on a stool near the counter. "Busy. My old supervisor was in to pick up a few things before leaving on a three month assignment to Africa. Let's just say he wasn't a happy camper."

"Why?" Staci pulled the glass baking dish with chicken breasts and sauce from the oven. "You didn't send him to Africa, did you?"

"True. But I have his job now. He wanted *me* off in Africa. It wasn't until I talked to the head honcho that I found out that my supervisor had never let them know I didn't want this overseas assignment. I planned to quit, but found out that my skills were valuable enough to the company that they honored my request and not only gave me a permanent job here, but a promotion as well."

"So…it's not your fault this guy's headed off for Africa." Staci placed the baked potatoes in a bowl and set them on the table. "Sounds like he dug his own grave."

"Yes, he did, but I looked at him today and felt sad for him. He's so full of anger, of bitterness, and I'm sending him to a continent I love. He'll never see the beauty in it." Eric sighed. "I just hope he doesn't do more damage over there. With the chip he's carrying on his shoulder, he'll never be able to communicate with the people there as he should."

"Daddy!" Sarah brought an abrupt end to their conversation, but Staci was more at ease now. His mood was understandable—even admirable. The self-centered person he'd been six years ago would have cared more about the fact that he'd gained a promotion than that another man was unhappy in his job.

"Hey, sweetheart." Eric swung her up in his arms, nuzzling her neck.

The tension that had radiated off him seemed to dissipate in the presence of his daughter. Though Sarah's energy could be draining at times, her excitement and joy could lift one of out of the darkest of moods.

"You staying here, Daddy? With me and Auntie Tori?"

"Yep, we're gonna try to survive without your mom for a few days." Eric set her down on her booster seat and glanced at Staci. "We ready to eat?"

Staci nodded. "What would you like to drink?"

"Water's fine for me," Victoria said as she settled in beside Sarah.

"And me," Eric agreed.

When they were all seated, Sarah said grace amid giggles and repetitions of requests.

Staci was glad they all carried on a conversation without her. Sitting this close to Eric had robbed her of words. His nearness pulled her back into the past and yet at the same time had her wishing for a future that couldn't be.

"I'm going to take you to the airport," Eric told her as he helped her carry the dishes to the counter when they had finished eating. "What time do we need to leave?"

"You don't need to drive me." Staci bent to slide the plates into the dishwasher. "I had planned to take my car and just leave it in long-term parking."

"There's no need for that. It's a waste of money when I can take you and pick you up."

Staci couldn't think of a logical reason and *I don't want to be alone with you* would reveal way more than she wanted to this man. She didn't want to protest too much. After putting the last of the cutlery in the basket, she straightened. "Okay. My flight leaves at nine. I need to be there before eight."

"We'll leave in half an hour." Eric took the dishcloth from her hand. "Go spend time with Sarah."

Before she could block it, warmth slipped into her heart. "Thanks."

"Ready to go?" Eric picked up the bag that sat on the floor in the front hallway.

Staci nodded. "Come here, baby." As her daughter approached, Staci stooped down to embrace her. "Be good for Daddy and Auntie Tori. I'll call you, okay?"

Sarah nodded. "I'll be good."

Staci kissed her cheek.

Eric could have rushed her but knowing that this was hard for her, he didn't. He could sense her reluctance and figured one word would have her canceling the trip. She needed to do this on her terms. Her timetable.

Sarah and Victoria stood in the doorway as Staci and Eric stepped out onto the porch. Even though it was cold, they stayed there until the truck had pulled out of the driveway.

For the first few blocks, Eric didn't say anything, but as the silence grew heavy, he asked the first question that came to mind.

"So, how exactly did you become a Christian?"

"What?" Staci's confusion was clear.

"How did you become a Christian? I don't recall you going to church."

"Oh. I don't know if you remember when I was approached to do a presentation at an elementary school. The woman who contacted me was a Christian and after the presentation, we kept in touch. One week she invited me for some meetings at her church. You were gone, so I figured why not?"

"And you became a Christian at those meetings?"

"Yes. It was a wonderful and horrifying thing."

"Horrifying?"

Her hesitation stretched several long seconds. "It brought to light several realizations."

Knowledge dawned. "Our relationship."

"Yes. I knew that I couldn't stay with you. At the time, I thought marriage would be the answer. I guess it was God's plan that you reacted as you did."

"I probably wouldn't have been very receptive to that news back then," Eric confessed. "I had become a Christian at a really young age, but I'd just chosen not to live the life because of some things that happened."

"Your dad's affair?"

Eric felt a bolt of shock. "How do you know about that?"

"Victoria told me. And explained some of what you went through having to leave Africa because of it. And how she felt you might have viewed her birth."

"She would know. We've had some long discussions about all that."

"Victoria mentioned a bit about how Brooke reacted, too, but is everything okay between you and your dad now?"

"Yes. I've had great talks with my dad. He in no way tried to justify his behavior which meant a lot to me. He admitted his mistake, took responsibility for what had happened and didn't diminish the impact it had on the rest of us. Though I don't admire what he did, I have to say that I admire how he's handled it. He's a very different man now. Humble and more of a father than he'd ever been in the past."

Staci didn't reply, leaving Eric to wonder if thoughts of her own father had come to mind.

"Have you talked to your parents lately?" he asked.

There were several beats of silence before she said, "No."

"Do they know about Sarah?"

Staci gave a humorless laugh. "Are you kidding? I would never expose Sarah to them. Perfection is everything to them."

"Your dad seemed nice, concerned when I called to see if they'd heard from you."

"You called my parents?"

Eric couldn't tell if she was shocked or annoyed. "I turned over every rock trying to find you. That included the boulder of your family."

"Did you talk to my mom?"

Eric glanced over his shoulder to check for traffic before pulling out onto the southbound highway. "Yep. Not nearly as concerned as your dad. Is that normal?"

"Very. My mom controlled everything. My dad had the money, my mom had the drive."

"But wouldn't they like to know about a grandchild?"

"How can Sarah be their grandchild when I'm no longer their daughter?"

Eric wished he didn't understand, but had he been any different? He'd basically disowned his family because of what his father had done. With God's help, he'd been able to right that wrong. Without God in their lives, Staci's parents would probably never extend her the love she deserved. He wondered how it had been for Staci to have parents who were that cold and uncaring. In spite of everything, Eric had always known—deep down—that his parents loved him.

"I never realized how bad your relationship was with your parents."

"I didn't realize that about yours either."

Eric sighed. "Yeah, we didn't talk all that much about our families." Nor about much else of importance, he realized.

Silence filled the vehicle, but there was no more time for conversation as the exit for the airport loomed.

"Just drop me off at the departure level," Staci said as he maneuvered his way through the turn-offs leading to the terminal.

He thought about protesting but decided a curbside goodbye would be less awkward than one at the security gate inside. As a hole opened near the curb, Eric guided the truck to a stop. He got out and unloaded the bag and hand-carry Staci was taking with her. She pulled the handle up and gripped it.

"I'll call tomorrow morning. It will be too late by the time I get in tonight."

Eric stepped up onto the curb beside her. "We'll be waiting for your call."

With a nod, she began to walk away but stopped when he laid a hand on her arm. Staci didn't turn around immediately, but when she did, Eric saw she was near tears. Without thinking, he touched her cheek. "She'll be fine, and we'll be here to get you Saturday night. If it gets too bad, I'll fly out with her. Okay?"

Staci swallowed then nodded. "I'll see you on Saturday."

Eric shoved his hands into his pockets and watched as she walked through the automatic doors of the terminal. When she'd traveled in her career, he'd never dropped her off at the airport. She'd never dropped him off at the airport for his trips either. It had just been easier to use a car service.

What exactly had their relationship been?

In the six years since they'd last been together, Eric's view of their time as a couple had fogged over. When he'd come home to find Ana gone, it had been pride more than anything that had driven him to try to find her. He'd told himself it was love, but now having seen loving relationships, he knew that wasn't the case.

Eric shook his head. Man, they'd had one messed up relationship. No wonder she was leery of letting him back into her life.

"Sir, you need to move your vehicle." Eric glanced over to see a uniformed man standing beside him.

"Of course." *Woolgathering*. What a waste of time. Eric rounded the hood of the truck and climbed in. The next four days stretched in front of him, exciting and yet intimidating.

Chapter Eleven

TRUE to his word, Eric answered the phone on the first ring when Staci called the next morning. He didn't waste time on preliminaries before handing the phone to Sarah. Hearing her daughter's sweet voice was the perfect start to her day. If Sarah was okay, she would be okay.

They only talked for a few minutes before Sarah was distracted by something on the other end and left mid-conversation. Eric came back on the line.

"That kid really likes the cartoon with the little girl and the monkey, doesn't she?"

Abandoned for Dora, Staci thought with a grin. Could be worse. "Yes, she does. You should watch it sometime. It has a certain appeal that you just can't ignore."

"I'll take your word for it. In a few minutes, I get to go off to work and brave tough men in suits."

"Have a good day," Staci told him.

"You, too. Will you call again tonight?"

"I'll try to take a break just before her bedtime to call. If not, let her know I love her and I'll call again in the morning." The two-hour time difference was easier to handle in the morning than the evening when one was trying to work around an early bedtime.

Staci hung up the phone, calm and at peace. She gathered up her music and slid it into her case. A car was due to pick her up in forty-five minutes, but she wanted a bite to eat before heading off. Lunch could well be forgotten if the recording was going well. Breakfast would keep her going until she could next eat.

With the knowledge that all was well with Sarah, Staci turned her thoughts completely to the music and the task that lay ahead.

———

"You want me to do what?" Eric froze with the coffee pot poised over his mug.

"Braid my hair," Sarah repeated. "Today is my swimming lesson, and Mama always braids my hair."

Eric glanced at his sister. Victoria stood on a small stool buttering toast. She glanced over her shoulder and gave him a grin.

"I'm sure your Aunt Victoria would do a better job."

"But I want *you* to do it." Sarah's chin lifted a fraction and Eric saw broad streaks of himself in her expression. His mother would probably die laughing at his predicament.

"How about I brush it then Aunt Tori will help with the braid, okay?"

Sarah nodded her head, and Eric finished filling his coffee cup. He shouldn't have to deal with stuff like this before he'd even finished his first cup of coffee. Wasn't there a law about that somewhere in the world?

"Why don't you lift her onto the stool?" Victoria suggested as she placed a stack of toast on the counter. "You want jam on yours, sweetie?"

"Yes, and peanut butter," Sarah informed her as Eric settled her on a stool at the counter.

He took another long swallow of hot coffee before picking up the brush Sarah had set beside her plate. Her hair stood out in a million different directions, it seemed. Bedhead at its worst. Gingerly, he set the brush to her hair and was rewarded with a loud yelp as he struggled with the first stroke.

Victoria came to stand beside him. "It's best if you gather the hair into your hand and grip it tightly. Then you can work the knots at the ends without jerking directly at her scalp."

Eric gave her a frustrated look. "Do they teach this somewhere or are you ladies just born knowing this stuff."

"Trial and error," Victoria announced as she headed for the coffee pot. "You're doing fine."

Fine? He doubted that Sarah would agree with that assessment if her yelps were any indication. Either he really was hurting her or she was just playing this for all it was worth.

After the fifth *You're hurting me* wail from the little girl, Eric rounded the counter and leaned his elbows on it to bring him down to her level. She immediately straightened and drew back as if she knew she'd pushed him too far.

"Sarah, I'm doing the best I can. You asked me to do this, and I'm doing it. If you want your hair braided, don't say another word." He gestured with the brush. "Do you understand?"

Sarah's eyes were wide, but she didn't appear frightened. That was good. It wasn't his intent to scare her, but he did want her to know he wouldn't put up with her shenanigans. As he took his place behind Sarah again, his gaze met Victoria's and she gave him an encouraging smile. He finished brushing her hair without hearing another peep from Sarah. And it couldn't have been too bad as she managed to finish two pieces of toast in that time.

"Your turn." He handed the brush to his sister. "This is as much as I can handle this morning."

Victoria laughed and pulled a chair over from the table. She stood up on it behind Sarah and began to braid the little girl's hair. It surprised Eric to see how quickly she worked, given that her fingers were shorter and not as nimble as a non-little person's were. He grabbed a piece of toast and, feeling the need of sugar fortification, doubled up on the raspberry jam and left off the peanut butter.

Three slices and another cup of coffee later, Sarah's hair was done to her satisfaction, and his nerves had finally calmed.

"I'm heading off." Eric drank down the last of his coffee and set the mug in the dishwasher. "Are you taking her to the pool?"

"Yep. According to Staci's schedule, her lesson is at eleven."

"Have fun," Eric said as he shrugged into his coat and picked up his briefcase.

"I'm not going anywhere near the water," Victoria told him. "But I'm sure Sarah will have a blast. This kid seems to love everything."

Eric caught the wistfulness in his sister's voice and wished that he could have changed how her childhood had been. It was interesting that Staci was doing a better job raising Sarah after having no children of her own and a dysfunctional family than his parents did after having two children before Victoria came along. He was glad his daughter had the mother she did.

Bending down, he pressed a kiss to the top of Sarah's head. "Be good for Aunt Victoria. I'll see you later."

Sarah gave him a jam-smeared smile and waved. "Bye!"

As he backed out of the driveway, Eric caught sight of himself in the rearview mirror and realized he was smiling. There weren't many days he headed for work with a smile on his face. Starting his day with Sarah was changing all that. He'd found that when he hit rough spots in his day he had only to think of her to gain some perspective.

He still didn't understand God's timing for bringing them together, but Eric was grateful it had finally happened.

Exhaustion hung on Staci like a heavy blanket. She couldn't escape it. The hours—though productive—had been long and intense. She hadn't slept well at night, and this morning she hadn't been able to call Sarah before leaving the hotel for the airport. Her flight was due to leave at twelve-fifteen and with the time change she would get into Minneapolis after five. Normally she didn't waste money flying first class, but she paid the extra this time around to get upgraded from economy. She needed the comfort for the three-hour flight.

The flight attendant offered her something to drink, and Staci took a bottle of cold water. The man next to her showed no interest in conversation for which Staci was grateful. She took a sip of the water and recapped it before leaning back against the seat. It was a relief to have the task of recording behind her. Now she just wanted to get home to her daughter.

Though only three hours in duration, the flight seemed to take twice as long. When they finally touched down in Minneapolis/St. Paul, Staci didn't wait as she usually did for others to deplane. She stood, gripping her purse and laptop bag, and stepped into the aisle when the man seated next to her moved back to allow her to exit ahead of him.

The tensions of the trip melted away as she spotted Eric and Sarah waiting for her. A huge smile wreathed her daughter's face as she ran toward her. Staci put her bag on the terminal floor and stooped to gather Sarah into her arms. It felt so right—so perfect—to hold her again.

Staci moved back. "I've missed you." She brushed a strand of loose hair from her face. "Were you good for Daddy?"

"Yep!" Sarah cupped a hand on each side of Staci's face and leaned in to rub her nose against Staci's. "Love you, Mama."

"I love you, too, sweetheart." Staci gave her another hug, tears pricking her eyes. In all her life, those words had only ever been said to her by this precious little girl. And that had always been enough.

"Glad to be home?" Eric asked.

Staci straightened and nodded. "You know, I don't miss LA at all. I did when I first left it, but not anymore."

"Well, we're glad to you have home."

"Did everything go okay?" Staci asked, picking up her laptop bag.

"It went fine." Eric glanced around. "Where's your luggage coming in?"

Staci pointed to the baggage carousel a few feet away. "That's the one."

Sarah took Staci's hand and then Eric's and together they walked to where the belt had begun to rotate. As they waited for her bag to appear, Staci glanced over at Eric and found him watching her. Warmth swamped her as she glimpsed the concern in his eyes.

"You look tired. Did the recording go okay?"

"We worked hard which meant I didn't get much rest, but I think this will be a great album. I ended up playing on a couple of songs that they had initially said they wouldn't need me for. I'm pleased with how it went, but also very glad this is my last commitment to them."

"And I won't talk you into another contract like that," Eric said with a grin.

Staci couldn't ignore her emotional reaction to Eric. Maybe it was because she was tired or just so relieved to be home. There had to be some reason why she felt drawn to him this strongly. Right then, she wanted him to pull her close and to rest her head on his chest as they waited for her luggage. It wasn't what she should want and most definitely wasn't what she should need, but it was there—strong and undeniable.

She turned her attention back to the carousel in time to see her own round the curve of the conveyor belt.

"Let me get that," Eric said when she started to reach for it.

Without hesitation, she let the bag go by. He retrieved it easily and set it on the floor. He pulled her suitcase with one hand and held her carry-on with the other so she was free to take charge of Sarah.

"You hungry?" Eric asked as they stepped out of the terminal into the cold air. So maybe there was one thing she missed about LA.

"Yes, I am."

"Why don't we stop for supper before heading home?"

"That would be wonderful."

"McDonald's?" Sarah asked as she skipped along beside Staci.

"I don't think so, sweetheart," Eric said. "We're going to a nice sit-down restaurant for your mom. One where they serve us."

To Staci's surprise, Sarah didn't even argue with her father.

Their dinner didn't last long. Eric could see the exhaustion written all over Staci's face. She didn't even argue when he picked up the tab for the meal.

"Go ahead and get in," Eric told her as they approached his vehicle. "I'll buckle Sarah up."

Staci climbed into the passenger seat, and he closed the door behind her. He marveled at how much like a family they were—and at how much he wanted that to continue. As he buckled Sarah into her seat, he wondered if it was time to talk to Staci about marriage. It would certainly nullify the need for joint custody, and he could see his daughter every day.

A glance at Staci as he climbed behind the wheel told him that now wasn't the time to broach the subject. She had her eyes closed, her lashes dark against porcelain pale cheeks. Her beauty twisted his gut, and Eric quickly turned away and started the car.

Once at the house, Eric freed Sarah from her booster seat then got Staci's bags from the back. "I'll come in and help you get her down."

Staci nodded, once again surprising him with her lack of objections.

"C'mon, kiddo, let's get your mom into the house."

Once Staci had unlocked and opened the door, Sarah scampered past Eric and up the porch steps into the house. The house smelled fresh and clean when he walked in. He and Victoria had worked hard all morning to get it into tip top shape before Staci came home. The last thing he wanted her to have to worry about when she got home was the condition of the house. Victoria had agreed.

"It's still standing," Staci commented with a small smile when he joined her in the hallway.

"We put it back together as best we could," Eric replied in a light tone. He set her bags against the wall. "Hopefully, you don't spend the next week trying to find where we put everything."

"Not a problem if I do." Staci headed for the kitchen with Sarah in her wake. "There are only so many places you can hide the cheese grater."

Eric stood in the entry of the kitchen and watched as Staci reached into the cupboard above the fridge and pulled down a bottle of acetaminophen. As she opened the bottle, he went and got a glass from the cupboard and filled it with water before handing it to her.

"Thanks." Staci popped the pills into her mouth and took a swallow of water. "Long day."

"Well, let me help you put Sarah to bed and get out of your hair."

"You don't have to do that," Staci protested, though even to Eric it sounded weak.

"Sit tight. We'll call you when she's ready to say her prayers." Eric took Sarah's hand and led her out of the kitchen and up the stairs.

He knew this routine well even though he'd only participated in it for four nights. Pajamas, brush teeth, potty, wash face and hands. The first couple of nights Sarah had tried to drag it out as long as possible but soon clued into the fact that her dad wasn't as dumb nor as gullible as she'd like him to be. She also seemed to realize that the more quickly this part of the routine went, the more likely she was to get an extra story once she was tucked in.

"Mama!" Sarah called down the stairs once she was all prepped for bed.

Staci joined them in Sarah's room. She knelt beside the bed and ran a hand over Sarah's curls. "Story?"

"Yay. How many?"

Eric reached for the top book on the pile on the bookcase at the foot of her bed. "Let's start with one."

He held the book out to Staci, but she shook her head. "I'll let you have this one."

Once that story was read, and another after it, Eric guided Sarah toward saying her prayers. He could see Staci was just about dead on her feet, and he still needed to speak to her before he left.

"Sleep well, sweetheart," Eric said as he bent and pressed a kiss to Sarah's forehead.

Staci continued to sit by the bed a while longer, her fingers feathering through Sarah's black curls. "Love you, baby."

"I love you, too, Mama."

Eric went down ahead of Staci then met her on the stairs as he returned with her bags.

"You don't need to do that."

"It's not a problem. I'll be back in a minute."

Staci nodded and continued on down the staircase.

Eric found her in the kitchen. She stood at the sink, her back to him, staring out the window.

"You okay, Staci?"

She turned and nodded. "So everything went alright while I was gone?"

"Everything was fine." Eric paused. "You interested in dinner at my folks' place after church tomorrow?"

Staci's face went blank momentarily then she nodded. "Okay."

"How about I come get you guys in the morning for church?"

"What about your own church?" Staci asked. "Are you not going there anymore?"

Eric shrugged. "I don't know. For now, I want to be where you and Sarah worship."

Staci was slow in reacting, no doubt because of her tiredness, but once again she nodded.

"I'll see you in the morning then." Eric turned and headed for the hallway.

Staci followed him to the door. Eric glanced once more at her tired face before he stepped out onto the porch. She said goodnight before closing the door behind him. He waited until he heard the thud of the lock before walking down the steps away from the house.

Once in his truck, Eric leaned with his arms on the steering wheel, staring at the house. How he wished he didn't have to leave. They should be together as a family. He should be able to care for both of them. If only Staci felt the same way.

Staci snapped the locks on the door then leaned her forehead against it. She inhaled a huge breath, held it and then let it out. So tired…she was so very tired.

She turned off the lights in the hallway. The medicine was kicking in, easing the headache that had been plaguing her since she'd gotten off the plane. Though exhausted, Staci didn't want to go to bed. She put a mug of water into the microwave and hit the button to heat it.

The quiet of the house embraced her. Being back in her own home was comforting.

The microwave beeped. Staci took the mug out and dumped some hot chocolate powder into it. When all else failed, chocolate—in any form—was the answer.

Before leaving the kitchen, Staci picked up the cordless handset and pushed the button to view the calls that had come in while she'd been gone. It scrolled from the most recent call. The top number showed Victoria's name. The second number sent chills down her spine.

Danners Family Law.

This wasn't her lawyer, which could only mean it was Eric's. Had he made the call to file for joint custody? Even after all she'd tried to do to accommodate him? Betrayal coursed through her though she wasn't sure why. He'd made it clear that was his desire.

Staci turned off the kitchen light and headed back to the living room. Though it was dark in the room, she was able to flick the switch for the fireplace. She stood staring at the flames before settling into her favorite chair. She pulled the blanket across her lap and cupped the mug in her hands.

The first sip of hot chocolate warmed its way to her stomach and for a few seconds, Staci allowed herself to just focus on the feel of it. She wanted to block all the thoughts and emotions battering her. But it didn't work.

It was hard to swallow that the only person in the whole world who loved her unconditionally lay upstairs in her bed, asleep. Oh, Miriam loved her as a friend, as did Denise, but she wanted more. She wanted the love of her parents. Of a man. And apparently her heart didn't want the love of just any man. As it had six years ago, it wanted Eric's.

But it hadn't happened then and wouldn't happen now.

Was there something so wrong with her that she couldn't be loved for who she was?

Her parents hadn't loved her enough to let her do what she had wanted. They'd tried to force her into the role they had for her. And while most people had fun memories of Christmas mornings, birthday parties and family vacations, the most vivid memory Staci had of her childhood was of begging for love.

Anastacia lifted her hands from the keyboard. "Do you love me, Mother?"

"What are you talking about?" Pamela Stapleton gave her a stern look from where she stood alongside the grand piano. "Play that last section again. It was too slow. It dragged."

Anastacia stared at her mother. She stood like a drill sergeant, ramrod straight, her white-blonde hair pulled back in a tight bun. Pamela Stapleton was all angles and sharpness. There wasn't an inch of softness in her appearance or her heart.

"Play it again," her mother snapped.

"Do you love me?"

"Stop with this foolishness." Her mother stalked behind her and gripped her shoulders. Anastacia winced as her mother's fingers dug into her muscles. "Play."

There had been no utterances of motherly love that night nor in the years that followed. Staci had vowed that never, ever, would Sarah have to plead for her love. She gave it freely and lavishly.

It wasn't a real surprise that she'd gone from one loveless situation with her family to another with Eric. Again she'd poured her heart out to him in the only way she'd known how—by trying to please him. If she pleased him enough, she'd thought, surely he'd love her then. But she'd been wrong. Just as she had been with her parents. Nothing she did had drawn the words she'd longed to hear from him.

Now he was back, willing to shower their daughter with love, but still had nothing for her. A shaft of pain shot through her chest and the mug of hot chocolate tumbled from her hands onto the gray carpet.

"Please, Lord, send someone to love me. I just need one man to love me enough to share his life with me. Please."

I love you, my child.

"But I want more. I need more."

I am sufficient for you.

"Oh God, please don't ask me to spend the rest of my life without someone to love me."

My will is perfect.

Tears fell in a torrent down her cheeks. Staci couldn't control the shaking in her body as sobs burst from her throat. It had been so long since she'd cried like this—the sobs drawn from deep down inside where her pain had been hidden for so long. How could she deal with this now?

She tried to take deep, gulping breaths in order to regain control, but it didn't help. Exhaustion had weakened the barrier that normally held her emotions in check. This was a tidal wave of emotion that had been suppressed for far too long and now that it had burst free, it would not be contained.

Chapter Twelve

ERIC pressed the doorbell for the second time and waited. Still no response. Concern won out over Staci's possible ire as he pulled out the key he'd conveniently forgotten to return and slid it into the lock. He punched in the alarm code before turning.

"Daddy?" He spotted Sarah standing in the archway of the living room. She still wore her pajamas and her hair was a tangled mess.

"Why aren't you dressed?" Alarm flared within him. "Where's your mom?"

"She's sleeping."

"Sleeping?" Eric moved toward Sarah. "Where?"

Sarah twisted to point into the living room. "And she made a mess."

Eric bolted past Sarah into the room. He immediately spotted the dark stain on the carpet and the mug lying in the middle of it.

What was going on?

He approached Staci and laid a hand on her shoulder. He gave her a shake. "Staci?"

She murmured in her sleep, so he knew at least she wasn't dead. "Staci! Wake up!"

Her eyes fluttered open, and he could see they were bloodshot and swollen. What on earth had she been doing? "Why are you sleeping here? You were supposed to be ready for me to pick you guys up."

Staci's gaze came into focus, and she stared at him for a moment before sitting bolt upright. The blanket pooled in her lap, revealing the same clothes she'd been wearing the night before. He dropped to a crouch beside the chair. "Are you okay?"

She rubbed her eyes and turned away from him. "I'm sorry. I guess I was more tired than I thought."

"And that?" Eric motioned to the spill of dark on the carpet.

"My hot chocolate." Staci straightened, swinging her feet to the floor. "I must have dropped it when I…fell asleep."

"Are you sure that's all?"

"Yes." Staci stood and moved a couple of steps away from him. "Why don't you go ahead to church? I don't think I'm going to make it."

Eric hesitated, still not sure she was telling him the truth. She looked fragile, as if she'd shatter if he said the wrong thing. "Is it okay if I still take Sarah with me? And then go on to my parents' place? Or we can come back and pick you up."

Staci shook her head. "I'll get Sarah dressed and you can take her for church and dinner."

Eric pushed back the edges of his suit coat and planted his hands on his hips. Something wasn't right. That was the understatement of the century. But how did he get out of her what was going on in her mind? He'd never taken the time to learn how to communicate with her before. She'd probably continue telling him that everything was fine. And until he figured out how to get past that, he'd have to continue to accept her word.

But one way or another, he had to figure out what was going on. If for no other reason than it scared him to think that Sarah had been up on her own with her mother seemingly passed out.

It wasn't long before Staci appeared from upstairs with Sarah in tow. The little girl's hair was neatly done, and her church clothes were tidy and pressed. He wasn't sure what to think after the last few minutes in Staci's house, but fear had given way to anger.

"Ready to go?"

Sarah nodded and went to the cupboard and got her coat off the low rack that had clearly been installed so she could reach it with ease.

His daughter preceded him out of the house, Staci standing at the door, her hand braced on the edge. Eric paused just outside the doorway, debating. Finally, he turned and pinned Staci with a firm look. "Use this time to get yourself together."

Staci's face paled as her eyes widened. Before she could respond, Eric moved down the steps in Sarah's wake. When he glanced toward the door after getting into the truck, he saw that it was closed. Should he have said what he did? Maybe not, but right then he was more interested in making sure Sarah was okay.

"Did you have breakfast?" he asked as he glanced in the rear view mirror.

"Of course!" Sarah replied indignantly. "Sometimes Mama lets me make my own."

"Make your own breakfast?"

"I asked her if I can, and she leaves me cereal and milk."

"And you like that?"

"Yep. I don't make pancakes though."

Eric smiled for the first time since arriving at the house. "I'm glad to hear that."

Anger coursed through Staci's blood. It had been building all day, fired by Eric's parting shot. Get hold herself? The man was going to get a piece of her mind, though truthfully, she felt like she could ill afford to part with any brain cells at that moment.

She paced to the living room window, pushing aside the curtain to stare at her still empty driveway. It was almost five o'clock. She would have thought that they'd be back by then. With a huff of disgust, she released the curtain and returned to the kitchen.

The phone rang. Thinking it was probably Eric, Staci grabbed the phone.

"Hello?"

"Staci?"

"Yes?"

"This is Pastor Evans."

"Pastor! I'm sorry. I didn't recognize your voice."

"Not a problem. How are you doing?"

"Fine."

"I'm glad to hear that." The man paused. "I wonder if Tannis and I could meet with you in the next day or so."

"Sure. Is there a problem?" She'd had to cancel their daughter's lesson that week, but she didn't think they'd have had a problem with that.

Another hesitation. "Not really. We would just like to touch base with you. It's been a while since we've chatted."

That was true. Between the hectic weeks leading up to Christmas and the New Year, Eric's reappearance in her life and her recording in LA, she hadn't had much time for anyone—or anything—else. "When were you thinking?"

"Whenever would be convenient for you," Pastor Evans responded affably.

Staci worked to flip her mind from her anger at Eric to what her week held. "I could see if Miriam can watch Sarah tomorrow morning. Would that work?"

"That would be great. Around ten."

"Sure, I'll see you then." Staci hung up the phone, her mind going back to Eric. The anger she'd been able to suppress momentarily while on the phone with the pastor came raging back. She stalked out of the kitchen and back to the living room.

The driveway was still empty but as she stood there, headlights swept across the front of the house. Staci watched the vehicle turn into the driveway. The lights on her garage illuminated it as it pulled closer, showing it to be Eric's truck. The headlights flashed off, but Staci only moved toward the front door when she saw Eric and Sarah walk away from the vehicle.

She opened the door as they approached. Sarah burst in, words flowing like a raging river from her. Eric stepped into the hallway and closed the door behind him. He stood there without taking his jacket off.

"I want to talk to you," Staci said. "Let me get Sarah settled first."

Eric nodded, his expression unreadable.

"C'mon, sweetie," Staci said and held her hand out to Sarah. "Do you want to play on the computer for a little while?"

"Yeah!" Sarah pulled her hand from Staci's and darted down the hallway to the office where her computer was.

It took Staci a few minutes to get the program running. It was Sarah's favorite pre-school learning program and would keep her occupied for a while. "Here, put the headphones on for the sound, okay. But don't turn it up."

Sarah nodded and settled the earphones over her head. Normally, Staci didn't like her to wear the earphones but right then it was more important that she not hear what Staci and Eric needed to discuss.

She rested her hand on top of Sarah's head for a moment and took a deep breath. Standing up to Eric was something new. In the past she'd never voiced a dissenting opinion or sought conflict with him. But it was necessary this time. She couldn't—wouldn't—let him get away with commenting on situations he knew *nothing* about.

The hallway was empty when she reentered it. She found Eric in the darkened living room, standing at the window where she'd stood only moments before.

She flicked on a lamp at the end of the couch.

Eric turned toward her. "Are you feeling better?"

"I'm feeling fine. And aside from exhaustion this morning, I was also fine."

"I didn't mean to insinuate—"

Staci slashed the air with her hand. "You insinuated plenty, Eric."

"Staci—"

"You have no *idea* what my life is like as a single mother." Staci took a step toward him. "You were worried about Sarah waking up while I was still sleeping?"

"Yes, I was."

"So am I supposed to stay awake twenty-four hours a day to make sure she never wakes up when I'm sleeping? Are you telling me that if she woke up in the middle of the night and tripped, or fell down the stairs that it would be my fault because I'd been asleep when she got up?"

"Well, no—"

"I was exhausted from my trip to LA, but Sarah was never, ever in any danger. The alarm is on so that she couldn't open any door or window without it going off. Loudly. The bathroom where the tub is is shut and secured so she can't get in there. Any and all dangerous mixtures are in secure locations that she can't reach. I do everything I can to make this house safe for her. You had *no* right to make me feel like I'd failed as a mother because I happened to sleep in a little this morning."

"Staci—"

"What do you want from me?" Staci's hands tightened into fists. She was on a roll now. "From the moment we met I have given and given and given to you. From the minute you walked back into my life I've done it again. You wanted to meet Sarah, I agreed. You wanted her to know you were her father, I told her. You asked that she get to meet your family, she did. You wanted to take care of her while I was in LA, I let you. All I needed in return was some recognition that I was doing what I thought was best for Sarah. Instead, you basically accuse me of being a lazy, unfit mother."

Eric frowned. "I didn't say that, Staci."

"*Get yourself together.* That's what you said. *Get yourself together.* Like I was sleeping off a hangover. If that wasn't a statement of judgment, what was it?"

Eric had the grace to look down.

"You didn't want to be a father. What gives you the right to march in here now and judge my efforts to be the best mother I know how?"

"You're right." Eric shoved his hands into his pockets and met her gaze. "I apologize. I should never have said what I did."

"You only said what you were thinking, Eric." Staci turned away, the pain of what had happened earlier washing over the anger. How come he still had the power to hurt her? She was a different person now. She'd moved on. His words should have bounced off her. Instead, they'd pierced her to the very core.

She heard movement beside her but didn't look up.

"Staci, you're right." Eric spoke, his voice low. "I had…have…no right to judge you for anything. Sarah is happy, well-adjusted and loving. Clearly, you've done all the right things."

"I did the best I could. Especially since I had no real example myself."

She felt a touch on her shoulder and glanced over to see Eric standing close. Too close.

"You're a wonderful mother. I never stopped to think about how it might be for you. Even with her this past week, I had Victoria's help. I'm sure I could never have done it on my own."

Staci crossed her arms, hugging herself tightly. It was all she could do to not lean in to Eric. She was relieved—and a bit surprised, actually—that he hadn't blasted her in response to her outburst. Her anger spent, she fought the urge to lean against him, to draw on his strength. Yes, she'd been a single mother all this time, but that didn't mean she hadn't longed for someone to share the load of parenting. And now Eric was there.

But he wasn't there for her. He was there for Sarah.

Staci stepped away from him. Living under delusions that he would ever be a part of her life the way she wanted would only lead to heartache. It had in the past, and she wanted to believe that she'd learned her lesson.

Eric knew he deserved all Staci had handed him and more. Emotions warred within him as he backed out of the driveway and headed for home. He was angry at himself for what he'd done to her. He should never have said anything—his mouth had run ahead of his brain. If he'd been thinking straight, he would have known that Staci had Sarah's best interests at heart, that she would never do anything to endanger their daughter.

He pulled to a stop at a red light, his hands gripping the steering wheel. But as much as he was disappointed in himself, he was proud of

Staci. He knew what it must have taken for her to stand up to him. It was something she'd never done before, but she'd done it well. He'd gotten her point.

A horn sounded behind him. Eric jerked his gaze back to the road and accelerated. He realized as he drove that his options were becoming more and more limited by the day. Staci's statement about how much she'd given rang hard in his gut. She had given so much, and he'd just kept taking. But he wanted to see Sarah first thing in the morning before he left for work and to be there each night to put her to bed. She was his daughter. It was the way things should be.

Unfortunately, that option would require more giving on Staci's part. And what would she get in return? Something told him that after this latest misstep, marrying him would be the last thing she'd want to do.

That left him with one option—one he'd never completely dismissed but had put on the back burner. But Staci would once again see it as him taking and her giving. And she'd probably hate him forever. But if marriage wasn't going to happen, he needed the next best thing. A guarantee that she could never disappear again.

The first thought in Staci's mind the next morning was of Eric. She sat up and swung her feet over the edge of the bed. Sleep had been a long time coming the night before, and she was dragging today. But she had things to do, places to be, and she would give Eric no reason to insinuate she was a bad mother again.

"Let's get going, sweetheart," Staci said as she poked her head into Sarah's room.

The little girl was awake, sitting on the floor playing with her Barbie dolls. "Where are we going?"

"To see Miriam. She's going to watch you for a couple of hours today." Staci helped Sarah do up the button on the pants she'd chosen and slip the sweatshirt over her head. "I think you'll have fun."

"Maybe she'll make cookies with me." Sarah handed her the hairbrush.

"I think she probably would," Staci said as she fixed her hair. They went downstairs and grabbed a quick breakfast before heading out.

Miriam let them in as soon as Staci rang the doorbell. "How's my doll?"

"Are we making cookies?" Sarah asked as she embraced the older woman.

Miriam laughed. "I think we can do that."

"I'll be back in about two hours," Staci told Miriam. "Is that okay?"

"Take as long as you need. I have no plans today." She took Sarah's coat and hung it in the closet. "Where are you headed?"

"I have a meeting with Pastor Evans and Tannis."

"Nice," Miriam said with a smile. "No need to rush back."

Staci gave Sarah a kiss and waved as she left.

The drive to the church didn't take long. As she walked through the door, it felt as if it had been ages since she'd been there.

"Hi, Staci," Annie, the church secretary, said with a smile. "You can go on in."

"Thanks." Staci walked through the open doorway into the pastor's office. Normally she wouldn't have been so well acquainted with the pastor and the staff of a church that large, but since she gave both Annie's daughter and the pastor's daughter piano lessons, she knew them fairly well.

He was seated behind his desk but stood as she came in. "Good to see you, Staci."

Tannis, his wife, stood and gave her a hug. "How are you doing?"

"Pretty good." Staci sat down in the chair next to the one Tannis had been sitting in.

"How's Sarah doing?"

"Great. She's with Miriam right now."

Pastor Evans settled back in his seat. He rested his hands on his desk, his expression serious. "I have something I need to talk to you about."

Staci felt a flutter in her stomach. Things that started that way were never good. "What's up?"

"A member came to me with a...concern."

Staci frowned. "A concern?"

"Last Thursday night they went by your place to drop something off. They saw a black truck pull in ahead of them and a man got out and using a key, let himself into your house. Figuring you had company, they didn't want to bother you. On their way to work the next morning, they stopped by again and noticed that the same truck was still there. This member had some concerns about a man staying overnight at your place."

Comprehension dawned. Staci felt a spurt of anger and frustration. Now having Eric back in her life was messing with her reputation, too? But she understood how it could appear to someone who didn't know what was going on. "It wasn't as it appeared."

Pastor Evans leaned forward. "I figured as much, but you know what they say about evil surmising."

Staci nodded and took a deep breath. "This all starts back several years. Do you have time for a little story?"

"Certainly."

"Six years ago, I lived a very different life. I wasn't a Christian—didn't even know what being a Christian meant. I was caught up in my music and the relationship I was involved in at the time." Slowly, Staci began to lay out the path her life had taken over the past six years. Starting with the revelation of her identity and ending with the reappearance of Eric in her life.

"That was Eric's truck the person saw in my driveway, and yes, he did spend the night, but I wasn't there. I had a commitment in LA, so Eric and his sister stayed with Sarah while I was gone."

"That's quite an amazing story," Pastor Evans said. "How did Eric become a Christian? From your story, it seems an unlikely possibility."

"To be honest, I don't know all the details. I do know that he was raised in a Christian home. His parents were missionaries, but somewhere along the way he rejected their faith. I haven't asked him about the details of how his life turned around. We've kind of had other things to work on since reconnecting, but I've heard from others that he was kidnaped in the Middle East when he was working on a project there."

"Wait a second. Eric," Pastor Evans said. "Eric McKinley?"

Staci nodded warily. "Do you know him?"

"Sort of. I was at a men's meeting where he was the main speaker. He shared his testimony—which is amazing, by the way—and I had a chance to speak briefly with him afterward. Quite a man."

"He is that," Staci said, knowing it was what they expected to hear.

"Are you two going to get married?" Tannis asked.

Staci dipped her head and stared at her hands. "I don't think that's going to happen." She looked up at Pastor Evans. "Is that wrong? I mean, just because we have a daughter together, does that mean we have to get married? What happened six years ago was before we were Christians."

"That's a tough question. There are consequences to sin, even after we've become Christians, even years after the sin was committed. I don't feel I can give you a definite answer. I think this is something you need to pray about."

"Believe me, I've been praying," Staci assured him. "But I'm not sure marriage is the answer for us."

"Well, don't dismiss it out of hand. Why don't you pray about it some more, and Tannis and I will definitely pray as well."

"Is he involved in another relationship at the moment?" Tannis asked.

Staci shook her head. "I think his most recent relationship ended a few weeks ago. It was before we met, but Eric hasn't mentioned marriage. His focus has been on Sarah."

"Let's take some time to pray about this right now," Pastor Evans suggested.

Staci bowed her head. As she listened to the pastor pray, she felt a bit more peace about the situation. Despite what had brought her to their office this morning, it was such a relief to have shared what had been going on in her life with him and his wife. What could have been a bad situation had turned out for good—at least on that day.

When they'd finished praying, both of them hugged her, once again assuring her of their support and prayers. "And don't hesitate to come to us if you need to talk or if things change. We'd even be willing to meet with Eric, too."

Staci thanked them and left the office, her steps lighter than when she'd come in. Once outside, she checked her watch. It was only a little after eleven. She phoned Miriam to see if she'd keep Sarah for a few more hours. The older woman agreed without hesitation. Her next call was to Denise to see if she could fit her in at her spa for the works. She felt in the need to pamper herself, so pamper she would.

Chapter Thirteen

"CAN you believe someone thought you were having an affair?" Denise tore a breadstick in half. "That is beyond insane."

Staci swallowed the mouthful of Zuppa Toscana she'd just taken. The soup warmed its way down her throat. "I guess you gotta look at it from their perspective."

Denise gave her an incredulous look. "Are you defending them?"

Staci shrugged. "Not defending them. Just saying that not realizing I was away and seeing a truck there at night and still there in the morning—well, I'd probably have jumped to the same conclusion."

"You are way too soft on people." Denise waggled half a breadstick at her. "But I'm glad you're that way. It's a great quality to have in a friend."

Staci smiled and pushed away her empty soup bowl. She was glad her friend had talked her into doing a late lunch after her time at the spa. It had been exactly what she'd needed after the week she'd had.

"So what's the latest with Eric?"

"He's getting along well with Sarah." Staci hesitated to bring in anything that would dampen the mood, but she had no one else to talk to. "But I think he's going to be filing for joint custody."

"Really?" Denise sat back, her brow furrowed. "Just legal or physical, too?"

Staci cocked her head, pondering Denise's question. "I'm not sure. He just said he wanted joint custody so that he could make decisions if he had to. Or that if anything happened to me, he wouldn't have to go through the courts to get custody of Sarah."

"That sounds like legal, not necessarily physical."

"I never really looked into it, to be honest. I'm not thrilled with the idea of sharing any type of custody of Sarah with anyone. I never thought it would be an issue."

"One of my employees went through a custody case with her ex and explained it all to me. Eric can't have joint physical without joint legal, but just because he has joint legal doesn't automatically mean he has joint physical custody." Denise tapped the table with her fingers. "You need to ask him what it is."

"But even if he's just going for legal now…Well, it just makes it that much easier to go for physical later on, doesn't it?"

Denise nodded. "Then I guess you need to marry the guy."

"Very funny." Staci tried to ignore the hitch in her stomach that Denise's words caused. For the second time that day, marriage had come up. "That's not going to happen."

"Just like you meeting up with him again wasn't going to happen either, right?"

Staci couldn't dispute Denise's logic. The impossible had already happened. But this required hope—and hope with regards to Eric had been something she'd given up on a long time ago. "Why don't we try discussing another topic? Like has Philip proposed to you yet?"

Denise rolled her eyes and motioned for the waitress. "Can you bring me the dessert menu please?" The waitress pointed to the plastic stand on the edge of the table. "Thanks."

"Is this a mega-chocolate discussion?"

"You betcha," Denise said and ordered the biggest chocolate dessert they had.

"We sharing or do I have to order one for myself?"

"I'm tempted to say order your own, but my hips are living in hope that I'll be wearing a wedding dress one day soon, so we're sharing."

"Well, I could be nasty and make you eat the whole dessert yourself and order my own since my hips aren't worried about a wedding dress."

"Don't be so sure."

Determined to push aside any thoughts of Eric, Staci dug her fork into the dessert as soon as the waitress set it down on the table.

Eric wondered if he'd be pushing his luck if he showed up at the house again so soon. He found it difficult to go for even one day without seeing Sarah. How long would it be until Staci got tired of him and told him to back off? He didn't want to be pushed into filing for joint physical custody, but if they weren't able to come to some sort of agreement, he'd be left with no choice.

A small selfish part of him longed for the Staci of old...Ana...she would have agreed to anything he wanted. He would have made a decision, and she would have gone along with it. But Eric couldn't deny that the person Staci was now was better for Sarah. His little girl didn't need a mother easily swayed by those around her. Sarah needed someone to stand up for her, to create a safe environment in a cruel world. There was no doubt in his mind that Staci had done that for Sarah. And because of that, he would do what he could to work things out with Staci without totally disrupting Sarah's life.

But that didn't mean he was going to stay away from her, Eric decided as he turned into the cul-de-sac and pulled into Staci's driveway.

He rang the doorbell and waited for what seemed like an eternity before it swung open to reveal Staci. She held a dishcloth in her hand and looked like she'd just been put through the wringer. In the background, he could hear ear-splitting shrieks.

"Is that Sarah?"

Staci nodded wearily and stepped back. Eric took that as an invitation to enter and stepped into the hallway. "What's wrong with her?"

"Too much sugar. Too little sleep. And, in her opinion, too much denial."

"I understood the first two, but too much denial?" Eric shrugged out of his coat and hung it in the closet. He waited to see some sign of protest from Staci, but she looked like she couldn't have cared less that he'd showed up unexpectedly.

"She is wanting everything under the sun, and I'm denying her. Cruel mother that I am."

As another shriek rent the air, Eric looked toward the kitchen. "Do you have her tied up in there?"

"She's in a high chair. I don't use it often since she associates it with babies, but when she's acting like this…well, she knows the punishment. Time-out in the high chair."

"Can I see her?"

Staci shrugged. "Just don't let her out of the chair. She's still in time-out."

Eric walked into the kitchen and came to an abrupt halt at the sight of his daughter. She was secured in the high-chair but clearly not enjoying it. Her hair had come loose from its braid and stood out in all directions. Her face was a bright red and at the moment, her eyes were squeezed shut. Her mouth opened as if to emit another shriek.

"Sarah. Stop."

At the sound of his voice, her eyes popped wide open. For a second, she seemed to be trying to decide the best way to play this. "Daddyyyyy. Mama is mean. She put me in this chair."

Eric advanced to where the little girl sat and pulled a chair around to face her. "Don't speak about your mother that way. Nothing, absolutely nothing, gives you the right to shriek the way you are."

"But…" Her lower lip trembled.

"No buts, Sarah. You're a big girl. You should *not* behave this way."

She regarded him for a long moment, her eyes suspiciously free of tears. Then a smile curved the corners of her mouth. "Okay, I'm all done. Can you take me out?" She lifted her arms to him.

Though it was a temptation to free her, Eric resisted. "No, you are in that chair until your time-out is over."

The smile—so like her mother's—faded. Her lower lip jutted out and tears formed in her beautiful dark eyes. She looked so wounded that Eric just about caved in. He heard movement behind him and looked over to see Staci leaning against the doorjamb watching with undisguised curiosity. He could tell by her expression that she was waiting to see what he would do.

As he stood and turned from Sarah, she let out a wail. Eric spun back around. She quieted immediately. "Stop it, Sarah. If you do that again, your time-out will be even longer. Do you understand?"

Wet eyes wide, Sarah nodded. This time when Eric turned to face Staci, the little girl remained quiet. "Has she been like this all day?"

Staci pushed away from the door jamb and walked to the counter. "No, she spent most the day at Miriam's. They made cookies, and I think she ate a few too many. Plus, she was up early and didn't have a nap. It's going to be an early night."

"Is she like this often?"

"Thankfully, no. I think she's a bit overwhelmed by everything that's gone on lately. Add sugar and tiredness to that, and it's a recipe for disaster."

"I'm sorry you're having to deal with it."

Staci shrugged. "It's not the first time and won't be the last."

A timer dinged. Eric turned back to Sarah. She sat with her hands folded on the tray. The redness of her face had faded, and all he could see now was her exhaustion.

"Is her time-out done?"

"Yes. You can take her out."

Eric sat down on the chair again and faced his daughter. She met his gaze straight on. "Are you going to be good?"

She nodded.

"I think you need to say sorry to your mom."

Another nod.

Eric set about releasing Sarah from the high chair. He lifted her up and held her for a moment. She rested her head on his shoulder, her arms wrapped around his neck. He moved to where Staci stood. "What do you say?"

Sarah straightened and held out her arms to Staci. "I'm sorry, Mama."

Staci stepped close and let the little girl hug her neck. She didn't try to take Sarah from his embrace so they stood there together. A family. Out of a habit from long ago, Eric shifted his hand to rest on the small of Staci's back. It surprised him when one of her arms slid around his waist while the other embraced Sarah.

The smell of her hair tantalized his senses. Memories swamped him. He should step back. End this embrace that had started out harmlessly enough, but was now threatening to drag his thoughts into a direction he'd tried so hard to steer clear of since coming back into Staci's life. But the feel of the two most important women in his life leaning on him was hard to surrender.

For the first time, Eric allowed himself to admit how important Staci was to him. And it had nothing to do with the fact that she was Sarah's mom. Their connection went back long before the little girl had made her appearance. He still felt everything he had six years ago, but now it was…more. He admired her. He respected the woman she'd become. And yes, he was still overwhelmingly attracted to her.

Was that wrong? He knew that a physical relationship was out of bounds before marriage, so he didn't dwell on that aspect of their relationship. Most of the time. But now…right now, he wanted the right to be close to her. To hold her. To show her what he had such a hard time putting into words. Rights he could only claim as her husband.

Staci must have sensed the change in him because her arm slipped from his waist and she stepped back. She kept her face averted from him as she turned away. "Have you had supper already?"

Eric swallowed and took a deep breath. "No, but I'll grab something on the way home."

"If you don't mind soup and toast, you're welcome to stay."

Common sense told him to run, but his heart held him firmly in place. "That would be nice."

"Why don't you go to the living room with Sarah while I get it ready? It won't be long."

Eric sensed she was trying to put distance between them. Smart woman.

He left the room still carrying Sarah. Distance was exactly what they needed.

Staci picked up the cloth from the counter and twisted it between her hands. What on *earth* had she been thinking? Getting that close to Eric was always a mistake. She'd just been so weary of dealing with Sarah that when he offered his strength, she'd leaned on him without a moment's hesitation.

She tossed the cloth down and moved to the fridge. The container of homemade soup she'd taken out of the freezer that morning sat on the top shelf. She took it out and stuck it into the microwave to heat it up.

And inviting him to dinner. What kind of dumb idea was that?

Staci dropped two slices of bread into the toaster. She wasn't thinking with her head. Her heart was beginning to override her common sense and, when Eric was involved, that was a very, very scary thing. But her love for him was so embedded in her heart that cutting it out would be impossible. If only he could love her back. But she was so different from the woman he'd known.

You're perfect.

Staci remembered the heat of his breath across her cheek as he'd whispered the words to her. If she'd been perfect to him six years ago, she certainly wouldn't meet his definition of perfection anymore. Would she be willing to change in order to try to be the woman he'd once wanted?

She couldn't believe that she was even entertaining that thought given all she'd gone through with him before. That mindset, that crazy desire to please him, had just about done her in. Why would she even think it was something to consider at this point? Particularly when she now had someone who was relying on her to make *good* decisions.

The toast popped up. With weighted movements, Staci pulled the bread out and buttered it before sticking another couple of slices in.

She tried to ignore the pain in her chest as she pulled the soup out to stir it before returning it to the microwave for a couple more minutes.

It wasn't fair that Eric always seemed to catch her at her most vulnerable. Tonight was no exception. The day had been going so well. If it had continued on that way, she would have been able to handle his presence tonight without any problem. But no, everything had fallen apart after they'd gotten home. It wasn't the first time Sarah had thrown a temper tantrum, but fortunately, they were few and far between. She'd certainly appreciated Eric's support, but since the price for it seemed to be her heart, Staci wished he'd never shown up.

She just needed to get through supper. Once he was gone, she'd do what she needed to do to shore up her defenses and make sure she was never as vulnerable to him as she had been earlier.

Grabbing on to her resolve with both hands, Staci set the table then called Eric and Sarah to supper.

It was a quiet meal with Eric and Staci doing most the talking for once. Sarah was either exhausted out of her mind or had figured she'd pushed her luck far enough that day.

"I'm going to be going out of town for a couple of weeks," Eric said as she handed him a second bowl of the cream of chicken soup.

Staci sank down into her chair. "I thought you weren't going to have to go away with your new position."

"No long term assignments, but I'm overseeing the overseas projects so this will be my trip through Africa and the Middle East."

Staci gripped her spoon. "The Middle East?"

"Yes. It will be my first time back."

"And you're not worried?" Staci hoped he didn't hear the panic in her voice.

"No."

"How can you not be after what happened before?"

"What happened last time was that the Lord put me in a situation where I finally realized I couldn't run from Him anymore. If something happens on this trip, I will accept that it's God's will."

Staci swallowed. "How can you be so blasé about it? You have a daughter to think about." *And me...I couldn't bear to lose you again.*

"And God will take care of her if something happens to me. He's been doing that through you already."

She looked down at her soup that suddenly seemed tasteless and unappealing. "When do you leave?"

"On Monday."

Staci, trying to keep her emotions under control, turned to check on Sarah. Her bowl of soup was empty and only the crusts remained of the piece of toast Staci had given her. "You done, sweetheart?"

Sarah nodded and pushed her bowl away. "Bed?"

"I think so." Staci stacked her bowl on top of Sarah's.

"Why don't you let me get her ready tonight?" Eric suggested.

"Okay, I'll just clean up here and be right there."

Eric lifted Sarah into his arms and headed for the stairs. Staci took her time clearing off the table and loading the dishwasher. Being part of what was becoming an all too common ritual weakened her. Kneeling beside Sarah's bed with Eric at her side made it all seem too much like a family. And they weren't.

When she'd finished cleaning up, Staci climbed the stairs to the second floor and found her daughter and Eric already in Sarah's room. Eric sat on the edge of her bed and looked up as Staci came into the room.

"Why don't you say your prayers first, then I'll let your mom read your stories tonight," Eric suggested to Sarah.

Without hesitation, Sarah nodded then bowed her head. The little girl's prayer wasn't as long as usual, yet another indication that she was one tired kid. When the prayer was done, Eric bent forward and pressed a kiss to Sarah's forehead. "Sleep well, baby. I'll talk to you tomorrow, okay?"

Sarah nodded as she reached for a book from her bookcase.

Without a word to her, Eric left the room. Staci pushed aside her thoughts of him. This was her time with Sarah, and he'd already intruded enough on their time together.

Just one story later, Sarah's eyelids were drooping, and she snuggled under her covers without complaint. Staci feathered her fingers through her silky curls for a couple of minutes before she pushed herself up from where she'd been kneeling beside the bed and left the room.

With Eric gone, there was no rush to return downstairs, so Staci went to her room and changed from the outfit she'd worn that day. She pulled on a pair of fleece pajama pants and a fitted long sleeve thermal top. The thick socks she slid on her feet guaranteed her warmth as the temperature in the house began to dip. Never one to enjoy sleeping in the heat, Staci always turned down the thermostat at night.

Staci checked in one more time to make sure Sarah was asleep then headed for the stairs. She rounded the corner into the kitchen and came to a screeching halt. At the table with a mug of coffee—if her senses were accurate—sat Eric.

Chapter Fourteen

He looked up and regarded her with an intense stare. Staci shifted from one foot to the other before going to the counter pulling down a mug for herself.

"I hope you don't mind that I made myself a cup of coffee," Eric said. She could still feel his gaze burning into her. "I know my way around the kitchen pretty well now."

Staci filled the mug with water and set it in the microwave. "I thought you'd left already."

"I thought about it, but we need to talk about a couple of things."

They did? She didn't like the sound of that.

When the microwave dinged, she set the mug on the counter. The hot chocolate powder she was spooning into her mug slid onto the counter when her hand shook. She took a deep breath and lifted another spoonful of the powder into the mug before getting a cloth to clean up the mess. The silence as she added the powder to the hot chocolate was deafening, but it was beyond her to know what to say to break it.

Was now when he'd tell her he wanted joint custody of Sarah? A pit yawned wide in her stomach and suddenly the hot chocolate didn't hold the appeal it once had.

Knowing she couldn't postpone the inevitable, Staci carried her mug to where Eric sat and slid onto the seat across from him. She stirred the dark liquid, the spoon clinking as it hit the edges of the mug. When Eric didn't say anything, Staci looked up again finding his gaze tight on her. The intensity in his expression as he looked at her was disconcerting. In their years together, he'd never looked at her intently unless they were in the midst of an intimate moment. Then the intensity had been edged with passion. Now, however, it was just a deep concentration, and it disturbed her.

What did he see when he looked at her? The woman she'd once been? Or the woman she was now? Or was he seeing her only as the mother of his child, the woman who stood between him and what he wanted? Her stomach clenched.

Afraid of what he might read in her own gaze, Staci looked down at her mug as she lifted it to take a sip. The warm liquid burned its way down her throat but did nothing to disperse the chill that had taken up residence in her body.

"I've discovered that I'm not happy with only seeing Sarah sporadically." Eric stated it bluntly, driving a shaft of pain through Staci's heart. "When I stayed here with her I realized that I want to be a part of her life on a daily basis."

"You already are," Staci pointed out, forcing the words past tight throat muscles. "You've been here the past two evenings."

"True, and I thank you for indulging me. It's just…" Eric hesitated.

Staci glanced up to see that he had finally looked away from her, his head now bent over his mug of coffee.

"I want more. I want to be a real father—full-time, not part-time."

Dread crashed over Staci like a tsunami. He didn't want joint custody, he wanted everything. Panic froze her vocal cords. Her hands clenched the mug. Had it been made of something less sturdy than stoneware, it surely would have shattered into a million pieces within her grip.

But she couldn't stop her heart from shattering. Her worst fears were being realized, and they were being wrought by the man she loved. This man knew her intimately—like no other person on earth—and yet he really knew nothing about her. For if he did, he would have known that taking her child from her would be a death sentence.

"Staci?"

She fought through the fog of emotion to focus on Eric's words. Though she didn't want to hear them, she knew she needed to.

"I've been trying to come up with a solution that will work for everyone and could find only one."

Only one? Surely there were other options. His taking full custody of Sarah wasn't the only one. She would fight him. She had the money. She had the history of being Sarah's mother for the past five years. She would win.

Full of new resolve, Staci straightened her shoulders and looked right at Eric. She was going to make him say it. Make him spell out that he planned to take her daughter from her. "And what solution is that?"

"Marriage. I think we should get married."

Shock swept away her resolve, leaving her once again frozen. *Marriage?* Of all the things she'd expected to hear him say, a proposal hadn't been one of them.

"No." The word was out of her mouth before she knew what she was saying. It stunned her into silence. For so long she'd dreamed of marrying this man. If he'd offered her marriage six years ago, she would have jumped at the chance. But now...*no?*

Eric's gaze flickered with emotion she couldn't recognize. "No? Why not? Sarah deserves both her parents. And we already know we're...compatible."

Staci didn't want to think about their compatibility. She had vowed to never put herself into another intimate relationship with a man unless he was her husband and he loved her. Though Eric would be by law her husband, the love wouldn't be there. Staci had seen a loveless marriage. She didn't want that for Sarah.

Yes, Sarah deserved both parents, but she was also entitled to a family where love flowed in all directions. Their love for Sarah couldn't be the glue that would hold them together. It shouldn't have to be.

Maybe love would come. But maybe not. He'd never told her he loved her though he'd defined her as his perfect woman over and over again. How could he love her now when in all the ways that mattered, she was pretty much the exact opposite of who she'd once been.

"Ana…Staci." Eric's harsh treatment of her name broke through her thoughts. "Why not?"

Staci took a deep breath. "It's not what I want."

Eric jerked back, his eyes going hard. In a heartbeat, he was the Eric she knew best. The one who kept everything hidden behind a façade. He gave her a sharp nod then stood and left the kitchen.

Staci blinked rapidly as she heard him open the front door. The firm closing of that door a second later sounded like a death knell. There was no doubt in Staci's mind that with this option of the table, Eric's next move would be custody.

Why hadn't she told him she needed time to think about it? With so much at risk, why had she blurted out *no?* Her answer had come from a wounded heart and now it had put her custody of Sarah in jeopardy. One thing she did know…her definitive answer had slammed the door shut on any future relationship between her and Eric.

∞

No.

It's not what I want.

Eric pulled the door of his truck shut with more force than usual. He sat in the cold for a few minutes staring at the window of the living room of Staci's house. Was this the way he was destined to live? On the outside looking in? He seemed to find himself in this position each time he left her home.

He started the vehicle with a rough twist of his hand. As he pulled away from the house, he wanted to press the gas pedal to the floor to burn some rubber. Only the roads were slick in spots from the latest snowfall. He may have been frustrated, but he wasn't stupid.

Or was he?

For some reason, he'd thought that Staci would at least take the time to consider what he'd been proposing.

No.

It's not what I want.

Without so much as a thought, she'd shot him down.

The embrace they'd shared as a family earlier in the evening had given Eric hope. Surely she could see that they would be better off together, the three of them. Okay, so their previous relationship hadn't been all that great. He hadn't realized it at the time, but in the light of God's place in his life now he could see that it hadn't been a good thing for either of them. But now…now they had the commonality of a daughter, a belief in God and he'd been willing to do whatever he had to in order to make their family work. To make their marriage work.

She hadn't even given him a chance. Was the prospect of marriage to him so abhorrent that she'd considered it and dismissed it even before he'd proposed?

For as long as he could, Eric tried to ignore the ache in his chest. He pulled into the underground parking lot at his building and wearily took the elevator to his apartment. The quiet that enveloped him as he walked in the door of his home was an embrace he didn't want.

He flung his jacket over the back of a kitchen chair. Without turning on any lights, he grabbed a can of soda from the fridge and went to stand at the large window of his living room. The cities of Minneapolis/ St. Paul spread before him, a twinkling blanket of lights that usually brought pleasure, but right then it couldn't touch him.

He couldn't figure it out. He hadn't offered a pledge of undying love to Staci—he was sure she wouldn't have believed it anyway—so why did he feel as if his heart had just been stomped on and kicked to the curb?

When the phone rang around five o'clock the next afternoon, Staci checked the call display and when she recognized Eric's number, she let Sarah answer the phone. Yes, she was a coward. She freely admitted it. But she wasn't up to another conversation with him just yet.

"Are you coming over?"

Staci held her breath at Sarah's question. From the frown creasing the little girl's forehead, she assumed that the answer had been negative. The sweep of relief made her feel rotten since her daughter was clearly disappointed.

Sarah talked for a few more minutes before handing the phone back to Staci. Taking a deep breath, she said, "Hello?"

Silence greeted her, and Staci realized that Eric had hung up already. He hadn't wanted to talk to her. Why that hurt was a mystery, since she hadn't wanted to talk to him either.

"Daddy's not coming over?" Staci asked, just to make sure. If he was going to land on her doorstep, she needed to shore up her defenses.

"No, he said he has to work late."

"We have to go to church tonight anyway, sweetie."

"I know." Sarah slid onto her booster, a morose expression on her face. "Couldn't Daddy come with us?"

"Not if he's working late." Staci studied her daughter's face and felt a pang of guilt.

Her answer to Eric had come from her own selfish efforts to protect herself, and yet here sat her daughter wanting to be with her daddy. It hadn't even been twenty-four hours since she'd last seen him, but it was clear that Sarah was missing him. Leaving her with Eric had sped up their father-daughter bonding and though Staci would have loved to class that as a mistake, after seeing Eric and Sarah together, she knew it had been the right thing to do.

Would marriage have been the right thing to do, too?

The question tumbled through her mind as she set a bowl of spaghetti noodles and sauce on the table. She helped Sarah fill her plate, letting her sprinkle a liberal amount of shredded cheese on top of it. Sarah prayed, most of it centering on Eric. Staci prayed silently for an extra measure of wisdom.

After they had finished supper, Staci gave Sarah a bath and dressed her for the mid-week meeting at the church. They arrived just a little before the service started, and Staci had just enough time to get Sarah settled in the children's class before going to the main sanctuary for the adults' service.

Usually, she participated in the prayer time, praying out loud for requests that others brought forward. That night, though, her heart was heavy, and she began to wish she'd just stayed home. There was no way God would hear her prayers. Selfish emotions crowded her heart leaving her restless and troubled. She needed to get herself together.

Staci was still trying to pull her ragged emotions back into place the next day as she worked at her studio. She had a few adult students throughout the afternoon. Her younger students came once school let out. The struggle to pay attention to each student was massive. She breathed a sigh of relief when the last one left just after five. Without delay, she packed Sarah up and headed for the sanctuary of home.

Once inside, she checked the voicemail on her cell which she'd shut off during her lessons and the drive home. While flipping through the mail she'd retrieved from the mailbox, Staci listened to the messages play back. One from Miriam. One from Denise and the last one was from Eric.

"I know it's late notice, but I was wondering if I could stop by and pick Sarah up and take her out for supper. Give me a call on my cell."

Staci stared at her phone then tapped the screen to bring up Eric's information. But she chickened out before connecting the call.

"Here." She handed the phone to the little girl. "Daddy wants to take you out for supper. You can call and tell him it's okay."

She showed Sarah where to tap on the screen then listened as Sarah told her father he could come pick her up.

"He'll be here in ten minutes," Sarah told her as she handed the phone back to Staci.

Staci listened to the phone and heard only silence as she had the night before. "Why don't we get you cleaned up then?"

Ten minutes later they stood in front of the living room window watching for Eric's truck. Sarah already wore her jacket and boots. As soon as she saw the black vehicle turn into the cul-de-sac, she raced for the door. Staci followed behind her and unlocked and opened the door.

Eric got out of the driver's side, his eyes guarded by a pair of dark shades. Sarah didn't wait for him to come to the door but scampered down the steps to the truck. Eric scooped her up and swung her around, hugging the little girl close. Staci blinked to clear the tears from her eyes. They both gave her a wave before Eric bent to put her in her car seat.

Unable to watch any longer, Staci stepped back and shut the door. She leaned her forehead against the wooden surface wondering if there was any way to make this work. This was rapidly disintegrating into something that would not be beneficial to any of them, most of all Sarah.

Staci spent the next two hours cleaning the house and trying to figure out how to do what was best for all of them. When the doorbell rang around seven-thirty, she still had no answers.

She opened the door to see Sarah standing there alone. Eric waited on the sidewalk at the bottom of the porch steps. He said goodnight to Sarah then turned on his heel and left. A giant hand squeezed Staci's heart, and even drawing Sarah into her arms didn't ease the ache.

As surely as she had rejected Eric's proposal, he was rejecting her.

Eric was wearying of the telephone tag he was playing with Staci. She was avoiding him. And if he was honest with himself, he was avoiding her, too, but that went against his usual manner of dealing with things. He'd decided that he needed to speak with her directly and still she didn't answer his calls. Stupid caller ID. No doubt she could see who was calling because without fail Sarah answered or the call went to voicemail.

He debated for a second before punching in the code that would hide the number he was calling from. It was underhanded and sneaky, but he needed to speak with her and he was running out of time. He was scheduled to leave in just two days, and he needed to talk with her before he left the country.

"Hello?"

Aha. It had worked. "Staci, it's Eric."

The pause on the other end of the phone confirmed his suspicions that had she known it was him, she never would have answered the phone. "Eric."

"Yes. I'm calling because I'm leaving for Africa on Monday, and I wanted to know if I could take Sarah for the afternoon after church tomorrow."

Another pause. "That should be fine."

"I also wanted to let you know that my cell phone will work world-wide, so if you need to get hold of me for any reason, just call. I'll try to call Sarah while I'm gone. Is there a time that's best?"

"Probably between five and six in the evening or eight and nine in the mornings. We're usually guaranteed to be home during that time. If not, try my cell. I'll keep it with me."

"Good. I'll see you tomorrow." No need to prolong the conversation since Staci's agitation was loud and clear even over the cellular connection.

Ending the call, he leaned back in his recliner feeling more at ease. The direct approach always worked best. Of course, he still had to use that approach to get the air cleared regarding his proposal. They couldn't keep going on like this. Middle ground was necessary. He'd wanted everything, had pushed for everything. That wasn't going to happen. At this point, he just wanted to make sure he didn't end up with nothing.

Chapter Fifteen

STACI scanned the foyer for Eric. Sarah wanted to see him before she went to Sunday school. When he didn't show up, Staci took her to the class.

"I'm sure he'll be here for the service. You can sit with him until you go to the junior worship, okay?" Staci hoped she wasn't lying to her. He'd come to the service in the past when he'd planned to pick up Sarah.

Settled in her seat for Sunday school, Staci waited for Eric to put in an appearance. When he didn't, she became concerned that Sarah was going to be disappointed that her father didn't show.

After Sunday school finished, she picked Sarah up from her class.

"Daddy here?" Sarah asked as soon as they left the room.

"Not yet, but he'll be here." Hand in hand they moved around clusters of people as they made their way to the sanctuary. "How was Sunday school?"

Sarah chatted about the lesson, but Staci could sense her distraction as she tried to look for Eric from her lowered vantage point. Staci toyed with the idea of phoning Eric on his cell. She hated seeing Sarah so anxious.

The prelude was playing as they took a seat near the back of the sanctuary. The song leader had just gone up on the platform when she heard a muted squeal of excitement. Turning, Staci saw Eric slide into the pew on the other side of Sarah. He touched the little girl's cheek and pressed a kiss to the top of her head.

There was no time for conversation before the service started. Once the children were dismissed for their worship, Eric moved over a little, closing the gap between them slightly. When he didn't look her way, Staci took a deep breath and turned her attention to the front where Pastor Evans had gotten up to preach.

"My text this morning is a short verse in Proverbs. Please turn with me to the sixteenth chapter, verse nine." A rustle of pages could be heard through the sanctuary. "And the verse says *A man's heart plans his way, but the Lord directs his steps.*"

Staci's hands clenched around her Bible. She wanted to get up and leave. She didn't want to hear this sermon. It scared her to think where the Lord might direct her, what He might require of her. She didn't want to think about that.

And is your way working any better?

Staci twitched. The sanctuary of a church was not the place for lies. Clearly, what she'd planned had not been so great. Things were worse now than they had been when Eric had first appeared on the scene. And the underlying fact was that she had not prayed for God's will to be done in this situation. She'd prayed plenty about what she wanted to happen. She'd beseeched God to make things turn out the way *she* wanted, but she hadn't given it all over to Him. Her faith, her trust had faltered.

She snuck a glance at Eric, wondering if this sermon was having the same effect on him. Or maybe he was better at this than her and had been praying all along for God's will to prevail. If that were the case, maybe she'd been wrong to turn down his proposal. Though she'd thought lots about it, she hadn't taken it to the Lord through serious prayer.

Eric sat looking straight ahead, his face a granite profile. Okay, so maybe she was the only one under conviction. That was nothing new. It seemed that this was one area she never could seem to come to grips with. After having someone else control her life for so long, it had been a thrilling freedom to finally begin to think for herself, to make decisions on her own. Giving that control over to anyone—even God—seemed to require giving up that freedom. Hard fought, hard won…it was a freedom that was hard to give up.

Head bent with her hair sliding forward to cover her face, Staci closed her eyes and began to pray. The rest of the sermon was lost to her as she placed the mess she'd made of things with Eric into God's hands. And she pled for the strength to leave it there. It would be way too easy to take it back, especially if it seemed things weren't going as she wanted.

As the service drew to an end, Staci had to fight the urge to tell Eric she wanted to talk with him. She wanted everything worked out *now*, but that was what had gotten her into trouble the first time around. No, this time she would wait and pray.

"You're okay with me taking Sarah now?" Eric asked as they stood in the foyer, people milling around them.

"That's fine."

"Do you need her back at a certain time?"

"Not really. Generally her bedtime is eight, but we can make an exception if you want her a bit longer."

"I'll try to have her home in time for bed."

"I have to pick her up from her class. Do you want to come?"

Eric nodded and fell into step with her as they moved down the corridor to the room where Sarah had gone for the children's worship. Staci didn't miss the looks people gave them as they walked together down the hallway. The ones who knew her were clearly curious about the tall, handsome man at her side.

When they appeared in the doorway, Sarah shot across the room and into Eric's arms. "Daddy! You came!"

"Yes, I was late though. Sorry about that." He kissed her forehead. "You ready to spend the afternoon with me and Auntie Tori?"

Sarah's ponytail bounced as she vigorously nodded her head. "And Mama, too?"

Staci reached out and touched her arm. "Not today. This is a special time for you and Daddy. He'll bring you back in time for bed tonight, okay?"

"What are you going to do?"

"I'm sure I'll find something," Staci told her with a reassuring smile. "You go and have fun."

They walked back to the corridor and found the cloak room where Staci had hung their coats earlier. Eric helped Sarah into hers and then they left the church. Eric had parked in a different part of the lot, so Staci said goodbye to Sarah and watched them walk away.

She crossed her arms against the sudden chill that gripped her. This was how she'd wanted it. She'd refused Eric's efforts to bring them together as a family. By saying no, she'd fractured their relationship and now his focus was just on Sarah.

Eric glanced back over his shoulder and paused when their gazes met. Staci quickly turned and headed for her car. Once inside the vehicle, she cranked the radio to drown out the silence.

With a twinge of regret, Eric pulled into Staci's driveway. He hated to drop Sarah off like this, but until something else was worked out, this was the way it would have to be. And knowing he'd pushed his luck by having Sarah all afternoon, Eric decided he'd not bother to ask if he could be part of her bedtime ritual. He climbed from the truck and opened the back door to get Sarah out. He'd explained to her earlier that he was going to be leaving for a couple of weeks. Victoria had made a calendar for her to cross out on to count down the days until he was back.

Eric couldn't help wondering if Staci would be counting the days down as eagerly as their daughter. Something told him that wouldn't be the case. He lifted Sarah into his arms. She laid her head on his shoulder, and Eric thought his heart would burst with love for this little girl. Somehow he had to figure out how to be a part of her life as much as his heart wanted. These goodbyes were killing him.

Staci opened the door before he knocked. She wore a baggy U of M sweatshirt and black sweatpants. Her hair was pulled back with just a few loose wisps framing her face.

"She asleep?" Staci asked as her gaze landed on Sarah.

"No, but she's definitely ready for bed."

"C'mon in." Staci stepped back without reaching for her daughter. "I think we can skip tooth brushing tonight. Why don't you just carry her upstairs and put her down?"

Eric didn't argue as he toed off his shoes and climbed the stairs to Sarah's room. He laid her on the bed and watched as Staci deftly removed her clothes and got her into a nightgown. Sarah snuggled into her pillow as soon as Staci was done with her. She bent over and kissed Sarah then straightened. "Go ahead and take your time."

Without glancing back, Staci left the room. Eric stared after her then shifted his attention to Sarah. He knelt beside her bed. "Remember that Daddy loves you. I'll try to call as often as I can."

"Love you, Daddy." Sarah's words were a sleepy whisper, but Eric heard them and leaned close to rest his cheek next to hers. This little girl had been conceived in passion, not love, and yet was so full of the emotion, so willing to love the father who'd been absent for all of her short life so far. How he wished he could cancel his trip, but he knew that maybe it would be best for Staci and him. They needed some breathing space from each other and, in the end, that would be better for Sarah.

The little girl's breath deepened and evened out. Eric stayed a couple more minutes before he stood and went back downstairs. Staci was in the kitchen folding laundry. He hesitated in the doorway, not sure what to say. Now was not the time to get into any sort of discussion regarding their future.

He cleared his throat, and Staci swung around.

"She down?"

"Yep. Sorry. We wore her out, I guess."

Staci gave him a small smile, just enough to give him a glimpse of her dimples. "Not a problem. She'll sleep well tonight."

Eric shoved his hands into the pockets of his jeans and shifted his weight from one foot to the other. "I leave early tomorrow morning." He frowned as he remembered Sarah's bag still out in the truck. "I have some stuff of Sarah's in the truck. I'll go get it."

He put his shoes on and went out into the cold night. Christmas lights still ringed the eaves of a couple of the houses in the cul-de-sac. Warm lights glowed from windows, and Eric wasn't all that eager to go home to his sterile apartment though he still had packing to do. He grabbed the bag from the seat and headed back to the house. Staci met him at the door and took it.

"Thanks again for letting her spend the day with me."

Staci shrugged. "You're her dad."

And what am I to you? Eric wanted to ask. "I'll see you in a couple of weeks. Call if you need anything. You can also call Trent if you can't get hold of me."

She nodded as she said, "Have a safe trip."

The conversation was so reminiscent of times in the past when one or the other of them would leave for business. As Eric stepped closer to Staci, she looked up at him, the light from the porch making her eyes glisten. He slid his hand along the back of her neck, beneath the heavy weight of her ponytail. His thumb traced her jawline right below her ear.

He waited for her to pull away. She didn't. In that instant, he knew without a doubt that his proposal had not been just for Sarah's sake. He wanted this woman in his life. In his arms.

I love her. Not the woman she'd been six years ago. Not the woman he'd spent years trying to find. But this woman right here.

The shock of his realization had him stepping back, his hand sliding from the satiny softness of her neck. Her hand went to her throat as tension strung between them like thick cords.

Eric swallowed, trying hard to keep his emotions from spilling over. All he wanted to do was take her into his arms and tell her how much he loved her. But if his proposal was unwanted, no doubt this declaration of love would be, as well. Given how he'd been with her six years ago, she was likely in no rush to get involved with him again. He took another step back then turned and headed for his truck. There was no way he could have said anything more with the frozen state of his vocal cords.

In addition to doing his business on this trip, Eric knew he'd be doing an awful lot of praying.

Staci shut the door and immediately went to the kitchen where she sank down onto a chair. Elbows resting on the table, chin propped on her hand, she could only wonder what on earth had been going through her mind. Or Eric's, for that matter.

Six years apart and still the moves were the same. And maybe that was part of the reason she hadn't pulled back. The familiarity of his touch was comforting…and yes, a little enticing, too. Okay, a *lot* enticing, if she was being honest. And wrong. She knew their physical relationship hadn't been the result of love six years ago, and it certainly wasn't now either. That was probably why Eric had pulled back from her. On some level, he was still attracted to her, but now he would know that lust was not a good foundation for a relationship.

Thankfully, one of them had had their head where it should have been. It was hard to ignore the things that drew her to him, even now. Though she'd come to hate how he controlled her life simply by withholding from her the one thing she'd ached for, there had been times when she longed for someone to help her care for Sarah. The weight of it was heavy at times. And being a single parent was just plain wearying. Much as she loved Sarah, she was a handful sometimes, but there was no reprieve from the responsibility. Having Eric take Sarah like he had earlier had been refreshing for her.

But the bottom line was that she didn't want to go back to having her life ordered by someone else. Would she be strong enough to not try to please him in order to keep him happy? To earn his love? In truth, it wasn't just Eric's control over her that she feared. It was her response to him. She'd viewed who she used to be in relation to him as weak, and yet here she was, six years later, fighting the same feelings. And in order to keep from slipping back into that old role, she was making decisions without thought or prayer. She just couldn't bring herself to trust who she was now in a relationship with him. And in reality, she still didn't trust him.

Trust.

Staci rubbed her forehead. *Trust.* Such a big step. Who was the last person she'd trusted without reservation? Probably Miriam or Denise. It certainly hadn't been her parents. And even Eric—then and now—didn't inspire complete trust. She felt like she was being forced to take a step over the edge a cliff, trusting that it wouldn't kill her.

In her own strength, she could never do it, Staci realized. Her trust had to be complete in Christ first before she could trust anyone else.

Could she trust that His will for her was the best?

Staci sighed. Clearly, she'd been relying *too* much on herself since the moment she'd laid eyes on Eric again. It was time to do what she should have done in the beginning.

"Are we going to church, Mama?" Sarah asked as she watched Staci make dinner.

"Not tonight, sweetheart." Staci finished cutting Sarah's chicken breast into small cubes. "There's a blizzard going on, and we don't want to get stuck on the roads. We'll just stay here for now."

The phone rang, and Sarah immediately raced for it. "Can I answer it?"

Certain that it was Eric, Staci nodded. He'd called regularly for the past two nights at exactly the same time. She hadn't spoken with him herself since Sarah seemed more than willing to share whatever news there was on their end and then tell her all the news from Eric after the call was finished. That usually consisted of him telling her about the funny animals he'd seen or the interesting people he'd spoken with.

Besides, what they had to say to each other couldn't be said over the phone anyway.

As Sarah chattered away, Staci put their dinner on the table. Grilled chicken breasts, roasted potatoes, and corn. All favorites of Sarah's.

"Mama, Daddy wants to talk to you." Sarah handed her the phone.

"Sarah tells me you're having a blizzard there," Eric said when she pressed it to her ear.

"Yep. They're forecasting at least ten inches or more." Staci tried to keep her heart from slamming out of her chest. Hearing his voice did weird things to her. "We stayed home from church tonight because I figured the roads would be bad."

"No such problem here," Eric replied with a trace of humor in his voice. "Probably a good idea to stay home. Listen, tomorrow morning at some point Trent will come by and shovel you out."

"That's not necessary," Staci told him. "I'm planning to stay home tomorrow, and it will probably melt within the next day or two."

"Don't argue with me on this, Staci. I will feel better if I know you have a clear path out of the house in case you need to get out with Sarah."

Staci couldn't argue with his logic, and she appreciated his concern. "Okay."

"He'll be by to shovel you out sometime in the morning. Look for a man dressed very brightly."

"Thanks. Shoveling snow has never been my most favorite thing."

"Wish I were there to help out, but Trent is my next best option."

"Well, enjoy your nice weather there. Think of us when you're sweating tomorrow."

"Have no fear, I'm always thinking of you…of you two."

Staci swallowed. "Take care."

The call ended, and Staci took a deep breath. "Let's eat, baby."

Sarah scrambled up onto her booster and launched into a long prayer with lots of mentions of her dad. Staci leaned back and watched Sarah as they ate. She could see flashes of Eric in her daughter as she talked. She truly was a mix of the two of them. Forever their lives were intertwined whether they wanted them to be or not.

Chapter Sixteen

THE next morning, true to his word, Eric's friend showed up. He didn't bother coming to her door but started right in on the heaping snow drifts in her driveway. Sarah watched with fascination from the window in the living room.

"He looks like a clown, Mama," she commented.

Glad that Trent wasn't within earshot, Staci murmured a soft reproof to her daughter. She had to agree, however, that with the bright red cap and sunshine bright yellow jacket, he did look a bit like a clown. "He's daddy's friend, and he's doing us a great favor by shoveling the snow. I don't care if he's dressed like Santa Claus."

"He's too skinny to be Santa Claus," Sarah pointed out.

Staci could only laugh at her daughter's observations. There were times that there was just no suitable response for them. She left the living room and went to the kitchen to put on a pot of coffee and some water in the kettle. Not knowing what Trent might like to drink, she was going to cover all her bases.

"He's done!" Sarah announced loudly as she came into the kitchen.

"Thanks, sweetie. Let's go invite him in."

He was climbing the steps to the porch when she opened the door.

"Hi, I'm Staci." She held out her hand which he took after pulling off his glove.

"I'm Trent." His gaze zeroed in on Sarah where she stood attached to Staci's leg. "And you must be Sarah." Trent dropped to a crouch that brought him closer to Sarah's low eye level. "Your dad has told me lots about you."

"Really?"

"You bet. All of it very good."

"Trent, why don't you come in for something hot to drink?" Staci offered.

Trent straightened and smiled. "That would be great. Thanks."

Once inside, she took his jacket while he doffed his boots. "Come on into the kitchen. Sarah helped me make some cookies, and she's a great little baker."

"I've heard that, too," Trent said as he followed them into the warmth of the kitchen.

The scent of the chocolate chip oatmeal cookies they'd made earlier still lingered in the air.

"Have a seat," Staci said as she motioned to the table. "What do you drink?"

"Whatever you have," Trent replied affably.

"I've got it all. Coffee, tea, hot chocolate."

"In that case, I'll have a cup of coffee. Black."

"That's easy enough." Staci filled a big mug with the coffee she'd made and carried it along with a plate of cookies to the table. "Help yourself."

"Can I have one too, Mama?" Sarah asked, her elbows braced on the table as she leaned forward in her booster seat.

"Sure. I'll make you some hot chocolate." She listened to Trent and Sarah chat as she prepared the hot chocolate for Sarah and poured herself a cup of coffee.

"So, you're pretty much like Eric described," Trent said, a smile lighting his gray eyes as she settled down across from him.

Staci felt warmth climb into her cheeks. "He described me?"

"Sure. I asked what you looked like, and he told me."

Staci figured she wasn't sure she wanted to know what the description had consisted of. "Well, you're pretty much like he described you as well."

Trent laughed, his eyes twinkling. "I suppose he wanted to warn you about the man dressed like a crazy idiot that was going to show up on your doorstep."

"He didn't say you'd be dressed like a crazy idiot, just that you would be dressed...brightly."

"Always the master of understatement," Trent said with a grin. "So," he turned his attention to Sarah. "You like your dad?"

"I *love* my daddy. He reads me stories and takes me to McDonald's."

"That pretty much guarantees a top place finish in her books," Staci informed Trent.

"As it should. Nothing like stories and french fries."

Staci found herself really liking this friendly man sitting across from her. She had a hard time picturing him and Eric as friends, and said so.

"We met three years ago when he started working at BlackThorpe. He needed some help with his computer, and I gave him a hand. Computers are kinda my specialty. We just clicked, and I count him as my best friend now."

"And I think he feels the same way about you."

"He'd better," Trent said with a scowl that lost all emphasis due to the humor sparking in his eyes. Then he sobered, the laughter fading. "He's been through a lot. Finding Sarah has been a wonderful thing for him. Thank you for letting him get to know her."

"I'd never have kept her from him. The only reason I didn't contact him before was because he'd made it perfectly clear he didn't want a family. Sarah needs a dad, and he's great with her."

"And what about you?"

"What about me?"

"Do you need Eric, too?"

Staci fought to keep her gaze steady on his. "I've been self-sufficient for the past six years so no, I don't *need* Eric. But since I'm sure you're not talking about that, I will say that I'm not sure about things on a personal level with him. He'll be the first to know—if or when—that changes."

Trent kept his piercing gaze on her for a moment then nodded. "Sounds good to me."

He turned his attention back to Sarah and managed to charm her with stories of Eric and the fun things they'd done together. Staci found herself enjoying the tales as well. It gave her a glimpse into who Eric was now.

"Much as I'd love to hang around, I promised Tori I'd stop by her place and shovel, too."

Staci stood when he did. "Thanks so much for doing that for us. It was great to meet you."

"And you, too."

They waited in the open doorway to wave to Trent as he drove his truck around the cul-de-sac and left. Staci closed the door, marveling at how Eric was still taking care of them even from halfway around the world. She shouldn't have been as grateful for it as she was.

So much for self-sufficiency.

The heat of the desert engulfed Eric as he stepped from the Baghdad International Airport. A frisson of unease slithered through his body as he took in his surroundings. Now that he was there, he could admit that it was a place he'd hoped to never visit again. Yet he knew that he had to confront what had happened there to make sure he was completely free of the fear that had ridden him since the day of his capture.

"Right this way, Mr. McKinley," the young man said as he motioned with his arm. He had identified himself as Aban Al-Jamil and he'd come from the company's Baghdad headquarters to pick him up. He led the way to a reinforced SUV with a guard and a driver.

Eric breathed a sigh of relief as he settled into the vehicle behind the tinted windows. It wasn't just a reprieve from the heat but also from the sights and sounds that turned his stomach. He had no idea if the three men in the car with him knew of his past, but none broached the subject.

"There's water here if you're thirsty, sir." Aban motioned to a cooler in the luggage area behind them.

"I'd like one. Thanks."

The man unscrewed the top of a bottle and handed it to him. He fought the urge to run the condensation over his face and neck. Even in the air conditioned interior of the car, he felt overheated and jittery. It didn't help any that the three men were now conversing in a language he didn't understand. The driver kept looking at him in the rearview mirror as he spoke to Aban and the large man seated across from him.

Trying to tune them out, Eric swallowed the cold liquid, his mind skittering back to the time when he'd had little water to drink and what he did get was tepid and awful tasting. He'd never taken water for granted again. Resting the bottle on his knee, Eric took a deep breath. Maybe he wasn't as ready to come back as he'd thought.

His knee bounced as he stared out the window. The press of humanity outside the vehicle closed in on him. Though the SUV had a bigger interior than his truck at home, it didn't feel big enough. Vehicles. People. Noise—though muffled—still too loud for his comfort. He reached into his breast pocket, pulled out a pair of sunglasses and slipped them on.

The trip seemed to take forever, but eventually the driver guided the vehicle to the front of the hotel where he'd been booked to stay during his week there. The man went inside with him and took care of the registration. When it came time to go up to his room, the man handed him a packet of papers.

"Here is your schedule for the week. The car will be here at eight tomorrow morning to pick you up." The man held out his hand. "If you have any questions or need information, my cell number is written on the top of your schedule."

"Thanks for your help." Eric shook the man's hand then headed for the bank of elevators, carrying his own bags.

Once inside the room, Eric set his bags on the floor. He walked over to the bed, turned around and dropped onto his back. Spread-eagled on the bed, Eric willed himself to relax.

Deep breath in. Deep breath out.

Exhaustion weighed heavily on him. He'd hardly slept the night before as he'd tied up loose ends. Then the route to get to Baghdad has been roundabout and long. Even though there was no such thing as a direct flight from Kampala, Uganda and Baghdad, Iraq, he was sure he could have gotten better connections. He'd be talking to someone in the travel department when he got back about this.

But here he was, and here he'd be for the next week. Surely he could handle a week.

When Eric woke the next morning, his suit was rumpled and he felt gritty. With a groan, he rolled to a sitting position with his feet over the edge of the bed and looked at his watch. Six-thirty. Hopefully, that was AM and not PM. He walked to the window, stretching as he went. His room faced east, and he could see that it was indeed six o'clock in the morning. He had enough time for a shower, devotions and a big breakfast since he'd not eaten anything substantial in almost twenty-four hours.

By the time the driver arrived to pick him up, Eric felt marginally more human and able to deal with the emotions of being back in the country where he'd spent the worst months of his entire life. But with his arrival at the office, he hit the ground running. He barely had time to breathe as he began to work through the appointments he had with several different company representatives. They were already working with some of them, but others were new and important contacts. The busyness was good, giving him little time to dwell on the emotional side of his return to Iraq.

"Is it him?" Sarah asked as she flew into the kitchen after the phone rang.

Staci shook her head and lifted a finger to her lips as she listened to the mother of one of her students explain why they'd be missing their next lesson. The disappointed look on Sarah's face broke her heart. And she didn't understand any more than her daughter why Eric hadn't been in contact with them.

Every day or so while he'd been in Uganda they'd gotten a call from him, but since he'd left for Iraq three days ago they'd heard nothing.

Staci tried to distract Sarah and would tell her that Daddy was probably just busy, but that did nothing to assuage her own worries. Given what she now knew about Eric's history with the Middle East, she couldn't help worrying about him being back there.

"Why don't you draw Daddy a picture?" Staci suggested after she finished her call. She reached into the cupboard to bring out the art box. "Then you can give it to him when he gets back. Or maybe I can take a picture of it with my phone, and we can send it to him."

Once Sarah was settled with paper and crayons, Staci picked up her phone. She debated calling Eric, but she'd already tried that a couple of times and it had gone directly to his voicemail. She hadn't left a message because she didn't want him to feel like she was hounding him. But she was almost to the point of not caring what he thought if it gave her and Sarah peace of mind. In the meantime, she'd try one other person.

"I'm going to the other room to make a phone call, sweetie," Staci told Sarah. She flipped on the small television in their kitchen and found a kids' show. "I'll be back in a couple of minutes."

Sarah nodded but didn't look up from the paper she was coloring on.

Staci picked up the business card Trent had given her when he'd come by to shovel them out. She tapped out his cell number, biting the end of her thumb as she waited for him to reply.

"Hause."

"Trent? It's Staci."

"Staci? What can I do for you?"

Staci suddenly felt a little foolish for having called. Clearly if something had been wrong, Trent wouldn't be sounding as calm as he did. "Well, I…um…was just wondering if you knew how things were going with Eric? He made sure to contact Sarah every couple of days while in Uganda, but he hasn't called since he went to Iraq."

There was a pause on Trent's end before he said, "I haven't heard that anything is wrong, and I'm pretty sure I would have. I think he's probably just really busy. I do know that there were changes to some things once he landed in Iraq that added to his schedule. He's likely just flat out busy."

"Okay, thank you, Trent. That's what I've been telling Sarah but just wanted to make sure nothing more serious was wrong. I mean, I realize I'm not entitled to information, but I was…concerned for Sarah's sake."

Another pause. "Actually, Eric told me he'd included you on his list of contacts if something happened. You will know if something comes up."

That information brought Staci a little bit of peace, but she still wished that Eric would call. She thanked Trent and apologized for interrupting his day before hanging up.

She went back into the kitchen and sat down across from Sarah. "I just talked to someone from Daddy's office." Sarah's head lifted at that news. "They said that he's just really busy. He'll call when he has the time. Anyway, he should be home in a few days."

Sarah nodded, but there was no smile on her small face. "I miss him."

Staci did, too, but she really didn't like admitting that. As she watched Sarah bend her head over the paper again, Staci realized again that she was being selfish in refusing Eric's suggestion of marriage. She couldn't bring herself to think of it as a proposal. That had romantic undertones and there had been nothing romantic in Eric's approach to it.

Seeing how much her daughter had missed Eric these past couple of weeks had made her rethink her knee-jerk response to his suggestion. Hard as it would be, Staci knew that when he got back, she was going to have to address it with him. Hopefully, he wasn't still angry with her about her outright refusal the first time he'd brought it up. And she also hoped he didn't delve too deeply into why her initial reaction had been to say no.

Eric opened the door of his hotel room and stood there for a moment. His gaze roamed the room looking for anything out of place or that shouldn't be there. Only when he was sure that things were as they had been when he'd left that morning did he step further into the room. The stress of not even being able to fully relax even in his hotel room was pushing him to a place he'd never been before. The panic and fear that had been riding him since his arrival in Baghdad made him realize he'd never completely worked through the emotions from his captivity four years ago. Coming on this trip, he'd really hoped that he would be able to face his demons and win, but instead, they were kicking his butt.

He dropped his jacket on the bed and went to stand at the large window of his room. Darkness had settled over the city leaving only a mass of twinkling lights. At any other time, he might have appreciated the view. His stomach growled, reminding him that he hadn't eaten much all day. Back to back meetings with different foreign companies looking to hire their security services in the region had taken up his whole day. Two more days and he'd be heading home.

Turning from the window, he found a menu for the room service and ordered a steak with all the fixings. He hoped that the taste of home might help ease the angst he felt.

As he waited for his meal to arrive, he set his laptop on the hotel desk. He'd seen that an email had arrived from Trent earlier but hadn't had a chance to read through it yet. Once the program had loaded, he clicked on the email to open it.

Hey, bro—just checking in with you. Your lady called me up today asking if you were okay. Seems she's a bit worried about ya. Of course, she said the little lady was the one wanting to speak to her daddy. Might want to touch base with her to let her know you're still alive and well. Hope things are going okay. –T

Eric sat back in the chair, his gaze still on the email. Staci had called Trent about him. Since arriving in Iraq, he'd actually tried very hard not to think about Staci and Sarah. He had so much more to lose now and thinking about that too much would have robbed him of the concentration he needed to be aware of his surroundings. When he'd been kidnaped four years ago, he'd had no one to worry about him but a handful of co-workers. As he'd sat in that dark room they'd kept him in, he'd realized that the way he'd been living his life had not really been living at all. He had no one who loved him enough to miss him. No children. His family hadn't known anything about his life or what had happened to him. The desolation of it all had weighed heavily on him.

Two weeks into his captivity, another prisoner had been shoved into the room with him. That man had been a soldier, and he had been tortured even worse than Eric.

His hand went to the left side of his torso. He still bore the scars of what he'd been subjected to. Though he hadn't been specifically targeted, the rebels had wanted to send a message to his company about the work they'd been doing in Iraq. He'd just made himself the most vulnerable with some really bad decisions. They had seemed to torture him just for kicks—never really asking for information or anything specific about the work his company did. He had figured it was just a matter of time before they killed him. The soldier, however, had been a different story. At least in their minds.

Each time the man returned—his body broken and bleeding—he'd sit in silence with his eyes closed. It hadn't taken long for Eric to discover that the man was praying. Slowly, they began to share their stories, and through Steven Johnson, Eric was faced with the power of his childhood faith for the first time in his adult life.

Though he had tried to ignore the draw to the faith of his family—of his father—in the end, he couldn't deny that he was weary of running. Of fighting the truths that lay deep in his heart. He'd been trying for too long to ignore the pull of the faith he'd rebelled against as a teen and rejected as an adult.

The words Steven Johnson had whispered through chapped and bleeding lips just before taking his final breaths were etched in his mind. Eric had held the man in his arms, tears dripping down his face trying to encourage him to keep going.

My race is over, man, but yours is just beginning. See you at the finish line.

Eric had never been faced with the reality of watching someone end their earthly journey and begin their heavenly one. Though horribly hard in that moment, it was a memory he now cherished.

As he thought of Steven now, Eric knew what he'd say about the fear that he'd been harboring since landing in Baghdad.

Fear is the devil's tool, Eric. He uses it to make you doubt that God is still in control and that He will take care of you. Don't let him deceive you. Even in your darkest hour, God is still there and nothing that happens to you takes Him by surprise.

The rebels had released him ten days later with a message for his bosses, but that hadn't been the only thing he'd taken away from his time in captivity. Eric had recommitted his life to God and had made the decision to make some pretty drastic changes in his life.

Now he was once again allowing fear to creep in and rob him of peace and his trust in God. He'd prayed about this trip. Had committed it to God. But now faced with so many triggers from his past, he'd allowed fear to eclipse everything else. Even contact with Staci and Sarah.

He'd been scared to call them. Scared that once he heard their voices, he'd be on the next plane out of the country. He had a job to do, but Trent's email and the memory of his time with Steven reminded him that he also had another important role in his life now. That of father.

Eric pushed up from the table and went to his jacket on the bed to pull out his phone. But before he could place the call, there was a knock on the door. He jerked at the sound and his heart rate picked up. Moving slowly, he walked over and peered through peephole, hoping it was just his dinner being delivered.

Recognizing the man in the hallway, Eric opened the door. Before he could greet him, two other men stepped into view in the doorway and reached for him. Eric tried to jerk back, but they pulled him from the room. He looked frantically down the hallway, hoping to see someone who would offer him help. Panic spread through his body. Two more men stood a short distance away but made no move in their direction.

"You have to come with us," Aban said. He gave a nod to the two men holding Eric, and they began to escort him roughly down the hallway.

Eric glanced back over his shoulder in time to see the other two men disappear into his room and shut the door. He still gripped his cell phone in his hand, and he hoped that they wouldn't notice. Maybe he could discreetly dial someone to alert them to what was happening to him, but as they entered a service elevator, the Aban reached out and took the phone from him.

"Don't do that, please," Eric said, trying to take it back.

The man shot him a look as he pushed a few buttons on the phone. He slid it into his pocket and said, "You won't need this."

Dread filled Eric along with regret. If only he'd taken the time to phone Sarah and Staci. How he wished he could have spoken to them one last time. His head dropped forward. How could this be happening to him again?

Please, God, send Your angels to protect me. Please.

Chapter Seventeen

STACI stared at the calendar on the fridge in frustration. It had seemed like a good idea when Victoria had made it. Make a countdown for Sarah so that she could mark off the days until Eric came home. Only she'd marked off the last day and there had still been no word from Eric. She'd hoped that after talking to Trent, he might give them a call at least, but there had been nothing.

Worry ate at her. Thoughts of Eric filled every hour. She wanted to know he was okay. Not just physically but also mentally. She could only imagine what it might have been like for him to have to return to the country that had been so traumatic for him in the past. What had Marcus Black been thinking when he'd sent him back there?

Staci took her mug of hot chocolate into the living room and sat down on the chair by the fire she'd turned on earlier. The house was so quiet that she could hear the clicking of the clock on the mantel. Normally, she would have put on some music, but tonight she didn't think that even that would ease her worries and restlessness.

Tomorrow she was going to phone Victoria and Trent again. Surely she had a valid reason if Eric still hadn't made contact. She would have understood him not calling her, but there was no way he wouldn't have contacted Sarah by this point. And if he'd arrived back today, she was positive he would have come right over.

The doorbell peeled, shattering the stillness. She jerked and hot chocolate spilled over onto her hand. She realized she was shaking as she set the mug on the table and stood up. Something held her back from the door as she wiped her hands on her jeans. But when the doorbell rang again, she knew it wasn't something she could ignore.

Maybe…maybe it *was* Eric. That was the thought that propelled her forward, but as she went up on her tiptoes to peer through the glass of the door, her heart shattered.

"Open up, Staci." Trent's voice was firm.

"No." She shook her head, clasping her hands in front of her. "No."

"We need to talk to you."

"Staci, please."

"Tori?"

"Yes. Open the door. We need to talk."

Even more alarmed that Tori and Trent were standing together on the other side of the door, Staci finally reached out and flipped the deadbolt. As the knob began to turn, Staci stepped back, wrapping her arms across her middle in hopes of keeping herself together.

"Let's go into the living room," Trent said as he slipped an arm around her shoulders.

Staci slumped into the chair she'd just vacated. Trent and Victoria took seats on the couch across from her. "What's happened to Eric?"

Trent leaned forward, his elbows braced on his thighs. "We don't know. Last time anyone saw him was when he was dropped off at his hotel…two days ago."

"Two days?" Staci frowned. "And it took them this long to realize he was missing?"

Trent shook his head. "We found out almost immediately. He'd ordered room service but wasn't there when they went to deliver it. The door was ajar, and all his belongings were missing."

Staci's heart pounded in her chest. "All his stuff was gone, too?"

"Yes. Which seemed very unusual. Usually in kidnapping cases, they take the person but don't bother with their things. We didn't let you know right away as we've been trying to follow up on some leads and see if we could figure out what happened to him."

"Were there no cameras at the hotel? I mean, he couldn't have just left with all his stuff without someone seeing him, right?"

Trent shrugged. "The cameras at the hotel were tampered with. There is no footage of him or anyone suspicious around the time he was taken. We honestly have no idea what's happened to him."

"You're a security firm. Surely you have resources that the average person wouldn't have. Doesn't he have GPS on his phone or something?"

This time it was Victoria who responded. "Believe me, Staci, Blackthorpe is doing all they can to find Eric. Whoever has him went to great lengths to cover their tracks."

"His cell phone appears to be disabled. There is a secondary GPS locator in all our phones that should still have been functioning, but it's dead. It all went offline while still at the hotel." Trent bent his head and cleared his throat. "Right now we're having to consider that it might be an inside job. There is just too much about this that smacks of information someone could only get by being part of BlackThorpe or having access to someone who works for us."

A sick feeling grew in the pit of her stomach. She'd read some articles detailing what Eric had endured the last time he'd been held captive and couldn't even imagine how he'd survive it for a second time. "Why would someone target Eric? Is it the same people as last time?"

"We don't think Eric was specifically targeted. Marcus was the one who was supposed to have taken this trip. Because of some intel we'd received, Eric convinced Marcus to let him go instead."

"Why would he do that? Put himself in danger?"

"I'm sure Eric didn't think he was doing that. From what we'd heard, the target was just Marcus. Apparently the man has made an enemy or two in the past. Unfortunately, the business that needed to be conducted on this trip was too important to be put off or to have to worry about Marcus's safety. Eric was the next logical choice given his knowledge of the area and his experience with corporate security."

"Still, I don't understand why Eric would do that." Staci looked to where Victoria sat, her face tense. "How is your family taking this? I'm sure this is hard to go through again."

"We didn't actually go through it last time. Right around when Eric was taken, other things were going on in the news that the media deemed more important. You know how it is. And Eric hadn't left any of us as his contacts, so no one from that company called to let us know. It wasn't until he was released and came home that we realized what had happened." Victoria sighed. "But in answer to your question, my family is doing okay. We know that God is with Eric wherever he is, and we're trusting that he'll be coming home soon."

As she sat there, Staci realized that for the first time in a long time, her faith was being tested on such a deep level. The last time had been when the doctors had outlined the possible struggles and health issues Sarah might face. The unknown of this situation—like the one with Sarah—was once again testing her belief that God was in control and that everything would work out.

"Knowing you were expecting Eric home, we figured we'd better let you know," Trent said. "I wanted to wait until we had more news, but you would have only assumed the worst anyway if tomorrow came and he didn't show up."

Staci nodded. "Thank you for telling me. I know this can't be any easier for you two than it is for me."

Victoria took a shaky breath and dipped her head. Trent slid an arm around her shoulders and pulled her close. Staci could see the resistance in Victoria before she sagged against him. The expression on Trent's face as he looked down at the small woman at his side distracted Staci momentarily from her own pain. She would have to take the time to process that at a later date.

Right then, she needed to figure out what to tell her daughter when she woke the next morning with no more days to X off the calendar on the fridge and still no sign of her daddy.

The next couple of weeks dragged by for Staci. Each day she woke with the anticipation that this would be the day when Eric resurfaced. Each morning Sarah would ask if Daddy was coming home. And each day Staci would struggle to keep her emotions in check as she lied to her daughter and told her that her daddy was tied up with his work and would be home soon.

But once the house was quiet each night, she'd sit in her chair and cry and pray that God would bring her daughter's father home. And this time she'd give him what he wanted. He wanted to be a full-time dad to his daughter and now, realizing how short life could be, Staci knew she was being selfish in denying him and Sarah that opportunity just because she was scared.

The box of chocolates he'd brought her still sat on the table beside her chair, a reminder of not just their most recent time, but of their time together years ago. Drawing her feet up as she leaned back in the chair, Staci wrapped her hand around the necklace she'd not taken off since she'd received the news of his disappearance.

All around her, life went on as normal. In lots of ways, she was being forced to go on as normal, too. She still had piano students wanting lessons. She still had a daughter who needed to be taken care of and whose emotional and physical needs had to come before her own.

Staci stared at the flickering flames and once again wondered where Eric was. Was he getting enough to eat and drink? Was it hot or cold where he was? Was he being subjected to the same tortures as before?

God, please no. Please protect him with Your almighty hand. You promised that if You are for us, no one can stand against us. Keep those holding him from harming him. And bring him home to us soon.

Staci kept her eyes closed and felt herself drifting off. Her sleep had been fitful since that night Trent and Tori had come by with the upsetting news. Both had made regular visits to check up on her and Sarah. They hadn't come together again, but Staci hadn't forgotten the exchange between them. She planned to talk to Eric about it when he came home.

Because he was coming home.

He had to.

She couldn't live with the alternative.

The doorbell rang, jerking her from drowsiness. She bolted out of the chair. Last time the doorbell had rung at this hour, it had brought bad news. Maybe this time it brought good.

Staci ran for the front door and pulled it open without even looking through the glass of the window. She gaped in shock at the man standing on her doorstep.

Bearded and looking exhausted, Eric stared at her.

"Oh, God, thank you!" Staci threw her arms around Eric's neck, her breath coming in gasping sobs. "You're home."

His arms closed around her waist as he pulled her tightly to his body. "Yes. I'm home."

She couldn't stop the hot tears that flowed from her eyes. Then she felt Eric lift her from the ground and take a few steps into the house. He set her down but didn't release her as he reached to close the door. She knew she needed to let him go, but she really didn't want to.

They stood there for several minutes not saying anything, arms tightly wrapped around each other. Finally, he stepped back and looked down at her.

"I told God if He got me home safe and sound, I was going to try one more time." He paused then said, "Staci, will you marry me?"

Without any hesitation, Staci said, "Yes. I also told God that if you gave me a second chance, I'd say yes."

Eric took her face in his hands and bent his head to press his lips to hers. With the facial hair he now sported, it almost felt like a different man kissing her, not the one she'd left behind six years ago. And he kissed her like he'd never kissed her before. It was gentle and loving in a way that made her heart clench.

When the kiss ended, Staci was reluctant to move away from him, but she couldn't be selfish. "Does anyone else know you're back?"

Eric shook his head. "I had to come here first." His gaze went to the stairs. "I need to see her."

Staci nodded. "Go ahead while I call Tori and Trent."

"I won't wake her. I need to deal with some other stuff before I can give her my full attention."

Staci watched him climb the stairs, almost afraid to move for fear of waking up. Surely this was a dream. She'd fallen asleep in front of the fire again and this was all just a dream. But the memory of his arms around her, his lips pressed to hers, was too real.

Turning, she went into the living room and grabbed her phone. She called Tori first.

"He's home," were the first words out of her mouth when Victoria answered.

Stunned silence filled the air between them for about two seconds. "He's there? He's back? And he's safe?"

"Yes, he's back and he's safe. You need to come over. And tell your family."

"I will. We'll be right there."

Next Staci phoned Trent and delivered the same message. His response was much the same as Tori's had been.

"I've got to tell the BlackThorpe guys. They're going to want to talk to him."

"That's fine, but maybe ask them to give him a little time with his family. They're on their way over here now."

"Okay. I'll let them know."

Eric stood in the doorway of the room, uncertain if he trusted himself not to wake the little girl sleeping in the bed just a few feet away. Until Staci had opened that door, he hadn't allowed himself to believe he was truly safe and that he would see his family again.

Slowly, quietly, he walked through the darkened room and sank to his knees beside Sarah's bed. She lay on her side facing him, her hands tucked up under her chin. His heart clenched at the sight.

Thank you, God. Thank you.

He allowed himself to reach out and lightly brush his fingertips across the softness of her cheek. She didn't stir, but he didn't touch her again. He really did need to deal with other things and when she woke he wanted to be able to give her his full attention. And he hoped to have showered and shaved by that point as well.

Pushing himself to stand again, Eric walked from her bedside. He paused in the doorway for one more look before descending the stairs. As he reached the main floor, he heard noises coming from the kitchen so turned in that direction.

Staci looked up from her phone as he walked in. Seeing her there, his heart felt as if something had just grabbed hold of it.

"Are you hungry?" she asked as he walked toward her.

Yes, in fact, he was starving. It felt like forever since he'd had a decent meal. "I am."

"Why don't you sit down while I make you something?" She lifted her phone. "I called Tori. Your family is on their way over. And I called Trent. He said the guys from your company would want to talk to you. I asked him to please keep them away until your family had a little time with you. I hope that's okay."

Eric lifted a brow as she detailed her actions. It wasn't like her to be so take-charge. "Yes, that's fine. Great, in fact."

She gave him a quick smile before opening the fridge and pulling out some packages of food. He slumped back in his chair and watched as she began to make him a sandwich.

There was so much Eric wanted to say. So much he wanted to share, but he knew that it would have to wait. The silence between them was deep and heavy, but not uncomfortable. He didn't feel compelled to break it as he might have in the past. Right then, he was just glad to be in the safety of her home, sitting at her table, being reminded that during his absence this time he had had family and friends praying for him. It brought tremendous peace to his soul after almost two weeks of upheaval.

She set the sandwich on the table in front of him. "Milk? Juice? Water?"

"Water. Cold water. Thank you."

After she had brought him a glass of cold water, she sat down across from him. He bowed his head for a quick prayer of thanks and found her still watching him when he looked up.

"Are you hurt anywhere?" she asked. "Should you be at the hospital?"

Eric shook his head as he chewed the first delicious bite of his sandwich. "It wasn't like that this time."

"Okay. I just wanted to make sure." She tilted her head to the side, her hair sliding across her shoulder. "I won't ask you to share everything now. You'll just have to repeat it." She paused. "Just know that we're very relieved you're safe."

Before Eric could respond, the doorbell rang.

"You'd better eat up. I have a feeling the family has arrived." Staci stood and left the kitchen.

A few seconds later, he heard voices that he recognized as his parents and Tori. He wondered if they understood why he had come here—to Staci's house—instead of theirs. He hadn't been entirely sure why himself, he just knew that when he left the airport and called a cab, this was the first address that had come to mind.

"Eric!"

He stood in time to feel his mother's arms around him. Fighting a rush of unexpected emotion at her tight hold on his neck, Eric wrapped his arms around her. "Love you, Mom."

"Oh, son, I love you, too." He felt her drag in a deep breath. Then she released him and stepped back, still not moving too far away. She reached up and touched his face. "And look at you. All furry-faced. But oh, so good to see."

"My turn, hun."

Eric smiled at his dad as he was pulled into his strong arms. And then it was Tori's turn. Brooke was missing, but that didn't surprise him too much.

As his parents pelted him with questions, the doorbell went again. Staci had been standing near the entrance to the kitchen, and he saw her slip into the hallway. When she reappeared a short time later, it was with Trent by her side. Since the man was the closest thing to a brother he had, and his family also embraced him as such, Eric waved him over to where they were huddled.

"Man, you had us *all* worried to death," Trent muttered in his ear as they shared a quick hug. As he stepped back, his eyebrows rose. "And you are a sight for sore eyes. Quite a sight, actually."

Eric gave him a playful punch in the shoulder.

"Can you tell us what happened?" his dad asked.

Eric sat back down as his family found seats around the table. He noticed Trent had set a piece of equipment on the counter and knew he was protecting their conversation. "There are a lot of details that won't make much sense to you, but suffice to say, I was taken for my own protection."

Trent turned from the counter to stare at him, and Eric knew that his friend understood the implications of that statement.

"For your own protection?" his mother repeated. "But why wouldn't they at least let you contact us to let us know you were okay? We were so worried."

"I know, Mom. And I'm sorry. I tried to convince them to let me get word out, but they were adamant. Maybe they were overreacting, I don't know, but what I do know is that I'm here now, and I'm safe. That to me is worth all we've been through these past couple of weeks."

Though the frown hadn't completely left his mother's face, she said, "That's true."

Eric knew it was hard for his parents to accept what they didn't truly understand, but they also were aware that due to the nature of his job that was often the case. Because of that, he answered what questions he could, which weren't many and even his answers to them were vague.

"Well, we'd better go," his dad said. "I'm sure your boss still wants to talk to you."

Eric nodded. "Yes. I need to touch base with him."

His mother stood and came to press a kiss to the top of his head, her hand cupping his cheek. "Come to the house for dinner on Sunday."

His gaze met Staci's for a moment before he said, "We'll be there." And hopefully would have an announcement to make. He needed to make sure that once the emotion of the moment wore off that Staci didn't change her mind.

Once his family had left, he sat back down at the table to finish his sandwich. Trent sat across from him. "The guys want to see you. Are you up for it?"

Eric nodded. "Definitely. But thank you for holding them off until after my family left."

The doorbell rang again, but as Staci moved toward the hallway, Trent called her back. "I'll let them in."

"Where they waiting outside?" Eric asked.

"Yep. A big black Suburban and a couple of trucks. Nothing too obvious," Trent said with a lift of the corner of his mouth.

Eric glanced at Staci as Trent left the room. Her gaze followed his friend as a hand reached up to touch her hair, a frown drawing her brows together. He couldn't help but smile at her reaction.

Her gaze met his, and she froze then lowered her hand. "Do I need to leave?"

He shook his head. "You might as well hear this. Saves me having to repeat it."

"Did you want another sandwich?" she asked as she approached the table.

"Maybe later," he said, handing her his empty plate. "But would it be too much trouble to put on a pot of coffee?"

"Not at all."

Eric watched her walk away, wishing he had pulled her into his arms. He had missed her as much as he'd missed Sarah. Would she believe him if he told her that?

Noise from the hallway drew his attention from the woman he hoped he'd soon call his wife.

Chapter Eighteen

THE testosterone in the room overwhelmed Staci. She tried to remember the names of each of the men Trent introduced her to.

Marcus—the only man she knew by name—seemed older than the others. Whether it was by age or from life, he had a hardened demeanor though he had been polite in their introductions. She knew he was co-founder of BlackThorpe and that Eric admired him.

"Staci, this is Alex Thorpe. He is the other founder of BlackThorpe," Trent said.

This man stood several inches above Trent and though he wore a pair of jeans and a t-shirt that said "Kiss me, I'm Irish" beneath a leather jacket, he exuded a quiet air of control. He nodded and smiled as he shook her hand. "A pleasure to meet you, Staci."

Next was Justin, a man who looked like he'd never met a piece of exercise equipment he didn't like. Like Alex, he was dressed in jeans and a t-shirt, but his shirt stretched tight across his chest in a way that his boss's hadn't. This guy was clearly the company muscle.

"And last but not least we have Than," Trent said as he jabbed at the man with his elbow. "He's our ladies' man so keep an eye on him."

Staci's eyes widened as Than winked at her. She shot a quick glance at Eric. Though he was watching them, he didn't seem overly concerned about his co-worker's introduction. The man looked to have some Hispanic blood with his dark eyes and hair and tanned skin.

"Pleased to meet you, Staci." His smile was infectious, and she found herself returning it.

It wasn't until the last of the men joined Eric at the table that she remembered she'd just greeted the head honchos of Eric's company in sweats and her hair all caught up on the top of her head in a scrunchie. So much for making a good first impression.

She glanced at Eric and found him watching her. He gave her a quick smile before Marcus drew his attention away. Butterflies fluttered in her stomach as she moved to where the coffee maker sat on the counter. Trying to be quiet, she started the pot and pulled out mugs from the cupboard.

"Our conversation is safe," Trent said as he settled into the chair beside Eric.

With a nod, Alex asked, "Who was it that took you?"

"Aban Al-Jamil," Eric responded without hesitation.

Staci glanced at the table in time to see Marcus scowl. "Aban? I talked to him every day. He said he had no idea where you were."

As she waited for the coffee to finish, Staci pulled out a container of cookies and began to put them on a plate.

"Yes, he told me he'd spoken with you." Eric paused. "He didn't trust anyone. I mean, he trusted you, Marcus, but he didn't trust that the phones and offices weren't bugged. That he wasn't being followed and being eavesdropped on wherever he went."

"Surely there was some way to contact us," Alex said. "We were going crazy trying to figure out what was happening."

"I told Aban I needed to contact someone, but he was afraid that the persons involved would get desperate." Eric looked at Marcus. "He had a feeling the driver was in on something. They had bugged the vehicle as well as putting a tracker on it, just in case. The man was asking too many questions when he picked me up at the airport. I couldn't understand what he was saying, but later Aban said he mentioned that he thought he was picking up Marcus Black."

"Does he suspect someone there or here?" Marcus asked.

Eric scratched his chin, as if the extra facial hair was aggravating him. "He never came right out and said, but given how he handled getting me out of the country, I think he suspected the person in charge was here. I traveled under false documents through a bunch of different countries before finally arriving back in the US. That's partly why he waited so long. He wanted my appearance to be different. Hence the beard."

"I'm still trying to follow all of this. Why would they take you and not try to let someone know what was going on?" This time it was Than who spoke. No longer the flirty ladies' man he'd been a few minutes ago, the dark-haired man leaned forward, his arms on the table. "He had to know we had resources to get you out safely."

As the coffee pot signaled its completion, Staci put cream and sugar on a tray along with the mugs and the coffee pot and took it to the table. Eric reached up to take the tray from her and slid it in front of the guys.

"Thanks," he said with another smile that set her nerves fluttering. "Help yourself, guys."

Staci wasn't sure if she should stay or leave, but she was very curious about what had transpired.

"I think Aban was afraid that we were wrong and that whoever had planned to take Marcus would be just as happy to take me instead. Either way, he'd have an advantage over Marcus. Apparently one of Aban's guys picked something up that led him to believe that it was going to happen soon since I was scheduled to leave in two days. But he didn't want whoever was behind it to suspect that I'd been taken by our own people. He figured I'd be safer that way."

"Then maybe they should have left your stuff in the hotel room," Justin remarked drily, speaking for the first time. "Having them clean out your room made it look a little less like a kidnapping and more like a planned departure."

Eric shrugged. "I think he was trying to make it easier on me. Honestly, I'm not ashamed to admit I was scared when they came to get me. He didn't let me know what was going on. Just grabbed me from my hotel room while I was waiting for my steak to be delivered."

"So what does Aban plan to do now? What are we supposed to do? Wait until someone moves on one of us here?" Marcus asked.

"I think Aban figured an attack was far less likely on our home turf, so to speak." Eric paused. "I guess what I'm wondering is who has it in for you, Marcus. And unlike Aban, I don't think we should let down our guard just because we're on familiar territory here."

Staci saw Alex and Marcus exchange glances, but it was Alex who spoke. "We may have a few suggestions on possible threats. And not all of them are here in the US."

There was silence at the table. Staci waited for either man to elaborate, and she suspected the other men were waiting, too.

Finally, Marcus drained the coffee from his cup and said, "Alex and I need to have a conversation about this then we'll all meet together again tomorrow at the office. We've got too many other things going on to allow ourselves to become too distracted by this, but it is definitely something we need to address. Obviously sooner rather than later."

When Marcus pushed back from the table and stood, Alex did as well. As if signaling the end of the meeting, the other men stood, too.

Alex and Marcus came and thanked her for the coffee before saying goodbye and leaving. Justin and Than stayed a little bit longer, asking Eric a few more questions, but soon they left as well.

"Do you need a ride home, bud?" Trent asked.

Eric nodded. "I want to get home and get this fur off my face before I see Sarah." He turned to Staci. "It looks like I'll be tied up at the office most of tomorrow, but can we plan on dinner together tomorrow night?"

Staci nodded, suddenly uncertain how to act. Technically, they were engaged, but it still felt a bit awkward. Particularly with Trent standing right there.

"Thanks for the coffee and cookies, Staci," Trent said. "I'm going to go start up my truck. Whenever you're ready to leave, just come on out."

Left alone with Eric, Staci felt self-conscious. "I...uh...hope they can figure out what happened."

Eric moved toward her. "We'll get to the bottom of it. It's what we do, and we're very good at it." He lifted her chin so their gazes met. "I know things are moving fast and sort of out of order with us. Just give me a few days, and we'll get this figured out. Okay?"

Staci nodded. When he moved a little closer, she found herself leaning into him. His hand slid around to the back of her neck as his lips pressed to hers. Her body immediately responded to his touch, as it always had. This physical pull was something that had always been there between them. At one time, she'd cherished it because it seemed to be the only connection they had.

Now it scared her. She wanted more from him. She wanted more for them. The physical intimacy could cloud everything. The memories of the past could impair her judgment as well as his. But if all he offered her was this physical connection and a shared love with their daughter, would it be enough?

The kiss ended, but the question lingered.

"Goodnight," Eric said, his gaze unreadable. "I'll call you tomorrow."

Staci wrapped her arms across her middle and nodded. "I think I'll wait to tell Sarah you're here until you can tell her yourself. She'll go bonkers wanting to see you if I tell her before then."

Eric smiled and emotion flooded his expression. "Yes, I'm sure that would be true. I hope you don't think I'm putting her second by not being here first thing tomorrow or even waking her up tonight. I just want to get this dealt with so I can focus on her. I will let the guys know that I need a few days off once I finish my debriefing with them."

"I understand. You do what you need to do. She'll be fine. I think just seeing you will put her mind at ease."

An awkward silence stretched between them again.

"Okay. I'll give you a call tomorrow."

Staci nodded then followed him into the hallway where he picked up his bag and opened the door. She stood in the doorway as he made his way to where Trent waited in his truck. It would have been nice if he could have stayed, but she knew that was just asking for trouble.

She gave a wave as the truck backed out of her driveway and then closed the door. After locking up and arming the alarm, Staci went back into the kitchen to clean up the remnants of the coffee and cookies. Maybe the mundaneness of it all would help to convince her that this was all for real.

As she placed the mugs into the dishwasher, her thoughts kept going to Eric's proposal. Even though she'd decided that if he asked again that she would say yes, she wasn't sure how she felt about it. There was no doubting that the physical connection still existed between them, but that hadn't been enough the first time around. Would it and their shared love for Sarah be a strong enough foundation for a marriage that would last? She wasn't even going to consider that their marriage would involve them not being intimate with each other. Something told her that would be next to impossible.

What about what God wants?

She paused, wet cloth in hand, and straightened from where she'd ben wiping the table. Eric had said that he'd asked God for a second chance, as had she.

Staci sank down on a chair, the dishcloth still clutched in her hand. Getting married would solve a problem for each of them. Sarah would have her mommy *and* daddy with her. Eric wouldn't have to leave his little girl every night. And Staci wouldn't face the prospect of having to share custody with Eric.

She could see that Eric had changed since they'd last been in a relationship. Staci didn't think it would be the same way it had been between them before. He might still not love her, but already she could see that he respected her in a way he hadn't six years ago. Oh, he'd had a slip-up here and there, but he'd apologized. Something else he'd never done back then. Maybe this time around would be different enough that she could live with it.

Maybe...

If she could only get past her fear of reverting back to how things had been for her six years ago.

Eric tossed his bag onto the bed and headed straight for his bathroom, shaving kit in hand. He'd understood why Aban had wanted him to grow a beard, but he was more than ready to be rid of it. He pulled off the t-shirt Aban had insisted he wear along with jeans for his trip home. Anything to make him less like a businessman. Less like a security specialist.

He picked up the scissors to trim a bit of the length before subjecting his razor to removing the rest. It would be good to feel more like himself again.

Though he still thought Aban had gone overboard with all the precautions, Eric couldn't deny that the outcome was a good one. He was home and safe. At this point, that was good in his eyes. Home to see his daughter.

Home to Staci.

He lowered his razor and stared at himself in the mirror.

They were engaged.

He gave his head a rueful shake. Though he had said if he'd had a second chance he'd ask her to marry him again, he had planned to do it a bit better the second time around. With a ring and a little more romance. Instead, she'd gotten a heated kiss along with the proposal then a request to see their daughter before having to deal with a kitchen full of family and strange men. He should have stayed so they could talk a little after everything had settled down. Hopefully, she'd give him that opportunity the next night after having dinner with him and Sarah.

He quickly finished removing the last of the hair from his face and then got into the shower to wash it all away. Not long after, he crawled into his bed and let out a long sigh as he settled down beneath the covers. Though it was technically *home,* it wasn't where he wanted to be. He was finding it hard to keep his past with Staci from spilling over into his present.

In the past, arriving home from an extended time away meant something far different than it did now. But that didn't stop him from wishing he was sharing a bed with Staci, just down the hall from where Sarah slept. The mental image of that felt right to him. It was where he belonged. Now it was just a matter of getting them to that point. At least she'd said *yes* to his impromptu proposal, so it didn't seem as out of reach as it had the last time he'd asked her.

And things would be different this time. The man he was now appreciated the changes in Staci in a way his old self wouldn't have. She had been a strange mix of timidity and strength back then. Around him, she had never voiced a dissenting opinion. Had agreed to do whatever he wanted. There had been times he'd sensed she wanted to disagree with him, but she never had. Put her at a piano in front of a crowd, however, and he saw a strength she didn't show when they were together in his condo. And she came to life as the music flowed through her. It had been mesmerizing.

A friend of a friend had introduced them after one of her concerts. Just watching her play with such passion and talent had intrigued him. He remembered that first meeting. She had been so dainty and her hand had felt fragile in his as they'd shook hands, though he knew that to play the way she did required incredible strength. Her blonde hair had been pixie short with frosted tips. With her icy blue eyes and flawless skin, she'd been striking in appearance, but his friend had told him that her nickname was the Ice Queen because she rarely showed emotion.

It had been something of a challenge to get her to go out with him at first. But he'd persevered. There was just something about her that had made him want her in his life. And in the end he had gotten what he wanted. But now looking back, he knew he'd had her body, but he wasn't sure he'd ever had her heart.

That was something he'd have to work on this time around with her. He didn't want Sarah growing up in a family that had parents who only tolerated each other. Though his parents had gone through a horribly rough patch in their marriage, they had persevered and seemed to love each other more now than they had back then. He wanted that same sort of family for Sarah. A family where their love grew stronger each day, drawing them closer to each other even as they faced rough patches.

As he lay there in the dark, Eric allowed himself to really dissect their former relationship. Between his schedule and hers and their social life, they hadn't had a lot of alone time outside of the bedroom. She had moved in with him three months after they'd started dating, and they'd lived together for two years before that day he'd walked into the condo and realized she was gone.

During that time, he hadn't been too interested in discussing his past, and honestly, he hadn't been terribly interested in her past either. They lived in the moment, really. No talk of their pasts and no plans for their future. Well, until the night she pressed him about marriage for the first time.

Maybe if she'd approached it more subtlety, he would have been receptive to the idea. But, then again, maybe not.

Probably not.

Staci found it hard not to tell Sarah about Eric's return the next day. The first phone call of the day already had Sarah asking about her daddy. Fortunately, that call was from a piano student so the conversation didn't alert Sarah to anything. Unfortunately, the call did derail Staci's plans for later in the day.

After she got Sarah settled playing her favorite game on the tablet, Staci went to the kitchen to call Eric. She was relieved when it went to his voicemail.

"Hi, Eric. It's Staci. I'm just calling about tonight. I forgot that I had agreed to meet with a student to help them with a piece they're playing at their church on Sunday. The only time they have available is six tonight, so it will just be you and Sarah going out for dinner, which I think Sarah would enjoy more anyway. I think she'd love to have you all to herself after missing you so much. Let me know what time to have her ready to go." She paused. "Talk to you later."

She switched her phone to vibrate after leaving the message and then slid it into her pocket so she'd feel it if anyone called.

Sarah had just finished praying for their lunch when Staci felt the phone vibrate against her leg.

"Your soup should be cool enough to eat, sweetie. I'm just going to go to the bathroom for a minute."

As soon as she was in the hallway, Staci pulled the phone from her pocket and tapped the screen to receive the call.

"Hello?" She kept her voice low as she was still within earshot of the kitchen.

"Staci?"

"Hang on." Staci slipped into the bathroom and shut the door. "Sorry about that. I didn't want Sarah to hear me talking to you."

"You're not able to come tonight?" He certainly didn't beat around the bush.

"No. I'm sorry. I had forgotten that I'd promised this student I'd help her. Tonight was the only time she could come."

There was silence for a couple of seconds. "That's okay. There will be other dinners out. I may ask Victoria to tag along. Could I take her to a movie or something as well?"

"That would be perfect. There's one she's been dying to see."

"Okay. I'll be by to pick her up around five-thirty. We should be wrapped up here by then."

"Everything going alright?"

"As well as can be expected," Eric said with a sigh. "More questions than answers so far."

"Well, like you said, you guys are good at what you do, so I'm sure you'll get to the bottom of it."

"Hopefully that's before anyone gets hurt."

Staci didn't like the sound of that. And Eric apparently didn't want to expound on it because the conversation ended shortly after. She slipped the phone back into her pocket and left the bathroom.

Sarah was still seated at the table and looked up as Staci slid onto a chair across from her. Hoping to distract her from questions about Eric, Staci mentioned possibly going to the movie she wanted to see.

"Really? We can go tonight?" Sarah's eyes sparkled with excitement.

"Yep. And maybe out for supper first." Staci figured that it would be easier to get her dressed later if she thought they were actually going out.

"I want to pick out my clothes," the little girl announced as she slid from her seat. "I'm done eating."

Staci smiled and nodded. "Make sure you put any clothes you decide not to wear back in the closet."

Alone at the table, Staci took a couple of spoonfuls of her soup before pushing the bowl away. She wondered how long she could avoid having to discuss the proposal with Eric. Without a doubt, he would want the wedding to happen sooner rather than later. She knew how much he wanted to be a full-time dad to Sarah. And she couldn't blame him. She just wasn't sure she was strong enough to have him back in *her* life full-time.

Would it have been the worst thing in the world to share custody with Eric? Families around the world did it all the time. They could probably come to an agreement on a schedule fairly easily. It would be a hard adjustment for her, but it would save having to deal with Eric on such an intimate level once again. It had almost destroyed her last time. She wasn't sure she was strong enough to deal with it again.

It had been several years since she'd last gone to her counselor, but perhaps it was time to make another appointment. In the meantime, a best friend chat might be the next best thing. And that night would be perfect since it looked like both Eric and Sarah would be gone for at least three hours. Plenty of time to work with her student and then chat with Denise.

"You're lucky," Denise told her when she phoned. "Philip is working late, so I was at loose ends. I'll be there at six-forty-five."

Feeling better already, Staci spent the next few hours trying to entertain a little girl who was already ready to head out the door.

"You doing okay, bud?"

Eric turned to see Trent in the doorway of his office. They'd finished the last of the debriefing twenty minutes earlier, and he was back in his office trying to answer emails that had come in during his two-week absence.

With a sigh, Eric leaned back in his chair. "I'm just feeling very frustrated. Like I should have more answers than I do. Believe me, I asked all those same questions to Aban. The man could be infuriatingly evasive. I think Marcus should fly him here and get more direct answers from him."

Trent settled into the chair across the desk from Eric. "Are you going out tonight with Sarah and Staci?"

Glad for the change of subject, Eric said, "Just Sarah. Staci forgot she had a student coming over at six."

"That's too bad," Trent said.

Eric nodded. "I assume she's telling me the truth and not trying to avoid me."

"Why would she want to avoid you?"

"I…uh…kind of proposed to her as soon as I walked in the door last night."

Trent let out a laugh. "You proposed to her?"

"Yeah." Eric shifted in his chair. "I decided that if I got out of the mess in Iraq, I was going to ask her again."

"Again? You've already asked her once?"

"Yeah."

Trent gave a shake of his head. "Still having those women troubles?"

"Shut up." Eric tossed a pen at his friend who easily deflected it. "This time, however, she said yes."

"But now she's avoiding you. That doesn't bode well," Trent pointed out.

"I didn't say she *was* avoiding me. Just that I *hoped* she wasn't. "

"Either way, dude, the fact you're thinking about it means you have some concerns."

"I always have concerns when it comes to Staci. She's already left me once and disappeared. She could do it again. Money's not an issue for her. So far, the only reason I think she's stuck around is that Sarah would be pretty upset if she couldn't see me anymore."

"Guess you need to treat her better this time around," Trent said.

"I really can't wait until you get a girlfriend," Eric muttered.

Trent grinned. "Just waitin' for that perfect woman."

"Good luck with that."

"I don't need luck. All I need is that one woman who may not be perfect for anyone else, but she's perfect for me."

Eric hoped his friend was right. In the time he'd known Trent, he'd only dated off and on, nothing serious.

"I'll leave you to your stuff. Maybe we can catch up on the weekend."

Eric nodded as his friend stood. "I'll give you a call."

Alone in his office, Eric finished up his work then headed home. He changed out of his suit into a pair of jeans and a sweater. Even though he knew he'd be early, he headed over to Staci's. He was more than ready to see his little girl.

Chapter Nineteen

THE look on Sarah's face when she rounded the corner to see him standing in the hallway filled Eric's heart until he thought it would burst. She flung herself into his arms and wrapped her arms tightly around his neck when he picked her up. It was like she was afraid to let him go.

"Daddy, you're home."

And those three words cemented in Eric everything he wanted. To be this little girl's daddy. And to call this house with her and Staci his home.

Eric glanced over to where Staci stood watching them, her arms crossed over her waist. "Hope it's okay I came a little early."

"It's fine. I was having a hard time keeping the secret anyway." The corners of her lips lifted in a quick smile. "Where are you guys going for supper?"

Eric grinned, trying to ignore the growing pit in his stomach at the distance she was keeping between them. "Where do you think? Unless things have changed since I've been away."

Staci shook her head. "Nope. Still the same."

Lowering Sarah to the floor, Eric said, "Well, kiddo, let's get your jacket and boots on so we can go get Aunt Tori."

"Aunt Tori is coming, too?"

Staci moved to open the closet beside Eric, and he had to resist the urge to pull her into his arms. Something about the way she held herself told him it would not be well received. And that concerned him. He could read nothing in her eyes. Nothing in her expression. The Ice Queen was alive and well.

"Here you go," Staci said as she held out Sarah's jacket so the little girl could slip her arms into the sleeves.

Sarah held Eric's hand in a tight grip as she shoved her feet into her boots. "You coming too, Mama?"

"Not this time, sweetie. I have to meet with Emily for a lesson."

Sarah frowned. "Can I still go to the movie?"

"Oh, yes. Your dad and Aunt Tori will still take you to watch it."

"Guess we'll get home a little later than usual," Eric said.

"That's fine. I think this is a worthy exception to her bedtime."

Staci bent to press a kiss to Sarah's cheek and then straightened. She didn't avoid his gaze as she said, "Have fun."

The need to talk with Staci grew as he drove to pick Victoria up from her place. None of his family knew of his proposal, so he couldn't even talk with Tori about it, but as Sarah ran off to play in the Playland, he knew had to do something.

"Would you mind terribly taking Sarah to see the movie on your own?"

Tori frowned at him. "I thought this was supposed to be your time with her after being away so long."

"It is, but I need to talk with Staci. And it's a conversation best had when Sarah isn't around."

His sister stared at him. "What's going on?"

"I'm not sure, to be honest. I think we just need to sit down and have a good conversation without having to worry about Sarah."

Though Tori hesitated at first, eventually she nodded. "You'll still have to drop us off and pick us up since I don't have my car."

"That's not a problem."

Thankfully, when they told Sarah about the change of plans, it wasn't a problem with her. She just wanted to watch the movie. And the promise of ice cream didn't hurt either.

It was around seven when Eric pulled back into Staci's driveway. He noticed that there was a car parked there and wondered if her lesson was still going on.

Not wanting to interrupt them, he let himself into the house with the plan of going into the kitchen to wait until she was done. But there was no music playing and the living room where the piano sat was empty. He heard the murmur of voices coming from the kitchen and headed in that direction.

"So you're having second thoughts?"

Eric came to an abrupt halt. He didn't recognize the woman's voice, but the question had his feet rooted firmly to the floor.

"Every single minute of every hour." Eric reached out to brace his hand on the wall. That was a voice he recognized.

From Denise's expression, Staci knew she had some explaining to do.

"What is making you have second thoughts? Was it more than Eric not being a Christian that broke you guys up before?" Denise asked. "It seems to me that if that were the only reason, you wouldn't be having second thoughts about it now."

"It was mainly his unwillingness to get married that broke us up, yes, but after I got out of the relationship and found out I was pregnant, I realized that it hadn't been a healthy situation for me. I know we're both different people now, but I'm still scared."

"Scared of what?" Denise lifted her mug of coffee and took a sip.

Staci looked down at the tablecloth as she contemplated telling her friend things she'd never told anyone but her counselor. "To help you understand, I need to go back to my relationship with my parents."

"You've never talked much about them in the years I've known you," Denise commented.

"That's because they're not in my life anymore." Staci ran a finger along the rim of her mug of hot chocolate. "My parents never wanted children, so they had a difficult time adjusting to having me in their life. They had lots of money though, so I spent most of my early years with a nanny. I guess I was about two when they realized I had a talent for playing the piano. I can't remember a time when I didn't play. I had all the best teachers and by the time I was ten, I was performing with world-renowned orchestras and conductors."

"I remember reading in a biography of you that you'd gotten your start young."

Staci nodded. "And I worked hard. Everything they asked me to do, I did. Every concert they scheduled, I performed. I did it all in hopes that one day I'd have done enough to make them love me."

Denise jerked back. "Your parents didn't love you."

Staci shrugged. This part didn't hurt her so much anymore. "I don't think so. They never told me or showed me in ways that I could understand. The worst part about that is that it made me ripe to fall into another unhealthy relationship. I was about twenty when I realized there was nothing more I could do to try to win their love. And it was around that time that Eric entered my life. When he suggested we move in together, I agreed. Immediately after that, my parents cut all ties with me."

"Why did they do that?"

"They didn't approve of my relationship with Eric. He was the first guy I'd ever dated, and my parents were sure he was just taking advantage of me. Plus, I wasn't the prodigy wonder kid I'd been since I was an adult. Frankly, I think it was just an excuse to get me out of their lives."

"Oh, my word, Staci, I had no idea." Denise reached out and covered her hand. "I'm so sorry."

Staci gave her a weak smile. "It's okay. Honestly, I was glad to finally be free of the compulsion I had to try to win their love. That lasted about a week before I found myself caught up in it again, only this time it was way worse."

"I don't understand."

"I'd only been living with Eric for about two weeks when I realized that he had never said he loved me. I'd been blinded by the way he'd wooed me, but it soon became apparent he loved things *about* me, but he never looked me in the eyes and said, 'I love you, Ana'." Staci swallowed hard. She was about to bare her soul in ways she never had before.

"Maybe he just didn't know how to say it?" Denise suggested.

Staci shrugged. "All I know is that it sent me into another very bad place. He loved how I played the piano, so if he asked me to play for him, I would. I would play until he said to stop. It wouldn't matter if I'd just spent eight hours at the piano already, and my back and hands were screaming in pain, I played for him. Always thinking that maybe that would make him love me.

"If he said he loved how my hair looked, I tried to duplicate that look every single day. If he told me he loved a certain dress on me, I would buy several in that style in hopes that would please him enough. He told me once my body was perfect. As soon as he fell asleep that night, I went into the bathroom and took measurements of every part of my body and weighed myself."

"Whatever for?" Denise asked.

"Every single day I would measure and weigh myself to make sure nothing changed. I needed to keep my body perfect for him. I never wore a t-shirt or comfy pajamas to bed. It was always lingerie, because surely that would please him more. I would wait until he fell asleep to clean my makeup off, and then I'd get up before he did to make sure my hair and makeup were done before he was up. I'm not sure he ever saw me without makeup. He always told me he appreciated how I never let myself get sloppy like the girlfriends of his buddies did."

"How could you live like that?"

The shock on Denise's face was hard to look at but, honestly, she wondered that herself, looking back. She pitied the girl she'd been back then.

"It was only because Eric would be gone for stretches at a time that I was able to survive. As soon as he left, I would crash. I would stay in the condo so I didn't have to face anyone. I would cry every day. And I would sleep a lot. I didn't know what more to do."

"And Eric never knew about this?" When Staci shook her head, Denise asked, "How could he not have known?"

"I hid it very well. He never knew the extent of my anguish during our relationship. I made sure he didn't. Because I loved him. He was a good man. He didn't turn me into that person. I turned myself into it because I loved him so much and all I wanted was to know that he loved me, too." Staci looked at Denise, felt the tears fill her eyes but did nothing to stop them from falling down her cheeks. "You don't know what it's like to go through each day knowing that there is no one in the world who loves you." She took a quick breath and swallowed hard. "Every day I woke up hoping that would be the day he'd say the words to me. The day when I'd finally done enough to earn his love. And each night I'd go to bed knowing that one more day had gone by and still no one loved me."

The sobs she'd tried to hold in escaped on gasping breaths. She buried her face in her hands, the pain of the past so very present in that moment. She felt an arm around her shoulders and looked up to see her friend.

"Oh, no, Staci." Denise's eyes were also filled with tears. "I can't even imagine that. I've just always taken it for granted that my parents loved me and that Philip does now, too."

Stacie brushed her fingertips across her cheeks and took a deep shuddering breath. "Then came the day when a woman told me that someone *did* love me. That God loved me and that I didn't have to do anything to earn His love. It was a huge revelation to me, and it was the beginning of my healing journey. Somehow I found the strength to leave Eric when he wouldn't marry me. When he brushed aside my request to talk about marriage, I think I finally realized that nothing I did would ever be enough to gain his love."

"Why did he stay with you if he didn't love you? I don't understand that."

Staci looked away. "I'm not entirely sure. I think there were several things, but all of them tied into my desperate need to please him. And the strong physical chemistry we shared. What guy wouldn't want to stick with a woman who catered to his every need?"

Denise scowled. "Well, that makes him sound like a selfish jerk."

"He only took what I offered. He didn't know about everything else I was dealing with, what prompted me to do all those things for him. I never asked anything of him. Like when my back, arms and hands ached and cramped at night so badly that I couldn't sleep, I never asked him to rub them for me."

"Why not?"

Staci paused. "Because I was afraid he'd say no."

"Well, I can see now why you're having these second thoughts." Sadness spread across Denise's face. "This is all my fault, isn't it?"

"What do you mean?"

"I should never have mentioned Sarah to him. If he hadn't found out about her, he might not be in your life now."

"For my sake, yes, it would have been much easier if you hadn't said anything, but when I see the joy on my little girl's face when she is with him...I can't take that away from her."

"Maybe it would be better for you to just try to pursue a custody arrangement instead of marrying him."

Staci nodded. "I've been thinking about that. But I'd like to think I'm stronger this time around. That the need for his love is gone. I know that I have people who love me now."

"You certainly do," Denise assured her. "But would you be able to live with a husband who doesn't?"

Pain shot through Staci's heart. Her shoulders slumped. "I don't know. Obviously, it wasn't what I'd hoped for when I started thinking about possibly getting married. Granted I hadn't dated any real winners, but maybe I would have met that one man who could love Sarah *and* me."

"Maybe you should talk to Eric about all of this."

Staci frowned as she stared at her friend. "Are you kidding me? I would never dream of sharing something like this with him. Do you share your most intimate thoughts with Philip?"

"Well, yes, actually. Philip knows me better than anyone else. I tell him everything."

Staci couldn't even imagine a relationship like that with Eric. "You don't worry that something you share might make him stop loving you?"

"No. He's told me that he loves me no matter what. And if something I told him did make him stop loving me, I'd rather find out now than later."

"It doesn't really matter. I mean, I've changed a lot since we were last together. I'm not his type anymore."

"How do you know that? Maybe he's changed, too."

"He's still got a physical type. We ran into an ex-girlfriend of his and she looked just like I used to. Short, blonde pixie-cut hair. Dainty figure. Even had blue eyes. If that's the type he's still going for, well, that's not me anymore. And I'm never going back there. I like myself a whole lot better now than I did back then. Both inside and out."

"And so you should," Denise said with a grin. "Bennett told me once that he wished he was older because he'd date you since you are—as he put it—a hottie."

Staci laughed for the first time that evening. "Well, my day is made. Your seventeen-year-old brother thinks I'm a hottie."

"Seriously though, Stace, I know you're thinking a lot about how this is best for Sarah, but what is also good for Sarah is seeing each of her parents in a loving relationship. That might not mean with each other. If there's any chance you'd revert to how things used to be…that's not healthy for Sarah to see. One of the things I loved to see as a kid was how my dad's expression would change when he saw my mom. I always said I wanted a man who had a special smile that he smiled for me and me alone."

"Oh, you've got that," Staci assured her. "I've seen Philip talking and smiling with people in a group, but the minute he catches sight of you…well, everything about him changes."

Denise beamed. "You need that, too. You deserve that, after all you've gone through in your life. You deserve to have that man who thinks you are his world and treats you like that as well."

Staci didn't respond right away then she voiced her one last fear. "But what if God wants this for me?"

"You think God wants you in a loveless marriage? To a man who almost destroyed you emotionally last time?"

"He didn't destroy me," Staci said, wondering at her need to protect Eric. "I did that to myself. And yes, I think God may be asking me to once again sacrifice my need to be loved by Eric and accept that His love for me is enough."

Denise shook her head. "I really don't want to believe that."

"I've read the Bible, Denise. I've read the stories where God asked people to do things that weren't easy and weren't things they wanted to do. Esther, for example."

"I don't want to think God is asking that of you. You deserve better."

"Do I? I've already got the best thing in the world in Sarah. I think Eric and I could have a respectful relationship. He knows I've changed, that I won't be the woman I was back then."

"And are you going to have a physical relationship with him? If that was the best part of your relationship before, is it going to be again?"

Staci stared down at her hands. Honestly, that was the one thing she couldn't seem to find peace about. Either way. "I don't know. I'll have to cross that bridge when we get to it, I suppose."

"So when is the wedding?"

Eric didn't stay to hear the answer to that question. He felt sick to his stomach, and he needed to get away before they discovered him lurking in the hallway. It hadn't been his intention to eavesdrop like that, but he hadn't been able to tear himself away.

Moving as quietly as he could, he went to the front door and slipped out into the cold night air. How could he have been so blind? So stupidly blind to not see what had been happening with Staci...Ana?

After he had climbed behind the wheel of the truck, he started it up and immediately backed out of the driveway. He needed time to think over what he'd heard, but he couldn't do it sitting in Staci's driveway. A glance at the clock told him he still had another forty minutes or so before the movie ended. He decided to go back to the theater and just wait in the parking lot for Sarah and Tori.

Once parked outside the theater, Eric closed his eyes and leaned his head back against the seat. Right then, he didn't know what he felt. Everything he thought about his relationship with Ana had suddenly been shattered. But it did explain one thing. He had never been able to figure out how she had been able to walk away from him so easily. He hadn't known about her becoming a Christian, which had partly explained it, but he'd had a perception of their relationship that she hadn't shared.

He *had* loved her. He still loved her. After discovering that his dad—in spite of telling his wife he loved her every day—had cheated on her, Eric had felt that the best thing he could give to Staci was his fidelity. He hadn't cheated on her, and he never would have. And he'd done his best to treat her well.

But he had to admit that his dad's affair had messed with his mind. How could you love someone and still hurt them so badly? How could you do loving things for someone then turn around and stab them in the back? His dad's words hadn't been supported by his actions, and his actions had belied his words.

Eric hadn't known how to love back then. He could see that now. He'd chosen to ignore the good in his parents' relationship and focus only on the bad. His own journey back to God and his family had taught him a lot. But had it taught him how to love Staci the way he needed to? In spite of what she thought, she shouldn't have to settle for a loveless marriage. He didn't want that for either of them. And he certainly didn't want her ever going back to that place she'd been when they'd been together before.

Bile rose in his throat again as he recalled her words of knowing that no one in the world loved her. He'd heard her sobs, and his heart had broken. He had done that to her. He hadn't meant to, but he still had played a role in it. In trying to protect himself, he'd wounded her so very deeply. As he'd heard her crying, Eric had realized that he'd never seen her shed a single tear in their time together. But clearly she'd shed plenty...just not around him.

Would he ever be able to convince her to trust him with her heart? With her emotions? Something told him that she would fight hard to never show any vulnerability around him. Somehow he had to show her that he wanted their relationship to be a safe place for her. For them both.

He knew that the engagement and marriage needed to be put on hold so they could work through all of this, but how could he do that without revealing what he'd heard? Should he tell her what he'd overheard? For now, he knew the answer was no. He wouldn't lie to her if she asked if he'd heard anything—not that that would happen since she didn't know he'd been there.

His phone chirped. Wearily, he lifted it to look at the screen.

Chapter Twenty

OVIE'S out.
He really wasn't in the mood to deal with his sister or Sarah, but took a couple of deep breaths and climbed out of the truck. He found them just inside the doors to the theater.

Though he knew it would give Tori the opportunity to question him, Eric decided to drop Sarah off first since it was late.

Staci greeted them with a smile, and Eric had a hard time reconciling her with the woman who'd spilled so much earlier. But then it was clear she was good at hiding what she was truly feeling.

"Can you put me to bed, Daddy?" Sarah asked after taking off her boots and jacket.

"Sorry, kiddo, but not tonight. I have to take Aunt Tori home." At the disappointed look on his daughter's face, Eric bent down and kissed her. "Another night, I promise."

"Okay." Sarah gave him another tight squeeze around the neck. "Goodnight, Daddy. I love you."

"I love you, too, sweetie." He straightened in time to see a strange look pass across Staci's face, but it was gone so quickly he wasn't able to identify it. "I'll give you a call to arrange a time to see her again."

Staci's brows drew together, but she nodded.

Back in the truck, he was able to brush off Tori's questions with vague responses, but he was still glad to drop her off at her place.

Unfortunately, being alone with his thoughts didn't help him solve anything with regards to Staci. He couldn't rid himself of the incredible guilt he felt for having eavesdropped the way he did. Maybe he needed to come clean about what he'd done and let the chips fall where they may. But he desperately wanted to make things right with her and had a feeling that if she found out what he'd done, she'd cut him out of her life completely. This was a lose-lose situation all the way around.

Please, God, give me wisdom to know how to approach this with Staci. I was wrong for what I did, please help me make things right with her.

∽

"Hey, Tori," Staci said when she opened her door the next morning. "Glad you could make it over."

Tori smiled as she walked into the house. "You know I love spending time with Sarah."

"The feeling is very mutual." Staci hung up her coat. "Sarah is in the kitchen getting started on the brownies already."

Staci followed Tori into the kitchen and offered her a cup of coffee.

"Thank you. That would be great," Tori said as she gave Sarah a hug. "So baking is on the agenda today?"

"Cookies and brownies. Mama said Daddy likes brownies, so I want to make him some."

Tory shot her a curious look. "That's true that your dad likes brownies. So do I, so he might have to share."

"I like them, too, so he'll have to share with me, too," Sarah said with a giggle.

As she watched them work together, Staci had to admit how wonderful it was for Sarah to have family around. It was especially great for her to have someone who could relate to the physical challenges she would face in her life.

"So, you and Eric were able to talk a bit last night?" Tori asked as she held the bowl for Sarah to stir the batter.

Staci frowned. "Not really. He left pretty quickly after he dropped Sarah off."

"No, I meant before that. When he left Sarah and me at the movie theater so he could come here and talk with you."

Staci felt a flutter of panic in her stomach. "I had a lesson with a student."

"Yeah, he said that he had a key and would just let himself in and wait if you were still busy."

"What time did the movie start?" Staci asked, trying hard to ignore the sick feeling growing within her stomach.

"Seven. He dropped us off around six-forty-five and said he was coming here."

"And he said he talked to me?" Staci asked.

This time Tori stared at her. "When I asked him how your talk had gone, he just said that it hadn't gone as expected. Didn't he come here?"

"Not that I know of. A friend came over after my student left." And if he'd let himself in and she hadn't heard him…

Stacie didn't even want to contemplate what may have happened.

Tori frowned. "I don't know why he didn't just say he hadn't talked with you. He did seem a little distracted during the drive to my place." She tilted her head. "Is everything okay between you two?"

"We're working on a few things. Trying to figure stuff out for Sarah." And possibly a whole lot more if he'd overheard even part of what she'd told Denise the night before.

Staci tried to push aside that possibility. She just didn't even want to consider it. But even though she tried to focus on helping Sarah and Tori get the brownies into the pan and into the oven, the certainty kept growing within her. Along with it came anger, humiliation, hurt…

Finally, she gave up. "Would you be okay here for a bit with Sarah?"

Tori looked up from the book she was reading with Sarah at the table while they waited for the brownies to finish. "Sure. Everything okay?"

"I just need to run an errand."

"No problem. I don't have any plans until later this afternoon."

"I'll be back way before then," Staci assured her as she grabbed her cellphone and purse from the counter. "Call me if something comes up."

She pulled on her boots and jacket and headed out into the cold. Once in the car, Staci found she could hardly get the key in the ignition she was shaking so hard. There was a part of her that was trying to get her to just stay home until she could think more clearly, but right then emotion was propelling her forward.

By the time she pulled to a stop in front of Eric's apartment building, anger had eclipsed every other emotion. She saw a couple headed toward the front door of the building and hurried after them. If possible, she didn't want to have to buzz Eric to get into the building.

As she came up behind the couple, she had her keys out as if she was preparing to open the door. When they spotted her, they held the door to let her in as well.

"Thanks," Staci said, hoping they couldn't see the emotion that was raging within her.

They got off on the floor before Eric's, leaving her alone in the elevator. When the doors opened on his floor, she hesitated but then continued out of the elevator and turned to look for his apartment number.

At his door, she didn't allow herself to think before lifting her hand and pounding on it.

Eric turned from where he was pouring a cup of coffee to stare at the door. No one just knocked on his door without buzzing first. Probably a neighbor needing something.

He picked up one end of the towel that lay across his shoulders and rubbed his damp hair with it as he walked to the door. He'd spent the morning with his weights, trying to work off the emotions he was dealing with. It had helped some, but he still had no answers on what to do with the situation with Staci.

His gaze widened as he opened the door and saw the woman occupying his thoughts standing in front of him. "Staci?"

She stared at him with more emotion than he'd ever seen on her face, and he knew that somehow...she knew.

He stepped back from the door to give her space to enter his apartment. Whatever was going to happen, he didn't want it going down in front of any neighbors who might venture out of their apartments.

She stalked past him then spun around as he shut the door.

All kinds of possible things to say tumbled through his mind, but he kept his mouth shut and waited for her.

Staci stood just feet from him, her hands fisted at her sides, anger blazing in her beautiful blue eyes. "You were in my house last night, weren't you?"

He had already decided that if she came right out and asked, he'd tell her the truth. "Yes."

His quick response seemed to take her off-guard, but not for long.

Her shoulders slumped. "How much did you hear?"

Eric gripped the ends of the towel in his hands and shifted his weight from one foot to the other. "Enough."

Anger blazed in her eyes again. "How. Could. You? You had no right. Absolutely no right."

"I know. I'm sorry." Eric didn't know what else to say. The situation was already so bad he didn't want to make it worse.

"How could you?" This time the words came out as a raspy whisper. Tears welled up and spilled over her cheeks. "That wasn't for you to hear. For you to know."

Pain pierced Eric. How many tears had she shed that he was responsible for? It broke his heart to see her like this. "I didn't mean to...I know I should have left...I'm sorry."

"I let you back into my life. Into my daughter's life. I gave you everything you asked for, but that wasn't enough. You had to take the one thing that I never wanted you to have."

"You should have told me."

"No."

"It would have made a difference."

She shook her head vigorously. "No, it wouldn't have. But that doesn't matter now. What matters now is that I trusted you and you took advantage of that."

"I didn't mean to." Eric felt desperation begin to well up inside him.

"I don't care. As soon as you realized I was having a personal conversation with someone, you should have left. If I had wanted you to know, I would have told you."

Eric held out his hands toward her. He wanted to take her into his arms and soothe her, make her understand how much he loved her. "What can I do to make it right?"

Her chin lifted and even through the dampness in her eyes, he could see determination. "Leave me alone."

"What? No. Please." Eric wasn't above begging. He couldn't lose her again. "Please, Staci, anything but that."

"Leave me alone," she repeated, crossing her arms. "I'm not saying you can't see Sarah, but I don't want to be around you. I don't know if I can trust you again."

"Please, Staci, don't do this. I'll do anything else, just don't cut me out of your life again. Not now."

She gave her head a final shake before turning from him and walking toward the door.

Eric stared after her as she opened the door, stepped into the hallway and shut it behind her. Agony pierced his heart, and he stumbled to the table to sink down onto a chair there. This hurt so much more than the last time she'd walked out of his life.

Last time he'd been angry to find her gone. He'd been convinced she was the one with the issues that caused her to end things with him. Only now, he knew he played a much bigger role than he'd been willing to accept back then. And this time around it was one hundred percent his fault.

The worst part was now he had information that could have helped him build a better relationship with Staci, but it was all for naught. He couldn't let her go without at least trying though. He wasn't sure how to go about it just yet, but Eric knew that it had to include him being as vulnerable to her as she'd become to him when he'd heard her share those things that hadn't been meant for him.

It was truly a miracle that Staci made it through the next week without completely falling apart. She'd had to stay strong for Sarah even though she was feeling weaker than she'd felt in a very long time. It wasn't a feeling she liked at all. The weepy, aching sadness she felt was far too reminiscent of the last time she'd ended things with Eric. It was like all the growth she'd experienced over the past six years was for nothing. In the blink of an eye, all the changes she'd undergone disappeared.

It was taking everything within her to keep herself together while dealing with Sarah. Each time Eric had come to pick Sarah up, he'd texted to say he was in the driveway and she would send Sarah out to him. Then he'd text again when he brought her back so Staci could be at the door to let her in. It was how she'd never wanted things to turn out, but he was respecting her wishes and leaving her alone.

Too bad her heart hated it.

She didn't know what Eric had told his family about what had happened, but they had backed right off in their interactions with her. She knew she should have felt relieved, but in reality, it hurt. It made sense though. It would have been difficult for them to maintain a relationship with her when she wanted nothing to do with Eric.

She was just putting together their things to take to the studio for her Monday afternoon lessons when the doorbell rang.

"Daddy?" Sarah asked, her eyes wide with anticipation.

"I don't think so, sweetie. Today is a workday for your daddy. Why don't you get your tablet and put it in the bag while I see who it is."

As Sarah headed for the living room, Staci opened the front door.

"Anastacia Stapleton?" the man standing there asked.

Staci stood frozen as much by the sound of the name as the large bouquet of flowers he held.

"Miss? Are you Anastacia Stapleton?"

"Uh, yes. Yes, I am."

"These are for you." He held the flowers out to her.

Slowly Staci took them, her gaze captured by their beauty evident even through their cellophane wrapper. When she looked up to thank him, he was already walking away from her down the driveway.

Taking a step back, she closed the door and went to the kitchen with the flowers clutched tightly to her chest. As she set them on the counter, a white envelope slid out from among the blossoms. She stood looking at the envelope for a moment before reaching for it.

The flowers couldn't be from anyone but Eric. The white roses and orchids with just the slightest blush of pink on them had been the first bouquet he'd ever given her. And they had been part of any bouquet he'd given her afterward. In the two years they'd been together, he had made sure that she had a bouquet after every concert. But those flowers had never come with a note. She'd just always known they were from him.

She slid the folded paper from the envelope, uncertain what Eric was hoping to prove with this gift.

Ana ~ When I saw you perform for the first time, I was completely in awe of your talent and the way you drew such emotion from the music you played. It was like it was just you, the piano and the music in your own little world. The audience—including me—was almost an interloper in your performance. Each and every time I would hear you perform, I wished I could communicate to you just how deeply your music touched me. I knew I could never find the words, so I left it unsaid. But just like the beauty of the roses and orchids I chose for you was rare and unmatched, so was your talent and beauty.

My mom loves music and plays the piano, too. She said that when she was pregnant with me, music always seemed to have a soothing effect on me. And once I was born, it was the one thing guaranteed to make me stop crying. She would use a wrap to secure me to her chest and then sit at the piano and play. Later on, I tried to learn how to play. Mom thought for sure that I'd be a natural given how much I loved music. But that wasn't to be. I was destined to be one who loved music, but could never create it.

I wish I could have found the words to let you know how much it meant to me that you would share your music with me. Nothing ever soothed me like listening and watching you play did. I bought each and every one of your releases after you left, but it wasn't the same. The

music without you was just…sound. Not the passion and emotion I
loved to see when you played for me.
I've missed that.
Eric

Staci let out a sharp breath. When a drop of wetness landed on the paper, she lifted a hand to her cheek to discover tears sliding silently from her eyes. What was she supposed to do with this? What was he doing? This wasn't leaving her alone.

She'd known he admired her talent and enjoyed her music. He'd told her frequently that he loved how she played. Sometimes she'd felt it was the main thing that drew him to her, aside from their physical relationship.

If he'd hoped to dissuade her of that notion with this gift…it hadn't really worked.

When the doorbell rang about the same time the next day, Staci wondered…but was still surprised to see the same man on her doorstep.

"This is for you," he said as he had the day before and held out a flat box.

"Thank you," Staci said as she took it. He smiled before leaving her again.

At the counter, she removed the paper and found a box of her favorite chocolates and another envelope. Again she questioned what he was trying to do. A little more wary of the contents of the note this time, she slowly slid it free and unfolded the thick paper.

Ana ~ I remember seeing you eat and savor one of these chocolates. From
that moment on, I knew it would be something I would gift you with
whenever I could. If I could give you something that gave you even a
fraction of the pleasure you gave me through your music, I would give it
to you at every opportunity.

However, I wondered why I never saw you eating them after I gave
them to you. You always seemed so pleased but never ate them when I
was around. Then one day, I went to your closet to find something and

instead found the boxes of chocolates. Perhaps every single one I'd given you. Out of each box was missing one chocolate. One and only one. I didn't understand then, just chalked it up to you being one of those women who closely watched what they ate. It hurts me to think that even as I gave you something to enjoy, I robbed you of the ability to find pleasure in it. I hope that you will eat each and every piece of chocolate in this box as the fancy strikes you.
They are for your enjoyment.
Eric

She didn't know he'd found her stash. Hidden so that he'd never know she hadn't eaten them and think she didn't appreciate his gift. She hadn't been able to bring herself to throw them out. Not until she had begun to pack up her things to leave him. She had taken only one with her...the one he'd given her most recently, but she'd never eaten any out of that box.

Staci picked up a knife and slid it through the cellophane wrapper so she could reach the chocolate. Picking one up, she put it in her mouth and savored the taste. And when that one was done, she ate another.

"What's that, Mama?" Sarah asked as she came into the kitchen.

"Chocolate. Do you want one?" It seemed fitting to share this particular gift with the little girl they had created together.

Staci lifted her up onto a stool at the counter and let her choose one from the box.

"There's a nut inside so make sure you chew it," Staci told her when the little girl put the chocolate she'd chosen into her mouth.

After letting Sarah snag a second one, Staci put the lid back on the box and looked again at the sprawling masculine script on the notepaper. It would have been so much easier for him to type it out, and yet he'd taken the time to write it. She traced the letters of his name at the bottom of the note.

What was he doing to her?

Chapter Twenty-One

BY the time the doorbell rang on Wednesday, Staci was no longer surprised, although she was still a little perplexed. It was as if Eric was showing things that had happened in their past together from his point of view.

This gift was another flat package, but when she removed the paper she found a plain white box. Curious, she opened the lid and saw a pastel colored t-shirt laying there. Not certain what to make of it, she lifted the shoulders of it and let it fall free of the packaging. She quickly realized it wasn't a t-shirt but a sleep shirt. The front of it had a picture of a teddy bear dressed in pajamas with the caption "Sweet dreams" on it.

Ana ~ I learned quickly to let you think I was asleep. I knew you would get up and leave our bed for a time. I wasn't sure why, but it happened every night. Once you came back to bed, it was my turn to wait for you to fall asleep. And once you had, I would turn so that I could see you. In the moonlight your hair shone like spun gold. You would sleep with your hands tucked up under your chin. So young. So innocent. So beautiful.

Part of me wanted you to open your eyes. I was sure that in those first few moments before you were completely awake there would be no wariness or reservation in your gaze as you looked at me. But I knew that seeing the wariness return would be difficult to see, so instead I had to be content to just watch you sleep. Sometimes I would touch your cheek and wish that somehow I would be less afraid of loving you completely.

I was as uncertain about our relationship as you were. My dad loved my mom and yet still hurt her in the most cruel way. I didn't trust love. It hadn't been enough to keep hurt from my parents' relationship. I didn't know that it would be enough to keep it from ours either. So I chose not to make that the focus of our relationship.
I'm sorry.
Eric

Glad that Sarah was in the other room, Staci wiped tears from her cheeks again. He had watched her sleep? She thought of the person she'd been back then and knew that if she'd opened her eyes to find him watching her, she probably would have tried to hide her face or leave the bed. What he didn't know was that there had been times when she'd also watched him sleep.

How was it that they had been two people both searching—longing—for love and intimacy…and yet had missed it completely? Both too scared to open themselves to each other. Eric because he'd been scared of being hurt. Her because she'd never felt worthy or certain of his love.

And then it had been over.

Thursday morning the doorbell rang a little earlier than usual. Staci had been afraid she'd miss the delivery—if there was to be one—because her lessons started earlier on Thursday. But somehow Eric must have known that and made sure the delivery arrived before she had to leave.

She wondered how long this would go on. Not indefinitely, for certain. But what would he expect when the last gift arrived? Staci's emotions were a mess. Eric was communicating with her in a way that he never had before, but the method he'd chosen didn't force her to respond immediately. For that, she was grateful, but she still didn't know what to do.

That day's delivery was another flat box, but it was heavier than the previous gifts had been. As she parted the tissue paper covering the item, she gasped at the ornate design on the oval shape. Staci grasped the handle, surprised at the weight of it as she lifted it from the box. She turned it over and immediately tears sprung to her eyes.

The other side held a mirror and written in bold black letters along the bottom of it was the word *Beautiful.* She traced it with a fingertip, surprised when it didn't smudge. She met her own gaze in the mirror, seeing there the dark circles beneath her eyes. The night before hadn't brought much sleep.

Eric wouldn't have recognized the significance of that day's date, but it had weighed heavily on Staci the previous night. Six years ago that day, she'd left the condo she'd shared with Eric for the last time. She'd spent that last night in their bed crying. She knew it was the right decision to leave, but the finality of it hurt so much. In her way, she had loved Eric as much as she had known how. And though she was learning that there was, in fact, someone who loved her without reservation, it was hard to leave yet another relationship having tried so hard to win their love and failed. First her parents and then Eric.

Last night she'd cried for the girl she'd been and the heartache she'd carried for so long. And now she bore the remnants of that sleepless night on her face and yet stood there looking into a mirror that declared her reflection *Beautiful.*

She looked down at the box and spotted the now familiar envelope. Already feeling a bit emotionally off balance, Staci wasn't sure she could handle what the envelope might contain. Still, she couldn't keep from pulling out the note and opening it.

Ana ~ No matter what you might see when you look in a mirror, you always were—always will be—beautiful to me. Eric

That one sentence struck hard at her heart, and Staci struggled to keep the tears contained. Each note this week had been like a balm to the wounds she'd discovered her heart still carried. Sharing them with Denise—and inadvertently Eric—had brought everything to the surface. She'd thought the pain would be with her forever, but each day her heart was healing little by little.

Unfortunately, she had no time to ponder what was happening in her heart right then. With one last look in the mirror, Staci set it down and went to collect Sarah to head out for their day.

On Friday, Staci's morning lesson cancelled so she hadn't been rushing out the door when the next gift arrived. This was the largest box so far, and it, too, had weight like the one the previous day.

As with every other gift, Staci opened it with a flutter of apprehension. Each one seemed to reach deeper and deeper into her wounded heart. Would there be one that would either completely break her? Or would it finally heal her?

After slitting the tape holding the plain cardboard box closed, Staci brushed aside the packaging material. The movement revealed the shape of a miniature grand piano. It was dark wood with a pattern inlaid with what looked like mother of pearl. Staci lifted it from the box, not caring when the Styrofoam popcorn packaging spilled to the floor.

She set the piano on the counter and lifted the lid slightly. It immediately began to play a song. The song she'd always played for Eric. It was her favorite, too, and he'd always asked her to play it.

Opening it a bit further to see if there was a way to prop the lid open so that the music would continue to play, she gasped. Not only was it a piano-shaped music box, it was also a jewelry box. And there, nestled between two ridges of deep purple velvet, was a sparkling diamond ring.

The breath squeezed from her lungs as she stared at it. With trembling fingers, she lifted the ring from the jewelry box. This was what she'd wanted back then. It was as if his agreeing to marry her would finally prove that he did indeed love her. When he'd brushed aside her questions about marriage in their future, it had been the final crushing blow to her dream of having someone love her. Of having Eric love her.

She slid the ring on then frowned when it wouldn't slide all the way to the base of her ring finger. Of course, he wouldn't know her ring size now. Staci slid it back off and returned it to the jewelry box, uncertain what exactly it meant. Was this a follow up to his proposal when he returned from his trip to the Middle East?

Maybe his note would explain it a bit more. She looked past the remaining packaging material to find the envelope she knew would be there.

Staci

The name made her pause as up to that point, it had been Ana. As if he'd been speaking to her past self. Suddenly more nervous than she'd been opening the other packages, she forced herself to read on.

I found this jewelry box while on my trip to Africa. I knew I was going to buy it for you just from looking at it, but if I'd had any doubt, when I opened it and heard the song—our song—I would have bought it no matter the price.

And the ring…I brought that back from Africa with me, too.

"No." Staci grabbed the edge of the counter as her legs suddenly went weak. "No. Oh, God, why?"

She sank to her knees and pressed her forehead to the cupboard. He'd returned prepared to propose, and she'd been gone. He had been ready to give her what she'd wanted, and she hadn't been there to receive it. That was why the ring didn't fit now…he'd bought it for her when she'd been smaller. It would have fit her finger back then.

Pain expanded within her chest until she thought she wouldn't be able to draw another breath.

She felt a touch on her shoulder. "Mama?"

Sarah.

"Mama? What's wrong?" The little girl maneuvered her way onto Staci's lap and raised a hand to touch her cheek. "Why are you crying, Mama?"

Crying? She hadn't even realized that tears had spilled down her cheeks. "I'm just a little sad about something, sweetie. Don't worry about it."

"Kiss to make it better?" Sarah asked, her head tilted to the side.

"Yes, a kiss would make it better," Staci said as she wrapped her arms around her daughter.

Sarah kissed her on each damp cheek before pressing her lips quickly to Staci's. "Better?"

"You always make it better, sweetie." And she did. Through the dark days following her departure from LA and Eric, the news of her pregnancy was all that had kept her going. And then once Sarah had been born—in spite of the health challenges she'd had—finally Staci had had a person to love without reservation. And over the years, that love had been returned a hundred fold.

Sarah sat with her for a bit, stroking her hair, but then seemed to feel she'd done what she could and scooted off her lap. "Can I play on the computer, Mama?"

Staci nodded. She still needed a bit more time to compose herself. Knowing Sarah could get to her program by herself, Staci stayed in the kitchen and leaned her head back against the cupboard.

She took a deep breath and let it out. Now that the initial emotional response had ebbed away, she was able to look at it a bit more clearly. Even though it hurt to think that Eric had been prepared to marry her, Staci knew in her heart that it wouldn't have been the right thing for them. Neither of them had known how to be in a relationship. Marrying wouldn't have changed that. In fact, it might have made it worse.

God had had a plan for each of them apart from the other. And then, when she'd least expected it, He'd allowed the paths of their lives to intersect once again. But was it just for Sarah's sake that He'd reunited them? Or could it really be a second chance at a relationship? This time around with love?

Realizing she hadn't finished reading the note, Staci pushed to a standing position and found it on the counter where she dropped it.

I had time to think while I was away and realized that if marriage was that important to you, I needed to step up or I would lose you. I know now that wouldn't have been a good basis for marriage. In fact, I can see that God had His hand on that whole situation. Sarah being born the way she was would have been devastating for me at that time. I needed you to leave me. I needed to become reckless with my own life in order to find God again. Sarah needed to be born to a mother who loved her and away from a father who might well have rejected her.

Does it hurt to say it was for the best the way things happened? Yes, it does, but I think what we would have gone through had things worked out like I'd planned back then would have led to far greater and lasting hurt.

I know you asked me to leave you alone, and I intend to honor that now. I just needed for you to hear from me how I perceived things back then. That the things you worried about where I was concerned were never how I viewed you or our situation.

I hope these gifts will show you that the way you were then—the way you are now—is just perfect. Don't change who you are in order to have someone love you. You are the best person to be perfectly you. I hope you'll remember that, and I hope you'll teach that to our daughter. Because she also is perfectly her.

Thank you for loving my daughter when I couldn't. She is the wonderful child she is today because of you. I can never repay you and never want to again inflict any hurt on you. To that end, I would still like to request joint legal custody just so that if something should—God forbid—happen to you, I would be able to claim her. I will leave physical custody completely to you, asking only that you let me spend some time with her each week.

Eric

Staci let out the breath she'd been holding. Why didn't she feel happier? He'd just agreed to everything she'd wanted. And yet, there was an ache in her heart that wouldn't go away.

"Please, God, help me know what to do."

Eric put his briefcase on the passenger seat before settling behind the wheel of his truck. He sat for a moment and blew out a long breath. The week had dragged on, each day feeling longer than the one before. And it had been emotionally draining. First with the continuing security issues from his trip to Iraq and then with the letters he'd taken the time to write to Staci.

When he'd decided this would be the best way to try to rectify the wrongs he'd inadvertently done to her in their past, he hadn't realized how much it would impact him. Reliving that time had been difficult. It had been hard to have to analyze their relationship now with Staci's view of it in his heart and mind as well as his own. They'd been together two years and had been no closer emotionally on the day she walked out than they had been the day they moved in together.

He'd hoped that putting it all down on paper for her would be cathartic for him, but as much as it had been that, it had also been a reminder of how much she'd meant to him. There was nothing more he could do now. All he hoped was that what he'd shared could bring some healing to her. That she would never again doubt that she was worthy of love just as she was.

With a sigh, Eric slid the key into the ignition and started the truck. But before he could pull out of his spot in the parking garage under the Blackthorpe building, his phone rang.

Victoria's number popped up on the screen. Frowning, he tapped the screen to connect with her.

"Can you come to Mom and Dad's?" she asked as soon as he answered.

"Why? What's wrong?"

"You need to come. I don't know what to do."

"I was going to pick up Sarah."

"Cancel for now. You need to be here."

Eric felt a spark of irritation war with worry in his gut. "Victoria. Tell me what's happened."

"There's a woman here. To see Dad." Victoria's voice had dropped to a whisper

"A woman?" *Please, God, don't let this be happening again.*

"She says she's his daughter."

"His daughter?" Eric stared blankly out the front window of his truck, his thoughts trying to process what Victoria was telling him. "How old is she?"

"I don't know for sure, but she looks around my age, I would say."

"How's Mom?"

"I don't know. She went upstairs." Victoria paused. "I don't know what to do."

"I'll be there as soon as I can. I need to let Staci know I can't pick up Sarah."

He thought about calling Staci, but this latest bit of news had rattled him. In the end, he settled for texting her.

Won't be able to pick up Sarah as planned. Something has come up I need to deal with. Will text when I know more. d

Without waiting for her reply, he left the parking garage and headed for his parents' home. He was trying to shake the feeling that the past had chosen this week to vomit its ugliness all over him. First he'd been worried about Staci, now he was worried about his mom.

It seemed to take forever to drive through the rush hour traffic to his parents' place. There was no vehicle that he didn't recognize in the driveway, so the woman must have arrived by cab.

Before he got out of the truck, he said a quick prayer for wisdom on how to deal with this. It was a situation he had never even contemplated, though he supposed it was always a possibility. Just never one he'd thought of.

He didn't bother ringing the bell, but let himself in the front door. Victoria met him in the entrance to the living room.

"Dad's in the kitchen with her," she said in a low voice.

"I need to check on Mom."

"I should've done that. I just didn't know what to say to her."

Eric gave her a quick hug. "It will be okay." He hoped that she was more convinced by his words than he was.

He quickly climbed the stairs to the second floor of his parents' home. The door to the master bedroom was open a crack but he still knocked. "Mom?"

"Come in."

Eric pushed open the door to see his mom sitting in a rocking chair by the window of their bedroom. She smiled when she saw him and held out her hand. Eric went to her and sank to his knees beside her. "Are you okay, Mom?"

He wasn't sure what he'd expected to find, but it hadn't been his mother looking so calm and peaceful. She laid her hand on his cheek. "I am fine, sweetheart."

"Who is she? Tori said she said she's his daughter?"

His mom nodded. "Yes, it appears that Sherry was pregnant when she left Africa. I don't know if she knew then or not."

Eric got up from his knees and settled on the edge of the bed a few feet from where his mom sat. "Why is this girl here now? After all these years, why now?"

"I'm not sure. We had no inkling until she showed up today."

"Why aren't you more upset about it?"

She shrugged. "To be honest, I always knew it was a possibility. You're old enough now to know that it only takes one time. Though it may sound strange, I had prepared myself for this and prayed that God would give me strength should it ever become reality."

"Why aren't you down there with Dad now?"

"When I realized who she was, I knew that she needed to talk first with your dad and make that connection before the rest of us were brought into the situation."

Eric stared down at the carpet, fighting the anger that had once dominated his relationship with his dad. He didn't feel any peace like his mother did about what was unfolding downstairs.

He felt a hand on his shoulder and looked up to see his mother had come to stand beside him. She looked down at him, an expression of understanding on her face. "She's an innocent in all this too just like you, Brooke and Victoria. She had no control over the circumstances of her birth any more than you three did."

"But she didn't need to come here and disrupt everything," Eric said.

"No, she didn't, but we don't know her story. Don't judge her without more information, sweetheart."

There was a knock on the door and Victoria poked her head through the opening. "Can I come in?"

"Of course, darling," his mom said. She motioned Victoria to her side and gave her a hug. "It's going to be okay."

Hearing his mom say the words filled him with more confidence than when he'd said them earlier to Victoria. As he looked at his sister, he could see the worry and fear on her face. She hadn't been around the last time they'd faced the consequences of his father's affair. Though she knew that they had survived that, it was different when it was suddenly right in your face.

"Has anyone called Brooke?" Eric asked.

Victoria nodded. "I tried but all I got was her voicemail."

Eric could only imagine his other sister's reaction to this latest bit of news. She continued to struggle in her relationship with their dad. Eric knew she still hadn't completely forgiven him for what he'd done. And it had only been made worse when she'd gone through something similar and had been left pregnant and alone.

"I'll try her a little later," his mom said.

As the room fell silent, Eric realized he hadn't checked to see if he'd gotten a response from Staci. He pulled his phone from his pocket.

Okay. Will let her know. Hope everything is okay.

Everything wasn't okay, but he couldn't spell that out in a text message. *Tell Sarah I'm sorry but I probably won't be over tonight. Will try to see her tomorrow.*

I'll tell her. We are home all day tomorrow so whatever works for you will be fine.

Eric let out a sigh. How he wished he could share this with Staci. He looked at his mom, who had settled herself back in the rocking chair, and wondered how she'd dealt with the feelings that must have come with learning of her husband's betrayal. Had she wondered if she could have done things differently? Or if there was something wrong with her that he'd turned to another woman? Though he'd never cheated on Staci, she had experienced those feelings in an attempt to earn his love.

"Caroline?"

Eric turned at the sound of his dad's voice. His expression was serious as he stood in the doorway to the bedroom.

Chapter Twenty-Two

ERIC stood up. "Did you need to talk to Mom?"

"Your mom and I will talk later," his dad said with a smile at his wife. "Right now I need to tell you a little about the woman sitting downstairs in the kitchen. Her name is Alicia and yes, she is Sherry's daughter. And mine as well."

"Why is she here, Dad?" Eric asked.

His dad settled into the winged armchair across from his mom. "Her mother died late last year and she has no other family that she knows of. And all she knew of me was a name on her birth certificate, but then she came across a journal in her mother's things detailing what had happened in Africa."

"So she's just here to meet you?"

"Something like that, yes." His dad glanced around at each of them. "Are you interested in meeting her?"

"Yes." His mother was the first to speak. "Yes, I would like to meet her."

His dad looked at him then at Victoria. "Just remember that as uncertain as you are about her, she's uncertain about you. She knew nothing about our family beyond my name."

As they walked downstairs, Eric tried to brace himself for meeting this woman who shared blood with him but whom he knew nothing about.

"I asked her to wait in here," his dad said as he led them into the living room.

The young woman seated on the couch jumped to her feet as soon as they walked in. Her gaze flitted over each of them but Eric noticed she didn't make steady eye contact.

"Alicia, I'd like you to meet my wife, Caroline," his dad said, lifting their entwined hands. "And this is our son, Eric and our daughter, Victoria."

Eric noticed that Alicia's gaze seemed most intent on his mother. She approached her slowly and held out her hand. "It's nice to meet you."

"You, too, Alicia," his mother said, her tone gracious.

"Why don't we sit down," his dad suggested. Once they were all seated, he continued, "I suppose you're curious about our family. Eric is our oldest and he works for a security company. He has a young daughter that we've just recently found out about. Her name is Sarah, and she's a real sweetheart."

Eric saw the spark of interest in Alicia's eyes at that revelation and didn't miss how her gaze dropped to his left hand.

"Next to Eric, we have another daughter, Brooke. She isn't here at the moment, but she too has a child. A ten-year-old son. And Victoria Grace is our miracle baby." His dad smiled at Victoria who beamed back at him. "Tori has her own company which provides equipment and resources for little people."

"It's nice to meet you," Alicia said, her voice soft.

Eric wasn't sure what he'd expected her to look like, but it was a bit unnerving to see some striking similarities in her appearance. She had the auburn hair like Brooke, but her eyes were dark like his and Victoria's. He wondered if she had the fiery temper and wild personality that Brooke had. Seeing her sitting there stiff and quiet, it seemed doubtful and that was probably a good thing.

Her auburn hair was pulled back into a braid so Eric wasn't sure if it was as long as Brooke's. She also had a softer appearance than Brooke did. As he looked at her, something his dad said came to mind. *She has no other family.* What he'd learned about Staci recently gave him an understanding into Alicia that he might not have had otherwise. Like Staci had with him, Alicia was probably trying to find a connection. To feel that love that was no doubt missing from her life now that her mother had passed away.

"Do you have a place to stay?" his mom asked.

"Yes. Thank you." Alicia looked down at her hands. "I don't want to take any more of your time. I just wanted to meet you, Mr. McKinley."

Eric waited for his dad to correct her use of his formal name, but he didn't.

"We would like to spend more time with you, if possible," he said. "Are you here for a little while?"

Alicia glanced at his dad and nodded. "Yes, I am. I can give you my number." She reached into her purse and pulled out a small notebook and a pen. After writing something on a piece of the paper, she ripped it off and held it out to his dad. "I really don't want to create any problems. If I have, please forgive me."

"There are no problems," his mom assured her. "We have worked through our past and what happened then is not a reflection on you. We are happy to have met you."

Eric stared at his mom, wondering if she really did feel that way. Glancing at his half-sister he found again that Alicia's gaze was tight on his mom. There was a mixture of curiosity and wariness in her expression. Almost as if she was waiting for the other shoe to drop. Like she couldn't believe what his mom had said. They had that much in common, Eric realized.

Alicia slipped the strap of her purse over her shoulder and stood. "I need to be going."

"Are you sure you can't stay longer?" his dad asked.

She looked around at them, and Eric wondered if she was going to change her mind but then she shook her head. "I think I should go."

"Do you need a ride someplace?" Eric asked. "I didn't see a car in the driveway."

She looked at him then, meeting his gaze for the first time. "I will just call a cab."

"That's not necessary," his dad said. "We can give you a ride."

"I'm fine taking a cab." Alicia pulled a small cell phone from her purse. "But thank you for the offer."

It seemed she was as overwhelmed by all this as the rest of them where. Although his mom and dad seemed to be taking it all in stride in a way that Eric just couldn't comprehend. Was it just a cover? When Alicia had gone and he and Victoria left, would they let down their guards and let their real emotions show? He wasn't sure if he should admire them or be worried for them.

"If you're certain," his dad said, apparently realizing that pressing too hard wasn't the way to go with this situation.

"If you'll just excuse me, I'll make the call now." Alicia left the room with her cell phone and purse in hand.

"Why didn't she just call here?" Victoria asked.

Eric wondered the same thing but before he could say anything, his own phone rang. He glanced at the call display and groaned. *Brooke.* He was half tempted to send it to his voicemail but knew that would only put her in a worse mood when they finally did connect. He wasn't too surprised that even though Victoria had left the message, Brooke had called him.

He stood as he connected the call. "Hello?"

"What's going on?" Brooke asked without any greeting.

Eric left the living room but went to the office at the back of the house instead of the kitchen where he assumed Alicia was. "There's been a development from the situation with Dad and Sherry."

There was a long pause before Brooke said, "What kind of development? Please don't tell me that woman made contact with him again. Or that he contacted her."

"Brooke, you know Dad wouldn't do that."

"Who would have thought he'd cheat in the first place." She sighed loudly. "Of course, he *is* a man."

Eric sighed. They'd been over this ground before, now wasn't the time to beat a dead horse. "Sherry passed away last year."

"Well, can't say I'm too sad about that. And why would that matter to us now?"

"A young woman showed up here at the house today and said she was Sherry's daughter. And Dad's."

"No. Freakin'. Way." Brooke bit out the words, making no attempt to hide the anger she clearly felt.

"Her name is Alicia, and she only found out about Dad when she went through her mother's things after her death."

"What does she want from Dad? Money?" Brooke laughed. "Good luck with that."

"Listen, Brooke, we're all aware of your feelings toward Dad and that situation, in particular. I don't expect you to want to meet the woman or anything like that, we just figured you should at least know what's going on."

"I appreciate the consideration. Any other news I should know about?"

Lots, but none Eric felt all that inclined to share with her. "Nothing you'd be interested in. How about with you?"

There was a pause on Brooke's end. "Nope, nothing new here either."

"Danny doing okay?"

"Danny's doing great." Eric heard the pride in his sister's voice and knew that there was at least one male in the world she didn't hate.

"That's good. Listen, I need to go. I'm still at Mom and Dad's."

When he returned to the living room, it was still just them and Tori sitting there.

"She left," his dad said when he saw Eric.

Eric let out a sigh as he sat back down in the chair he'd vacated earlier. "That was Brooke." He saw the look his parents shared. "I told her that she didn't need to meet Alicia but that we just thought she should be aware of what is going on."

"All I want you three to understand," his dad began, "is that Alicia bears no responsibility or blame for what happened twenty-six years ago. That falls directly on me and Sherry. Though I realize it's unlikely that Brooke will be able to separate Alicia from those events, I hope that the two of you will. In whatever form of relationship she wants with us."

"Does she not have any other family?" Tori asked.

"Apparently, her mother never married though she did have some relationships over the years." His dad sighed. "It sounds like everything that happened with the affair and then the pregnancy turned Sherry quite bitter. Her family cut her off after the disgrace of what happened. It doesn't sound like Alicia had an easy life growing up. I don't want to add to that now."

"Are you going to ask for a DNA test, Dad? Just to make sure?" Eric asked. With his security background, he couldn't help fearing the worst. And though he wouldn't tell his dad about his intention, he planned to run a background check on her as soon as he could.

"She offered one, so yes, I will do that just to put everyone else's concerns at rest. I have no doubt in my mind that she is my daughter. The similarities with you three are pretty striking."

Eric glanced over at his mom. She'd remained quiet during this time. Her gaze was on her husband, but there was no readable expression on her face. Anger again rose from deep inside him. As it had been twenty-six years ago, his mother was the innocent being forced to accept events over which she had no control. Could his dad not see how hard it must be for her to be faced with the prospect of being reminded every single day of what had happened to completely derail their lives all those years ago?

If Alicia wanted some sort of ongoing relationship with their family, his mother would constantly be reminded of that horrible, horrible time. Eric wanted to do all he could to protect her, but he didn't know how he could do that. Particularly when she seemed so determined to accept this turn of events and welcome this young woman into their lives.

A familiar feeling of helplessness swamped him. First Staci. Now his mom. The women he loved were hurting and there was nothing he could do to take it away. He remembered being nine years old and suddenly being told they were leaving the only home he'd ever known. He hadn't understood then why. There had been tension evident between his mom and dad, but he'd been too young to understand what had caused it. The realization of why they'd had to leave and who was responsible came when he'd turned fourteen, and had changed his world forever. The man he'd admired for so long fell off the pedestal his young son had put him on, leaving Eric disillusioned, hurt and angry. How could his father have put his own selfish desires before everything else? And how could he have done that to his wife? Eric's mom? At fourteen, he hadn't been able to understand any of it.

Truth be told, he still didn't understand all of it, but he'd forgiven his father. Or at least he thought he had.

"I was supposed to take Sarah out tonight. I think I'm going to see if I can stop in before she goes to bed." Eric felt an overwhelming need to escape his parents' presence.

"I'm sorry you had to cancel that," his mother said as she stood when he did. "We'd love to have her come over again soon."

"I'll arrange something with Staci," Eric said as he gave her a hug. "Call me if you need anything."

His mom cupped her face in his hands. "Truly don't worry about me, sweetheart. Your father and I will deal with this together as we do everything else."

Eric nodded his understanding though he really didn't. "I'll give you a call tomorrow."

After saying goodbye to his dad and Tori, Eric let himself out. Though mentioning going to see Sarah had just been an excuse to get out of the house and the tense situation there, Eric knew he needed to see her. And Staci. He had promised to leave her alone, so if she told him to leave, he would.

Staci slumped down on the bench of her piano. Bracing one hand by her leg, she picked out a random tune with just one finger of her other hand. She was glad to finally have a few minutes of peace. Sarah had once again flipped out when she'd heard that Eric wasn't coming to pick her up, and it had been a miserable few hours. She'd finally sent her to bed early in hopes of giving them both a break.

Though she really didn't want to admit it, Staci was worried about Eric. She'd had mixed feelings when she'd received the message from him. Part of it was relief at not having to deal with him, but there had been concern for him she couldn't ignore. Even now she wondered what had happened and wished she had the right to ask him about it.

She lifted her other hand to the keyboard and began to play, not thinking of the keys and chords her fingers chose. Slowly the chords and melody came into focus for her, and she recognized the song her fingers had chosen. It was the song from the music box. It was as if she wanted to offer the music to Eric even though he wasn't there. She sensed that he would have needed it.

She knew the music wouldn't disturb Sarah. She was used to hearing Staci playing after she'd gone to bed. It wasn't every night, but there were times when Staci had needed the music after the day was over, and she was alone with her sleeping child.

Letting herself get lost in the music, Staci closed her eyes and suddenly she was back in that condo in LA. In her mind she could see Eric in his favorite chair, his legs stretched out, head tipped back and fingers intertwined across his abdomen. He would close his eyes as he listened and often she'd watch him as she played.

As she reached the end of the song, the doorbell rang, shattering the memory she'd wrapped herself in with her music.

Blowing out a long breath, Staci got up from the piano and went to the front door. She looked out the glass pane in the door and, in the dim illumination of the porch light, saw Eric. Her heart skipped a beat, and she gripped the handle for a moment before turning it to open the door.

Eric stood there, his head bent, arm braced against the door jamb. He looked up at her, and Staci could see weariness on his face. The emotion in his gaze took her breath away.

"I know I said I'd leave you alone and if you want, I'll go, but I was wondering if I could see Sarah."

Staci stepped back from the doorway to let him in. "She's in bed, but you're welcome to go look in on her. She might even still be awake. We had a bit of an unpleasant evening after she found out you weren't going to pick her up."

Pushing back the sides of his jacket, Eric braced his hands on his hips. "She gave you a rough time?"

Staci shut the door and nodded. "Eventually it was best for both of us that she go to bed."

"I'm sorry to hear that. Perhaps I should have spoken to her when I cancelled to let her know myself. She seems to get upset when you pass on the message to her."

"Yeah, not sure if she thought I was the one who cancelled the plans or what, but she was one unhappy camper."

"I'll just go look in on her. I didn't mean to interrupt your...playing."

Staci's gaze jerked to his. How much had he heard of her music before ringing the doorbell? From the look of his expression, quite a lot. Perhaps the whole song. "Take your time. Especially if she's awake."

"Thank you," Eric said with a nod of his head. He slipped off his shoes then turned to go up the stairs.

Staci watched him leave before letting out the breath she'd been holding. In light of all the gifts he'd sent her way with the notes, she wasn't exactly sure how to act around him. She thought of the piano jewelry music box sitting upstairs on her dresser, the ring still in its place between the velvet folds. How was she supposed to react to him now that she knew he'd planned to propose to her once he returned from his overseas job assignment?

Not wanting to have him come back down the stairs to find her in the same position, Staci first turned toward the living room but then didn't want to be near the piano either. Finally, she went into the kitchen and began to go through the process of making a cup of hot chocolate. She set out a second mug but didn't put anything into it yet.

She had just taken the first sip from her mug when she heard movement on the stairs. Nerves battled inside her. She had thought she'd have time to work through the emotions that the week had stirred within her before having to deal with Eric, but here he was, mere hours after the final emotional gift.

As she turned from the counter, Staci saw Eric walk past the kitchen to where he'd left his shoes. He was going to leave? Just like that? She wasn't sure what she'd expected him to do, but she didn't think he'd leave so quickly.

Cupping her mug in her cold hands, Staci walked to the entrance of the kitchen and saw him putting on his shoes.

"Was she asleep?"

Eric straightened and turned to face her. "Yes, but thank you for letting me see her."

Staci hesitated then said, "Is everything okay?"

Eric stared at her, his expression unreadable, but he didn't reply to her question.

She wasn't sure what prompted her to say, "Would you like a cup of coffee?"

He stuck his hands into the pockets of his leather jacket and dipped his head. "I thought you wanted me to leave you alone."

What could she say to that? She was still scared of the power he'd held over her in their relationship before, even though it hadn't been power that he'd taken but that she had given him. He pulled at her emotions on so many levels, but he'd been willing to end this with her so maybe whatever he felt for her back then wasn't something he felt any more. Maybe his explanation of how things had been back then for him had been for her benefit not his.

"Yes, I did." She gripped the mug tightly. "It's just that for Sarah's sake, we need to be able to interact. I realize it was unrealistic to ask you to leave me alone when we need to parent her together."

Again Eric looked at her. This time his jaw was set and he gave a quick nod of his head. "Yes, that's true."

Staci held her breath, waiting to see if he'd agree to stay and talk, but her heart sank when he turned away.

"I'll give you a call tomorrow to arrange a time to pick Sarah up, if that's okay."

Swallowing hard as emotion rose up inside her, Staci struggled to keep it from her face. Right then she hated herself for being weak and still loving a man who didn't love her. And yet she hated him for still having so much effect on her.

Pulling her shoulders back and lifting her chin, she said, "Sure. I know she'd love to see you tomorrow."

Eric opened the door, letting in a cold blast of air, but it didn't even come close to touching the chill invading her heart. He turned back to her. "You still play as beautifully as ever." Then he stepped out into the darkness of the night and shut the door behind him.

Feeling as if she'd just been stabbed in the heart, Staci braced a hand on the wall beside her. It was still about the music for him. Always about the music. Why had she thought it would ever be anything different? The sooner she accepted that this time around, the better it would be for all of them.

With a sigh, she headed back to the living room but ignored the piano. She set her mug down on the table next to her favorite chair and sank into its softness. Would she ever learn? Nowhere in the notes he'd sent did he say that he loved her. At no point during either of his proposals had he mentioned loving her. She apparently hadn't been able to get over her feelings without him around six years ago, how on earth was she supposed to do it now when he was present in her life? No wonder she hadn't been interested in any of the guys she'd come in contact with over the years. Her heart was still tied to Eric, and she had no idea how to break that connection.

Tears dripped down her cheeks. Tomorrow she'd be strong again for Sarah, but right then she let her sadness and heartache take control of her emotions.

⌒⌇⌒

Eric sat in his truck, staring at the slices of light showing through the curtains of Staci's living room. He was still trying to figure out why he'd said no to her invitation to have a cup of coffee. It had been an opportunity to connect with her again. Maybe open the door to building something they'd never had before. Something that might lead to the love he wanted to share with her.

As he'd looked into her beautiful blue eyes, he knew he couldn't stay there without revealing how he felt. The offer for him to stay had sparked hope in his heart. Hope that maybe she didn't hate him after all. But hope so quickly could lead to heartache if he pushed her too soon.

And yet he had to know.

He pushed open his door and stepped back out into the cold.

One way or the other, he had to know.

Back at the door, he pressed the button and waited. It seemed to take forever but then the door swung open to reveal Staci once again. The hall light behind her cast her face in shadow so he couldn't see her expression.

"Eric? Did you forget something?" she asked, her arms wrapped across her waist. This time she didn't move to the side to let him in.

He struggled for the words to say to her. "I just need to know...so I can figure out what to do."

"To know? What?"

"Is there a chance that someday you'll forgive me for what I did? Not just for the other day but for back in LA, too." Eric swallowed. "And consider giving me...us...another chance?"

This time she did take a step back, but Eric got the feeling it was more a reaction to his words than it was to let him into the house. Still, he stepped in and closed the door. She took another step away from him, allowing the light to fall on her face. Her eyes were swollen and the sadness in her expression crushed his heart. He had hurt her. Yet again, he had hurt her.

He held out his hands toward her. "I know I don't deserve a second chance. I seem to keep hurting you, but all I want is to be able to love you the way my heart wants to. The way I should have six years ago. But if you don't want that, just say the word and I'll never bring it up again. I just need to know."

"You want to love me?" Staci whispered as she lifted a hand to her mouth.

"I *do* love you. I want to be able to show you the way I should have before." He took a step toward her, encouraged when she didn't step back from him. "I know our relationship before was bad for you, but I think we can make it good this time around. If God is part of it the way He should be, if you'll trust me with your heart, I promise I will do my best to honor and cherish you the way you deserve."

When she still didn't say anything, he continued, "I just need to know. Just be honest and I'll accept whatever your answer is. I let you slip out of my life six years ago because I was too scared to say anything, but not this time. If there's even the slightest chance, I don't want to miss it. If the door is closed, I'll move on. I promise. This will be the last time I bring it up."

"How can you love me?" Finally, she spoke, but they weren't the words he'd expected her to say. "I'm not her anymore. Everything you thought was perfect about her. Everything that you loved about her. That's not me anymore."

"I'm not the man I was back then either."

"But you still look the same. I don't. And I'll never go back to looking like that."

Eric frowned at her. "You think this is about how you look? You think I loved you only because of how you looked?"

As she stared at him, he sensed Staci was trying to figure out if she should share something. "You only ever used the word love in relation to two things about me." She gestured to her body. "My appearance and my talent."

He couldn't deny that he was attracted to her physically or that her music moved him as much as it ever had. Just hearing *their* song earlier had proven that. But how did he make her see that it was so much more than that.

"You want to know what I love about you? I love the way you stuck to your convictions. Even though you were a new Christian, you knew that the way we were living our relationship was not glorifying to God. I love how you were strong enough to walk away from our toxic life and build a safe one for yourself."

He took another step toward her. "I love how you love our little girl. There are some who might have rejected her because of who she is, but you love her the way every child should be loved. And you did that without ever having experienced that kind of love for yourself." And another step. "You're strong. You're determined. You've picked up the pieces of your life and made something better for yourself and Sarah. I admire and respect you for that more than you'll ever know."

Eric reached out and touched her cheek with his fingertips, tracing down along the soft curve of her jawline. "And I'd be lying if I didn't also say that you are the most beautiful woman I've known. Inside and out." His fingers slipped down the softness of her neck, feeling the flutter of her pulse. Memories began to seep past the boundaries he tried so hard to keep in place. He jerked his hand back as his gaze met hers. Was she remembering, too? That was a dangerous path to venture down. He couldn't let the intense attraction from the past cloud what he was trying to accomplish right then.

"This," Staci said as she motioned between them. "Scares me. I can't lose myself again."

"I won't let that happen. I know you have reason not to trust me when I say that, but what we had back then wasn't any better for me than it was for you. I don't want to go back to that. I don't want to have you hiding yourself from me. And more than anything I desire, I feel that against all odds God brought us back together. Sarah needs us both in her life. I need you both in my life. You even more than her. You make me want to be a better man. A better father."

He struggled to find the words. The ones that would wipe the apprehension and fear from her face. When she turned away from him, Eric's heart sank. But if this was the end, he could walk away knowing he'd tried his best. He laid it all out for her. Laid his heart bare. Though he could hardly bear the pain in his heart, Eric stepped back and turned for the door.

He knew he'd laid the foundation for this moment six years ago when he'd looked at her when she'd asked him about marriage and stabbed a knife in her heart with his words. No other woman would touch him like she had. He would live the rest of his life bereft of her presence in his life in that way.

When he walked out the door this time, it would be over for him. He wouldn't pressure her about this again. He would move forward, his only connection to her would be their daughter.

The door shut behind Eric with a resounding thud. Staci stared at it. Fear paralyzed her, but she couldn't let it win. She knew he was different now. He'd proved that to her over and over. And she was different now, too. She had to have confidence in the changes she'd made to herself over the years.

And as Eric had pointed out—against all odds—God had brought them back together. He'd said he loved her. Something he'd never told her before. And she loved him. Why was she letting fear keep her from what she'd always wanted?

Reaching deep for the strength Eric said he'd admired in her, Staci ran for the door. She jerked it open and darted out onto the porch. Eric's truck was backing out of her driveway already.

Frantic, she ran down the sidewalk, calling his name. Cold bit into her sock-covered feet as she raced along the snowy walkway. When she saw the truck come to a stop, she continued down the driveway toward it. The door opened as she neared it, and Eric stepped out.

"Staci?"

Finally feeling free of any doubts, Staci threw herself at him, wrapping her arms around his neck. Instantly, his arms encircled her and he pulled her close, lifting her feet from the cold ground. She buried her head in his neck, surprised by how much his embrace felt like she'd just come home.

"I love you, Eric." She whispered the words, but he must have heard them as his arms tightened even more securely around her.

Slowly he lowered her, but instead of setting her feet on the ground, he settled her on the tops of his boots. Staci looked up at him, her arms still around his neck.

He stared at her for a long moment before saying, "For real, Staci? I need you to be certain. I can't handle losing you again now that you've said the words I've longed to hear from you."

"For real, Eric. I've loved you all along. I was just too scared to take another chance with you."

"You won't ever have to wonder if I love you." He lowered his head toward her. "And you'll never have to earn my love. It's yours. Always and forever, it's yours." His lips touched hers, and the cold of the air vanished as warmth flooded her.

This kiss was different from the way he used to kiss her. There was no desperation in this kiss. Only gentleness. Tenderness. A promise of the love he had for her.

When the kiss ended, he swept her up in his arms. With strong strides, he walked up the driveway and along the sidewalk to where the front door still stood open. As he set her on her feet inside the doorway, he said, "I'm going to park the truck. Wait for me."

Gazing up at him, Staci nodded. "I'll be here."

Though the air still held a bite to it, Staci stood in the open doorway watching him pull his truck back into the driveway. When the headlights snapped off, her heart skipped a beat. She moved back to let him into the house when he approached the front door.

He took her hand and led her into the living room. Staci sank down into her chair when he gestured to it. Then he got down on his knees in front of her. Taking both of her hands in his, Eric looked at her.

"Staci, I want to be there for you in the good and bad. I want to raise our daughter together and maybe have one or two more. I want you to always know that your place in my heart is secure without you having to do a single thing to earn it. I love you and plan to spend my life showing you that over and over." He took a deep breath. "So, for the third—and hopefully final—time, will you marry me?"

Staci gripped his hands tightly, afraid she was going to wake up and find it was all a dream. "Yes. And this time it is a definite yes. I want us to be together again. This time with love."

THE END

OTHER TITLES AVAILABLE BY

Kimberly Rae Jordan
(*Christian Romances*)

Marrying Kate

Faith, Hope & Love

Waiting for Rachel (*Those Karlsson Boys: 1*)
Worth the Wait (*Those Karlsson Boys: 2*)
The Waiting Heart (*Those Karlsson Boys: 3*)

Home Is Where the Heart Is (*Home to Collingsworth: 1*)
Home Away From Home (*Home to Collingsworth: 2*)
Love Makes a House a Home (*Home to Collingsworth: 3*)
The Long Road Home (*Home to Collingsworth: 4*)
Her Heart, His Home (*Home to Collingsworth: 5*)
Coming Home (*Home to Collingsworth: 6*)

A Little Bit of Love:
A Collection of Christian Romance Short Stories

For more details on the availability of these titles,
please go to

www.KimberlyRaeJordan.com

CONTACT

Please visit Kimberly Rae Jordan on the web!
Website: www.kimberlyraejordan.com
Facebook: www.facebook.com/AuthorKimberlyRaeJordan
Twitter: twitter.com/KimberlyJordan

Printed in Great Britain
by Amazon